Revenge
Fires Back

[2nd Edition]

JR THOMPSON

[i]

This is a work of fiction. The characters, incidents, and dialogues are either products of the author's imagination or are used fictitiously.

Cover design by Indie Book Cover Design.

Discover more about Christian Author JR Thompson and his writings at www.jrthompsonbooks.com

All scriptures quoted and referenced in this book are taken from the Authorized King James Bible.

ISBN: 1546624158
ISBN-13: 978-1546624158

I would like to dedicate this book
to my son, Justin Shaw Thompson,
and to all of the children and families
who have struggled through the
foster care system.

TABLE OF CONTENTS

1

SHADOW MONSTERS

LIGHTNING-FASHIONED strobe lights presented eerie shadow monsters creeping across the Clark's tent. The frightening show was intensified by earsplitting crashes of thunder which rattled the ground beneath them. Wind gusts of nearly thirty miles per hour shook the tent so violently that the youngest child thought the shadow monsters were coming in. *What if they aren't just shadows after all?*

"I'm scared, Mommy," Derrick whispered into the night. Scared was an understatement. The eleven year old was terrified. Out of all of the places he could be with a storm of this magnitude brewing, why did he have to be trapped in Nowheresville?

"It's okay," Roxanne spoke softly as her fingers caressed the boy's shaggy caramel colored hair. "This will all be over soon."

How does she know? Derrick thought. *And why does that drummer keep giving his snare drum the beating of a lifetime just beneath my pillow?* The rat-a-tat rhythm being pounded out by the heavy rainfall combined with the constant BADABOOM of thunder was filling him with misery. He dreamed of snuggling in his warm, cozy bed at home.

A few hours prior to the storm rolling in, Roxanne had told him how excited she was about this trip. She had never gone camping before and it had only taken Trevor sixteen years of their marriage to convince her to try it.

Derrick knew his mom had been trying to be an optimist. That became obvious when his dad, Trevor, got her to laugh with his crude humor about the family having to use a chocolate filled port-a-potty in the middle of the woods. Even though she had pretended to be proud of the fact that she was going to survive a few days without electricity, Derrick knew better.

Once the first crack of thunder had ricocheted across the mountaintops, the look on Roxanne's face made it obvious that Derrick was right—there was no more faking that optimism!

Following his mother's gaze upward, Derrick's eyes caught sight of the most frightening storm clouds he had seen since the tornado he and his family had survived back in 1991. It had been three years since that funnel cloud had touched down, but in his mind it seemed as though it had taken place only a few days before.

Derrick listened intently as his mom began to express her concerns. "Trevor, I'm not so sure this is a good idea. Perhaps we should go home and try again some other weekend."

Derrick observed as that playful smirk he loved to see on his dad's face made its way to the surface. He had to chuckle when Trevor replied with, "Where's your sense of adventure?"

Even though his dad's humor was known for lightening the mood in any given situation, Derrick also knew his dad had no clue what the word "fear" meant. The only thing he was afraid of was not living life to its fullest.

Getting no response from his better half, Trevor added, "A little bit of wind and rain never killed anybody. Dalton and Brady seem to be enjoying themselves. I haven't heard a complaint out of either of them yet."

Derrick didn't give his mom a chance to respond. "Wind and rain did too kill people! Don't you remember the story about Noah and the ark? And the reason Brady and Dalton haven't been complaining is because they're too busy sleeping, Dad."

As usual, Derrick was right on target. As soon as the tent had been set up, Brady and his buddy from school, Dalton, had changed clothes, crawled inside, and drifted off to La La Land. The guys passed out so quickly they didn't even know a storm was brewing.

"Honey, do you suppose we should pack up and go home with the weather turning so fierce?" Roxanne asked.

"This is what memories are made of. We would be crazy to

run off now. What would you like the boys to remember twenty years from now? The trip where Mom and Dad chickened out because of a few rain showers or the time their entire family braved a savage thunderstorm under the protection of a thin canopy?"

"If it was up to me, we would have left an hour ago," Roxanne scolded. "I appreciate where you're coming from, but I'd rather play it safe than sorry. Please Trevor, let's go home!"

"Yeah Daddy, she's right. I think we should go home," Derrick chimed in. "It's dangerous out here."

After waiting more than a decade for his family to accompany him for a night in the wilderness, Trevor was not going to retreat effortlessly. "No way. We're staying put. I have been on hundreds of camping trips—in the rain, sleet, and snow. Not once have I ever backed out due to bad weather."

With sprinkles beginning to fall on their heads, the three made their way inside the tent.

Just after Trevor, Roxanne, and Derrick crawled into their warm sleeping bags, Brady woke up and grumbled, "Who did that?"

"Whatever it was, I didn't do it," Trevor chuckled.

"Who did what?" Roxanne asked.

"Somebody just dripped water in my eye."

Just as the words fell from his tongue, another bead of water plopped just above his upper lip. "The tent's leaking," he groaned.

Why me? Brady thought. *Why is it that every time something bad happens, it happens to me?*

It had only been one week since he had sat on a yellow jacket—one who was quick to let him know he didn't appreciate the gesture. He sat on a package of frozen veggies for about two hours after that ordeal. One month before that, his bus broke down on his way home from school. Now, he wouldn't have minded if it had broken down on its way to school, but on the way home was a completely different story. Now this! He was the only one getting dripped on.

Seeing the frustration on Brady's face was enough to shove Roxanne over the top. With a cold sounding voice, she told Trevor enough was enough. She was no longer in the mood to make suggestions—it was time to go home.

"Yeah Daddy, we need to go back to the house," Derrick agreed.

Of course Derrick would agree with Mom, Brady thought. The boy rarely had an opinion he hadn't stolen from his mother's lips.

Just as predictable as it was for Derrick to side with Roxanne was the notion that Brady's opinion would be in opposition to his whiny little brother's. "I don't want to go," he fussed.

Trevor and Roxanne looked at each other, but their looks didn't match very well. Trevor's expression was one of delight. Of fun. Of adventure. Roxanne's, on the other hand, was an expression of disbelief in her husband's and her oldest son's insistence of braving the weather.

After a brief stare down, Trevor turned toward the boys and said, "That's the right attitude, Brady. When the going gets tough, the tough get going."

Brady appreciated the fact that he and his dad could almost always see eye to eye on important matters like this one. For whatever reason, it seemed their house was regularly divided into teams—Mom and Derrick versus Dad and Brady. *I'm glad I'm always on the winning team!*

Before the boy could say a word, Roxanne replied with sarcasm, "No argument there. Let's get going."

Trevor began to put his two cents in the bucket, but Brady beat him to it. "If we go home, we'll be a bunch of sissies. I'm fourteen years old now and I'm a man. I told all of the guys I was roughing it for the weekend. They'll call me a coward if we come back early."

Another bead of water plopped on Brady's forehead. Using the sleeping bag, he wiped it off.

[4]

This is going to be a long night, he thought. *But I'm a man. I got this!*

He and Derrick listened as Trevor and Roxanne continued their debate—as humorous as it was from time to time.

Trevor insisted a man's reputation was worth more than all of the luxuries they had at home. When people heard the name Clark, he wanted them to think of a family who worked together as a force not to be reckoned with. That reputation could be ruined at the drop of a hat.

Roxanne found it rather absurd that Trevor considered his reputation to be more valuable than their lives. She argued that they could die out there. She had made a mistake in allowing Trevor to talk her into such an outing and more than anything, she wanted to return to civilization.

Trevor was not about to give in so easily. He told Roxanne they would be much safer in the woods than they would be if they were traveling in the van, where they could hydroplane or collide with an overloaded coal truck.

When is Mom ever going to learn? Brady thought. *She is nowhere near as stubborn as Dad.*

Tuning out their argument, Brady thought back to some of the other disagreements his parents had had—like the time he got caught shoplifting a pack of baseball cards back in the fifth grade. Roxanne had insisted it would be the right thing to do to call the police. She said getting the law involved would make him think twice before ever looking at another pack of baseball cards. Trevor, on the other hand, argued that for a first offense, that would be taking things to the extreme.

Brady ended up having to return the stolen goods to Dale's Sports Mart, along with volunteering to clean the store from top to bottom for an entire month of Saturdays.

Then there was the time when Trevor wanted to go fishing for a whole weekend with a couple of guys from the church. Roxanne said weekends were important family time. She argued with Trevor for a week before and a week after the trip—but it was Trevor who won that debate.

[5]

Looking back, Brady could only count on one hand the number of times he had seen Mom come out on top of any debate she had with Dad.

Why does she even try?

When his mind finally returned to planet Earth, he heard his mom bark, "Fine, you stay here. The tent is already leaking. Yeah, I'd like to take a shower, but not in our tent! While you're busy catching pneumonia, I'm gonna be catching up on my beauty sleep in the van. Who wants to keep me company?"

Uh, not me! Brady thought. *Talk about being a sissy. I can see it now—Dalton and Derrick spreading it around town that I went to sleep in the van because I was too big of a baby to put up with a few raindrops. Over my dead body!*

When no one volunteered, Roxanne turned to her protégé. She told Derrick she knew he was petrified of the storm and suggested he would feel better sleeping in the van with his mommy.

She was shocked when Derrick didn't go along with her. He said he thought it would be better if all five of them stayed together. He didn't care if they were in the tent or in the van, but staying together was of vital importance.

"Why? What good will staying together do?" Roxanne asked.

"Mom, don't you ever watch the movies? We're in the middle of nowhere. There's no one around but us. If three people stay in the tent and two people go to the van, some psychopath murderer will come and kill the two who are by themselves. You've already lived your life, Mom. I'm just a kid and I'm too little to die."

Brady struggled to withhold his laughter. He knew exactly what was going to happen next. If there was anything his mom hated more than the outdoors, it was horror movies. Trevor never allowed any of the really gory ones in their house, but anything with even the most remote form of a fear factor always sent Roxanne scurrying off to her room where she would curl up with a good book.

Just as he expected, Roxanne said she would stay in the

tent—just to make Derrick feel better, of course.

The storm continued for hours. Trevor and Brady drifted back to sleep within minutes of the debate. Roxanne and Derrick, on the other hand, did not receive even an ounce of rest until the thunder and lightning finally subsided and the winds died down.

At 9:30 the next morning, Dalton woke up to a very unpleasant surprise. *My sleeping bag's completely saturated! It's not just my sleeping bag—my clothes are wet.*

The fifteen year old glanced around the tent. Thankfully, no one was awake. Reaching further into his bag, he felt the front of his jeans. *Oh, man. There's no way. I did not. I could not. It's just not possible. Not here. Not now. What are the Clarks gonna think of me?*

Completely unaware of the storm that had taken place, he glanced over toward Brady and saw that his sleeping bag was drenched as well.

"Brady, Brady, you awake?" Dalton asked quietly.

"I am now. What's up?"

"We have a serious problem here, dude. It looks like you wet the bed. That's sick!"

"I didn't wet the bed. I haven't done that since I was five."

Shifting the blame, Brady wasted no time in pointing out that Dalton's sleeping bag looked wetter than his. He returned the accusation and added that it wasn't his fault Dalton was too afraid to admit he had an accident.

Neither of them was ready to take the rap for this one. How were they going to justify how their clothes and sleeping bags had gotten sopping wet? Everyone appeared dry except for the two of them.

Looking around the tent, Dalton came up with an idea. "We could just pour a cup of water on Derrick's crotch and say he did it," he chuckled.

Derrick was always the scapegoat. Being the youngest and the smallest made him easier to shift the blame to. Since Dalton

[7]

and Brady had buddied up, they had gotten the little booger in trouble for all kinds of things he didn't do: leaving a piece of chewing gum in the floor, breaking Roxanne's flower pot, egging the neighbor's house, and then there was that time when he caught the garage on fire. Poor kid.

"I didn't do it," Derrick fussed. His eyes were closed, but he had been listening to every word.

"You are such an eavesdropper. You were supposed to be asleep," Dalton told him.

Derrick told the guys about the storm and that neither one of them had wet the bed. The older boys pretended they knew that the whole time—they had only been messing around. Dalton said they were just using sarcasm and asked Derrick if he knew the meaning of the word.

"I don't know. What is it?"

"I guess you're still too little and don't need to know," Brady teased.

Derrick's blood was boiling. "Who are you calling little? You're the bed wetter!"

"You better shut up before I give you such a tremendous wedgie that a crane'll have to pull it out for you!" Dalton threatened.

He knew that would make Derrick close those fat lips of his. The last time he had given the boy a wedgie, it was one none of them would ever forget. All of the boys had been hanging out at the park and every time Dalton or Brady tried to talk to a girl, Derrick blew it by doing something childish like passing gas as loud as he could, making noises with his armpits, or joking with the girls about how much the older guys liked them.

Having enough of that, Dalton, with a little bit of assistance from Brady, lifted him up and hooked the back of his shorts on a thick tree branch. He let him go kind of slow, just in case the tree branch or his drawers gave way.

Derrick had squirmed and tried to fight his way out of it the whole time he was being raised up. When Dalton let go, he started crying and yelling for help.

By the time another parent came to his defense, his shorts

had begun to rip and he was dangling sideways off of the tree. A small fragment of his behind was hanging out on public display. It was the ultimate wedgie.

"Mom! Wake up!" Derrick demanded, knowing good and well that Dalton wouldn't lay a hand on him if his mom had anything to say about it.

"You are such a sissy!" Dalton whispered.

"What's going on?" Trevor asked when he heard the commotion.

Shew! At least it's Trevor and not Roxanne, Dalton thought.

Derrick wasted no time in sharing a slightly twisted version of what had taken place. He claimed both Brady and Dalton had wet the bed during the night and had planned to blame it on him.

Please stay asleep, Roxanne. Let Trevor handle this. You would buy into every word of his story. I know you would.

Trevor didn't think twice about it. It was obvious the boys were soaked because of the leaking tent. He was certain Brady and Dalton were only teasing about making it look like Derrick had wet himself and he told the boy he needed to learn how to take a joke.

That didn't fly with Derrick—not at all. Determined to get the last word, he continuously insisted the other guys were not playing.

That kid is so annoying! Dalton thought.

Trying to lighten the mood, Trevor laughed. "Boys, I don't think you can blame the storm for wetting your sleeping bags after all."

"Dad, come on. You don't really think we wet the bed?" Brady asked.

"No, but look at your mom. She's over there drooling away. It's probably all that slobber that plastered your sleeping bags and clothes."

"Ewww!!!!! Gross!!!!" Derrick looked as if he was going to

blow chunks.

The girlish sounding squeal woke Roxanne from her sleep. "What happened? Is a tornado coming in?"

"No Mom, you were drooling!! Dad pointed it out. You had so much slobber gushing out of your mouth that Brady and Dalton are covered."

Looking at her pillow, while slowly bringing her hand up to feel her face, Roxanne turned ten different shades of red. Even though her pillow was wet and her face felt slightly sticky, she insisted she had not been drooling.

Trevor wouldn't let it go. He told her she most certainly was drooling—so much, as a matter of fact, he claimed the Titanic could have sailed on it.

Even though all three of the boys found his comment hysterical, Roxanne didn't. "I don't believe this," she shrieked. "You saw me drooling and told all of the boys to gawk at me? Why would you do that?"

"Why not? It was funny," Trevor snickered while winking at Brady.

Sometimes I think I could kill that man, Roxanne thought. *What did I ever see in him? He is so immature and pathetic. Dad told me it would be a mistake to marry him. Boy was he ever right!*

When they were dating, Trevor's sense of humor was quite charming. His jokes and sarcasm had been hilarious. But that's when they were teenagers. She had matured, with or without the man she had married. *How on earth have I put up with him all of these years?*

Swiftly gathering her belongings, she threw her slippers on and unzipped the tent.

The moment she stepped out, however, she was bowled over by the sight of a tree lying across the top of their mini-van. *I don't believe this! Was there a full moon last night?*

"How am I going to get home now?" she shouted.

Roxanne barely had time to finish her question before Derrick poked his head out of the tent. "Mom, I have an idea. Why don't you go to sleep in front of the van and drool again and then maybe it'll float home like the Titanic."

"That is not funny, Derrick," Roxanne scowled.

Still not understanding his mother's frustration, Derrick was not ready to stop talking yet. "Was it hilarious then, Mommy?"

"No. It was rude, Derrick."

Tears began to form in the corners of Derrick's eyes. "I'm sorry, Mommy. I wasn't trying to be mean. Besides, didn't the Titanic sink? That probably wasn't such a good plan anyway."

Roxanne didn't even reply. She scurried to the van and clutched the tree trunk with both hands. She heaved as forcefully as she could, but the tree wouldn't budge. She climbed up on top of the van and attempted to thrust it off. Still, it wouldn't move an inch.

She demanded Trevor hand her the keys, but wasn't too surprised when he refused to do so and reminded her there was a tree on top of the van. Sarcastically, he asked her if she really thought she could drive home hauling that thing on the luggage carrier.

Why not? Roxanne thought. *People drive home with Christmas trees on their cars all of the time!*

Even though she thought she had only said those words in her brain, apparently they had slipped out and Trevor had heard them. He again insisted he would not give her the keys and told her he feared she was having a nervous breakdown.

"Fine. Whatever. I'm going to take a walk. I need some alone time," Roxanne grumbled as she stomped off. She hoped that while she was away, the others would calm down and stop making fun of her.

Twenty minutes later, a startling sound caught the ears of Trevor and the boys. There was a scream. Not just an ordinary scream, but one that sent shivers down the spines of everyone who heard it. It was a long, piercing cry. The voice definitely belonged to Roxanne. She was either hurt, scared, or in some sort of danger.

2
THE SEARCH IS ON

TREVOR CALLED OUT, "Roxi, where are you?" To his dismay there was no answer.

As seconds turned to minutes, tears streamed down Derrick's face. "Mommy, are you okay?"

Still there was no response. Trevor felt helpless. *Should I have the boys stay at the camp while I search for Roxi? Perhaps I should send one of the guys to find help while the rest of us search for her. What if there really is a violent predator or a wild animal is hunting us? I don't even know if Roxanne is okay. Something terrible had to have happened to her.* Trevor's entire body trembled with anguish. Whatever had happened, only he could accept the blame.

The whipping Trevor was giving himself was soon brought to a halt. Rubbing his belly, Brady said, "Dad, I know it's a bad time to talk about it, but I'm hungry."

Kids! Trevor thought.

"How can you jabber about food when your mother just screamed bloody murder?"

Derrick's eyes grew as wide as quarters. "Murder? No!!!" he squealed. "Mommy!!!"

"Mommy wasn't murdered," Trevor said calmly. "That was just a figure of speech."

"Daddy, why did she yell like that then? Do you think that psychopathic murderer is torturing her before he kills her?"

Frustrated, Trevor insisted there was no psychopathic

murderer on the loose. He was hopeful he would be able to answer Derrick's question about Roxanne's whereabouts in the near future, but the only way to know why she screamed was to go out and find her.

With the appetite of a hog being raised for the slaughter, Brady voted they wait until after breakfast to search for her.

Dalton, whose gut size made it clear he was more than capable of out-eating Brady any day, seconded the motion.

I can't believe the rudeness of these guys. I can't even imagine thinking my appetite is more important than a person's health.

Trevor gave the boys a stern lecture, which was quickly refuted by his youngest son.

"If we don't eat breakfast first, our bodies might get too weak and when we find Mom we won't have any strength left to help her," he whined.

Oh my! You would think these guys hadn't eaten in weeks. It's three against one, Trevor thought. *If I take them in the woods on empty stomachs, they're not going to be doing anything but complaining. We probably won't even be able to hear Roxanne if she calls out to us because of all of their belly-aching.*

"Okay fellas, you stay here and stuff your faces all you want to. I'm going to find your mother—even if I have to go alone."

Trevor wasn't about to waste any more time debating about the food. He darted off into the woods, leaving the three boys to fend for themselves.

"Mom sent a bowl of chocolate chip cookies and brownies. We could eat those," Dalton said. His mouth watered at the thought of those scrumptious chocolate chips melting on his tongue.

"Mom definitely would not approve," Derrick mumbled.

"But she's not here," Brady reminded him.

"But we're supposed to honor our parents. That's what the preacher says."

"Ah, shut up," Brady replied. "We're gonna eat the goodies. If you don't think that's the right thing to do, don't eat then."

Chuckling, Dalton slipped into the tent and returned with

an oversized bowl jam-packed with snacks. Brady and Derrick couldn't wait to chow down. They each licked their lips in anticipation.

To their surprise, Derrick snatched the largest brownie Mrs. Ryan had baked, along with three cookies before they even had a chance to think about what they wanted to start with.

"Did you guys hear that?" Derrick asked.

"Hear what?" Brady replied.

"A twig snapped. I heard it as plain as day. Be quiet. Listen."

Even though they didn't believe him, Brady and Dalton got quiet for a moment just in case. They didn't hear anything except the breeze blowing some leaves around.

"I did hear something. I really did," Derrick whined. "What if whatever happened to Mom happens to us? Or even to Dad?"

"Grow up," Brady said. "You're such a baby. Mom's fine and nothing's going to happen to anybody else."

Derrick's teeth began to chatter as he peered all around them.

The boy's fear was contagious. Before he knew what hit him, Dalton found himself a tad on the scared side as well. "Why don't we hear anything? Shouldn't we hear your dad hollering your mom's name or something? What if Derrick's right? What if something terrible is going on out there?"

Brady chuckled. "Like what? An invasion by zombies?"

"Come on, man. This is serious. I think we should have went with your dad."

"Me too," Derrick fussed.

Brady, suddenly realizing how selfish and inconsiderate they had been, told his brother and Dalton they were right. They had to head out to find his parents.

That didn't, however, mean Brady was taking the situation quite as seriously as he should have been. "Maybe we should leave Derrick here," he said. "I mean, just in case we find Mom's carcass. Derrick wouldn't be able to handle it if he saw her body half-eaten by a pack of wolves or something."

Dalton couldn't help but to snicker. *That is messed up!*

"I'm not staying here by myself," Derrick argued. "Even if a pack of wolves chewed Mom up and spit out her dead body, I could handle it. I'm tough."

"Yeah, sure you are," Brady said.

"If Mom's still alive, do you think she's awake or asleep?" Derrick asked.

"Awake, I suppose," Brady replied. "Why do you ask?"

"Good thing. I still haven't learned to swim yet. If Mom is asleep, she might flood the whole forest with all that drool."

"Look, Derrick. Mom doesn't like it when we talk about her drooling. It makes her very uncomfortable. We're gonna have to stop talking that way."

"Yes, sir!" Derrick said, saluting his big brother.

Dalton was the most worried of the bunch. He had never seen Mrs. Clark as angry as she was when she stormed away from the camp. He had never heard her scream so wildly either.

There was no time for panic. "Okay guys," he said. "It's time to get this show on the road."

"Uh, Dalton," Brady said. "We have a slight problem." Brady had left all of his clothing in the van the night before. With the tree weighing heavily on the vehicle, it was not possible to open any of the doors.

Like it or not, both Dalton and Derrick told him there was no choice. Brady would have to walk around in his pajama bottoms; he had to forget changing clothes and hurry up and get his shoes on.

That was a difficult thing for Brady to do—more difficult than it would have been for anyone else in their party. At the age of fourteen, the boy was obsessed with his image. He worked out five days per week and had a reputation of being the toughest jock in Washington High. He was at the age where everyone was watching every step he took. Where that one

[15]

misplaced zit could ruin the upcoming dance. Where the wrong brand of shoes could end his popularity.

Brady insisted he couldn't leave the campsite wearing teddy bear pajamas.

Even though Dalton and Derrick could understand where he was coming from, they insisted Brady get his shoes. They had already wasted enough time and both of the adults on the trip were quite possibly in serious danger.

"My shoes are in the van too," Brady complained.

Running out of patience, Dalton snapped, "Shoes or no shoes, you're going to have to go with us to find your mom. I don't care if you have to go barefoot—we have to get going. We've wasted too much time already."

As much as he hated to, Brady gave in and the three boys wandered into the woods.

"MR. CLARK?" Dalton called out.

There was no answer.

"MRS. CLARK?"

Still no answer.

"What are we gonna do, Brady?" Derrick asked.

"We're going to keep walking and looking. That's all we can do."

A branch suddenly fell from a tree behind them and landed on the forest floor with a thud. All three boys jumped and spun around in a heartbeat.

"Whew! Just a fallen limb," Dalton said.

"Yeah, but what made it fall?" Brady asked, gazing into the tree fearfully.

"How am I supposed to know? Let's keep looking," Dalton said. "Maybe we should split up so we can cover more ground."

"Split up? Are you crazy?" Derrick squealed. "Mom went out by herself and disappeared. Dad went out by himself and now we can't find any traces of him either. We have to stay together."

"Brady, looks like you have the tie-breaking vote on this one," Dalton said.

Brady didn't even have to think about that one. "We're

[16]

sticking together… MOM? DAD?" he shouted.

Still no answer came.

The boys combed the woods for another fifteen minutes before finally hearing Trevor hollering his wife's name. They ran toward his voice and were relieved to find him alive and well.

"It's about time you guys got out here," Trevor said before telling the guys they had to cover as much ground as possible in a short period of time. He said everyone would have to pay close attention and follow directions precisely. It would be necessary for all of them to spread out a bit, but to stay close enough to hear one another's voices.

With one accord, Trevor and company began their search anew. From time to time, they would all stop walking and take turns hollering Roxanne's name. Just like before, their cries went unanswered.

"Mommy! Where are you?" Derrick yelled.

If she won't respond to anyone else, she'll respond to Derrick, Trevor thought. It wasn't necessarily that his wife loved Derrick more than anyone else in the family, but the boy definitely held a soft place in her heart. *She might be able to hold a grudge against me, Brady, and Dalton, but not Derrick.*

With no response, Trevor's worries escalated. He and Dalton marched forward looking under every bush and behind every boulder. Whether she was dead or alive, if Roxanne was out there, she was going to be found.

Why had we been so foolish to tease her? Trevor thought. *Roxi didn't deserve to be treated that way. She wouldn't have gone out alone had I just kept my fat mouth shut.*

Barefoot, the soles of Brady's feet were bloody and bruised from stepping on briars, rocks, acorns, pinecones, and sticks which were left lying in his path. Still, he moved forward. "Mom!" he yelled. "Mom, we're going to find you. Please call out and let us know where you are!"

Normally, Brady was the tough guy. Never would he be seen showing any signs of fear. Never would you see him crying—not because he was hurt, not because he was scared, not because someone close to him died. Never. This was different. Even in the corners of Brady's eyes, tears could be seen forming.

"Guys, I think I found something!" Derrick hollered out suddenly, with a voice full of excitement.

The other three went running in his direction, anxious to see what clue had been uncovered.

When they got there, Derrick pointed to the bottom of a tree and asked if it was his mother's guts.

He was disappointed to learn it was only a mushroom.

Brady and Dalton were aggravated. For a moment, there had been a shimmer of hope. For a split second, they thought Derrick had actually found something that would point them in the right direction. Now, that little glimmer of hope had disappeared.

"Wait a second," Derrick whispered. "Do you guys hear that?" Putting his hand behind his right ear, he tilted his head to listen more closely.

"Okay, that's enough, Derrick," Brady grumbled. *I knew we should have left him behind. He's already slowing us down.*

"Derrick, this is serious. We need to find your mother. We don't have time for games right now," Trevor scolded.

"Wait, I think I hear something too," Dalton said. "Listen." *Sure Dalton, just like the time you heard a chimpanzee in the yard next to your house. You have quite the imagination.*

Just in case he and Derrick did hear something, the search party grew quiet. If it would have been possible, they would have kept their hearts from beating.

Derrick had been right. Something was moving by the water. All four of them took off running.

Brady was the first to arrive at the river's edge. *There she is— in the water. Did she fall in? Is she drowning?* With no time to lose, Brady dove in head first.

He went under, but kept his eyes closed. Feeling around

[18]

with his hands, he eventually touched something—it was an arm. *Got her!*

Reaching out, he clasped the arm with both hands. *I hope I'm not too late.* Holding her tightly, he kicked his legs while moving toward the water's surface. To his surprise, Roxanne started fighting him. She was trying to pull away and kicked at him with her legs. *What is her deal?*

Regardless, Brady was proud of himself. *I just saved Mom's life. They're going to plaster my face all over the newspapers. I'll probably even be on TV—nationwide!*

That thought train suddenly had a head-on collision with reality.

"Cindy?" Brady gasped. It wasn't Roxanne he had pulled from the water after all. *So much for being a hero!*

His ex-girlfriend slapped him right in the face. "You nearly scared me to death, Brady Clark!"

"Sorry, Cindy. Honest."

Cindy punched him in the eye and told him his apology was not accepted.

She did not just hit me. That actually hurt. She packs a more powerful punch than a lot of the guys on my football team. "Cindy, will you please listen to me?"

"You mean like the last time I listened to you? Like when you told me you were breaking up with me to date Tia Landers? Why should I listen to you?"

From his place on the river bank, Dalton interrupted and told Cindy about Roxanne's disappearance.

As soon as Dalton spoke, Cindy blushed and asked him how long he had been standing there. It was obvious that even though Cindy hated Brady, she had a bit of a crush on his best friend.

The feeling was anything but mutual. Brady knew that was the case because Dalton never had anything positive to say about her. Usually, whenever her name came up, Dalton would refer to her as Little Miss Priss. Or The Stuck-up One.

[19]

As Cindy attempted to admire Dalton, she couldn't help but to see Derrick and Trevor standing next to him. *Should I be ashamed of myself for being so hardcore?* she asked herself. *Nah, Brady deserved that black eye. More than that, he deserves the humiliation stemming from being beaten up by a girl. Actually, I'm kind of glad there were some witnesses.*

She knew it was wrong to gloat. Especially considering the fact that Brady's mom was missing in action. Instead of continuing her aggression, she asked for more details.

Brady began telling her everything he knew, but of course he was not able to finish the story without help from Derrick. Derrick had lots of information he felt needed to be included— especially the part about his mom drooling.

"Sorry Brady, I forgot you said not to talk about that," Derrick apologized immediately afterwards.

"Boy, you couldn't keep your mouth closed if your teeth were cemented together and your lips were glued shut, stapled, and covered with duct tape," Brady told him.

When Cindy learned about Mrs. Clark, she volunteered to go back into town for help. She ran as fast as her petite legs would carry her. Part of the reason she ran so fast was so she could help Mrs. Clark as quickly as possible. The other reason was because she was afraid. *If whatever made Roxanne disappear is still out here, I'm probably in danger. I'm the only other female out here and I'm alone. As long as I move fast enough, I should be okay.*

While Cindy was making her way back to town, the search continued. Dalton, Brady, Derrick, and Trevor combed the woods for another hour looking for any trace of Roxanne before a rescue party arrived. Dozens of townsfolk showed up on four wheelers and dirt bikes. "Mrs. Clark!" A man yelled.

Just as before, there was no answer. Everyone began searching and yelling. Some people even brought dogs with them to try to sniff her out. After about fifteen or twenty minutes of the search party's efforts, the sound of a gunshot echoed off of the mountains. Everyone knew what that meant. Something had been found.

Every member of the search party rushed toward the shot. When they drew in close, they saw Roxanne's body lying completely still on a bed of grass. Her eyes were closed and there was no sign of foul play.

"Daddy, she's dead!" Derrick screamed.

"No, baby," Trevor said. "I think Mommy's sleeping." *I hope.*

The crowd came to a hush as they waited to see if Mrs. Clark was indeed alive. "Wake her up, Daddy! Hurry before all these people get washed away by her drool! Remember how much saliva she spit all over the tent last night?" Derrick asked.

That stupid boy of mine. Really? In front of all of these people!

Derrick's voice was as loud as could be. Everyone turned to look at the boy, and then to his mother lying on the ground. Sure enough, there was a small stream of drool trickling from the corner of her mouth.

"Mommy! Wake up!" Derrick yelled. "You're gonna flood the place!"

Slowly, her body began to move. She opened her eyes. "What's going on? Where'd all these people come from?"

"They all came out to help us find you, Mommy," Derrick said.

Blushing, Roxanne told the crowd she hadn't been lost. She had been mad at the world and hadn't gotten much sleep during the night so she had simply gone out in the woods to take a nap.

Right, Trevor thought. *It's perfectly normal for a person to take a nap in the woods and even more so, to let out a horrific yell first.*

"Roxi, we heard you scream," he said.

"Oh, that. Well, like I said before I was mad at the world, especially at you, Trevor. Before I laid down to take my nap, I decided to give you a scare. I screamed as loud as I could possibly scream. You know what? It felt pretty good too."

They couldn't believe their ears. Mrs. Roxanne Clark had pulled off a stunt like they had never seen. She had scared her

[21]

husband, sons, and even neighbors into thinking she had been killed or tortured. Still though, they were thankful she was alive.

Within minutes of learning the whole ordeal had been a gag, the crowd dispersed. All of the families who came out to look for her returned to their respective homes. It was an event none would soon forget.

One thing that had been temporarily forgotten, however, was that the Clark's van was out of commission and they had no way of getting back home. The Clark's had been so concerned about their family being the laughing stock of the whole state that they hadn't even taken the time to ask for help.

3
STOLEN MANHOOD

AFTER EVERYONE LEFT, Roxanne informed Trevor she would not be spending another night in that tent. One day of living like a cavewoman was enough. She had no intentions of losing another night of sleep.

Giving her a hard time, Trevor responded by asking if she planned to sleep under the stars all by her lonesome.

Even though Roxanne was not amused, Derrick's face filled with excitement. "I want to do that too! Can I, Dad?"

He had always enjoyed stargazing. Practically every night he watched for the first star to appear in the sky above him. When his eyes fell on that star he would say, "Star light, star bright, first star I see tonight, I wish I may, I wish I might, have this wish I wish tonight." It was a saying his mother had taught him. He always wished for the same thing—a baby brother. So far that wish had never come true, *but if I wish for it enough times, it's bound to happen,* he told himself.

"No one is sleeping out under the stars," his mother replied. "That would be far too dangerous."

"So you're going to sleep in the tent with us, Mom?" Brady asked.

"No, we're going home. I don't know how, but we're going."

For whatever reason, Derrick's eyes looked his mom over from head to toe. She appeared to be worn out. Her hair was a mess, she had no make-up on, and she was wearing the same clothes she had slept in. It was the only time in her adult life that she had went twenty-four hours without taking a shower.

"I'm hungry," Dalton blurted out.

"Is that all you think about?" Brady asked.

"Shush, Brady," his mother snapped. "I'm hungry too. I haven't eaten anything since last night." Her stomach rumbled as she spoke.

"We did," Derrick said excitedly, rubbing his tummy and smiling like a rat who had stealthily stolen the peanut butter right off the trap that had been set for him. "We had cookies and brownies for breakfast."

Roxanne's eyes looked fierce. "You did?" She turned to face Trevor. "You mean to tell me that the four of you heard me scream a horrific scream like that and you thought eating a bunch of junk food was more important than my life?"

"No, the four of us did not," Trevor said. "The guys were complaining that they were starving to death so I left them and their bellyaching and started searching for you. I haven't eaten either."

The boys were silent. What could they say? She was right; they had been selfish and thoughtless. They would have been furious if things were the other way around. How could they put their own personal desires in front of the safety of another human being? Especially the human being who had given birth to both Brady and Derrick.

Since the boys weren't ready to speak, Roxanne continued. "I suppose the four of you now expect me to fix lunch for everybody now too? Am I right?"

"Yes!" Derrick blurted out instantly. *I hope it's a juicy T-bone steak,* he thought.

"No!" Trevor snapped back immediately while giving Derrick a look that told him he had better not utter another word. "We're gonna fix you lunch. You deserve to eat a lot more than we do, dear. We're really sorry for the way we've been

[24]

treating you on this camping trip."

"Good, you should be sorry."

"Mr. Clark," Dalton said. "I have a question."

"What is it?" Trevor asked, hoping Dalton wasn't going to make any snide remarks which could lead to an even uglier conversation.

Fortunately, his question had nothing to do with Roxi or her drooling. Instead, he asked how they were going to cook when they didn't have any food in the tent.

At first, Trevor thought it was a silly question. He knew his wife had packed sandwich meats and bread. Even if they couldn't cook, they could at least make sandwiches.

That theory went out the window pretty quickly when Derrick reminded him that the sandwich meats, like everything else, were locked in the van.

How could Trevor keep forgetting such an enormous detail? Practically everything was stuck in the van. There was no way that all of them together could get that tree down without a chainsaw. He did bring a saw, but he had secured it just behind the backseat of the van. Wouldn't do much good there.

Brady, always looking for an opportunity to play the part of the macho man, suggested his father and the boys gather wood and start a fire. He would find a way to get the food and he could have it out in no time.

He was shocked when his dad actually agreed to the plan.

Brady waited until the three had disappeared further into the woods. His mom was still close to the tent, but she was not paying any attention to what was going on as she was in a world all of her own. A world where nothing mattered. Where no one existed, but herself.

He didn't know how, but Brady was going to prove to his family that he was a man. *One way or another, I'm going to get that*

[25]

food out of the van, he thought while walking around their smashed up vehicle and the tree that had attempted to crush it like an ant. He examined both carefully, hoping to find just the solution to the problem at hand.

That's it! I've got this!

Behind the van was a gap between the tree and the ground—just big enough for him to squat and waddle his way under it. Once in position, he raised his body up so the tree trunk was resting on his right shoulder. He counted out loud to three before attempting to stand up. He strained, his whole body trembled, he grunted and groaned, but the tree was too stout for him. *It didn't even move an inch.*

Brady slowly crawled back out from under the tree. He walked to the side of the mini-van to have a closer look at his enemy. "Okay big guy," he said. "You're gonna get off our van whether you like it or not."

With that being said, Brady wasted no time in grabbing the first branch he could get to with both hands. Turning his body sideways, he pulled with all of his might. *I'm gonna play tug of war with you until you fall to the ground. I will get the victory. I think I can. I know I can. I will!*

"Come on you stupid tree, move it!" Brady yelled as he continued pulling and tugging. However, the tree was extremely stubborn. Perhaps it just didn't like the hateful tone of voice Brady was using.

When Brady let go of the limb, he noticed his hair and upper body were completely drenched with sweat. His hands were beginning to blister and his shoulder was sore. His pants were filthy. He was still barefoot and his feet wouldn't have felt worse if he had just walked across an ocean of broken glass.

Maybe I should just give up and ask Dad for help, he thought. *Then again, that's what Dad expects me to do. That's the only reason he told me I could get the food. He thought I'd give up and then he could show me how it's done. I refuse to give him the satisfaction. Ain't gonna happen.* Brady had to tackle that tree all by himself. He just had to.

[26]

He sat on the ground to rest and brainstorm. After a few minutes of intense thought, a silly idea came to mind. He had heard a saying before, "Mind over matter." Perhaps, just perhaps he could think the tree down off the van.

He needed to pick one part of it to concentrate on. Looking it over, he decided to stare at a hole a woodpecker had pecked in a part of the trunk. "Tree, move off this van," he said. He meant it too. He wasn't asking this time, he was telling. "Come on tree. Fall off the van, NOW!"

The tree ignored him.

"What's your problem? I said MOVE! I don't have all day! Fall off the van RIGHT THIS INSTANT!"

The tree still didn't move. "Fine, have it your way." It was time to get down to business. If he had to knock a window out of the van, that's exactly what he was going to do. On the movies it always showed somebody either kicking a window out with his feet or taking off his shirt and wrapping it around his hand to bust glass. *I don't have any shoes on. Kicking out the window would be foolish. I don't even have a shirt to take off. I don't have a glove. I have nothing.*

Looking around, he saw no one but his mom and she wasn't paying any attention to him whatsoever. "Come on tree, please move off the van. I really don't wanna do this."

Even hearing the word "please," the mean ole tree didn't shake a single leaf. "Tree, I'm giving you one last chance. Move off the van now or you're gonna be sorry."

Still, nothing happened. "Okay, we'll do it the hard way, Mister!"

Brady quickly put his hands in the waist band of his pajama pants and slid them toward his feet. About the time they hugged his ankles, he heard giggling behind him.

"What do you think you're doing, Brady Clark?" A laughing voice said.

As Brady turned around, his eyes met with those of Cindy.

[27]

She came back, but she wasn't alone. She brought her new boyfriend, Jordan, along. Cindy laughed hysterically.

"I'm just trying to get our stuff out of the car," Brady said before realizing how he was dressed. How humiliating. *I'm standing in front of my ex-girlfriend and her new boyfriend wearing only my boxer shorts—and dirty ones at that.* He was certain the teddy bear pajama pants around his ankles didn't count for anything. *So much for being a man.*

As quickly as possible, Brady bent over to pull up his breeches. The second he was bent over, Jordan gave him a push and Brady fell to the ground. Cindy burst out in another episode of giggling. Brady, however, did not think anything was funny.

I'll kill him. By the time I'm finished with that jerk, he'll regret the day he was born.

Brady jumped up off the ground and was going to bust Jordan right in the nose. However, when he got back to his feet and started to charge his attacker, he tripped. His feet were still shackled together by his teddy bear pajamas. Brady fell flat on his face and his nose landed right between Jordan's feet.

This time Cindy's giggles turned into loud, hysterical laughter. Jordan laughed out loud as well before sitting on Brady's back. "Hurry, grab his pants," Jordan said. Jordan loved being a bully. It was what he did best.

Brady squirmed around trying to free himself and to retain a little bit of dignity. *I'm gonna turn the tables on this dude and he's gonna regret the day he messed with Brady Clark.*

Unfortunately, thoughts and reality aren't always the same thing. Before he could free himself, Cindy managed to slip his pajama bottoms off his feet.

"I can't wait to show your drawers off at school!" she laughed. Cindy held his jammies high in the air. "What cute little teddies."

Their fun came to an abrupt end when they heard Trevor's booming yell. "Hey, what's going on over there?"

Before Trevor had time to drop his armful of firewood,

[28]

Jordan and Cindy, as well as Brady's pajama bottoms, were gone; they had vanished without a trace. Brady just lay there on his stomach—too embarrassed to get up. *Again, I must ask myself why. Why do things like this always and only happen to me? Here I am minding my own business, trying to do something productive. What did I do to deserve to be treated like this? Seriously, how many things can go wrong in a weekend. Oh my. It's only been twenty-four hours since we started this adventure. Twenty-four hours. Wow! Unbelievable. I bet nobody in the world has to face so many problems in such a short amount of time. Well, then again, I guess maybe Job did. But that was back in the Bible. This is too much. I thought God said he wouldn't put more on us than we can bear. I can't bear this. It's too much!*

"I've seen London, I've seen France, I see Brady's underpants," Dalton teased.

Brady felt like his manhood had been stolen. He was too embarrassed to do or even say anything back to Dalton. He just lay there trying to bury himself in the dirt. He didn't want anyone to see the tears that were now slowly making their way down his cheeks. Never had anything embarrassed him like this before.

"Look, Brady has skidmarks on his underwear!" Derrick yelled. He laughed so hard his stomach hurt. He didn't know what was going on, but he found the sight of rough and tough Brady Clark being brought down to a state of nothingness to be absolutely hilarious.

Still, Brady remained motionless.

"No he doesn't," Trevor said. "You boys run along and play while I have a talk with Brady, okay?"

Derrick and Dalton followed his command, though still looking over their shoulder from time to time, laughing at the site of Mr. Macho Man lying in the dirt in his boxers.

Brady didn't feel like talking—he made that abundantly clear. *I wish I had my own spaceship. I'd just fly off to Jupiter or somewhere and be completely alone.*

[29]

At first, Trevor started to insist on his son opening up and talking to him, but he decided that was not a battle worth fighting. He knew Brady would come around eventually.

Trevor walked away, leaving Brady to continue his pity party there on the ground.

Brady wasn't quite sure why he didn't get up. Maybe he thought if he couldn't see anyone else, they couldn't see him either. Maybe it was just because he was so ashamed of not being able to defend himself that he couldn't face anyone. Perhaps it was because he just wanted some time to think and he was afraid if he got up everyone would start picking on him again. Then again, maybe it was a combination of all of those things.

"Dad, how are we gonna eat since Brady still hasn't got the food out of the van?" Brady overheard Derrick ask.

Seriously? he thought. *After everything I've been through, that little brat is talking about food! Creep!*

This was quickly becoming the most intense, unbearable camping trip Trevor had ever been on. *All I wanted to do was to show my family how much fun camping can be. After this, they'll never step foot inside of the woods again.*

Lying on the ground a few feet away from the van, Trevor saw a small boulder. *Perfect. Just what the doctor ordered.* Picking it up, he bombed it through the windshield of the van.

The ear shattering sound of breaking glass brought Roxanne back to her senses. "What on earth was that?"

"Daddy beat up the van!" Derrick tattled, while biting his tongue to keep from giggling.

"Trevor, why did you do that?"

Looking at his angry soulmate, Trevor smiled from ear to ear. "You wanted to eat, did you not?"

"Yes, but—"

"And I needed to calm down."

[30]

"Oh, really? I need to calm down too," Roxanne said, heading toward the van.

Oh no! This is gonna be good, Trevor told himself.

He watched intently as his normally calm and collected wife walked around to the front of it, turned backward, and kicked out the driver's side headlight.

I can't believe she had that in her, Trevor thought.

"You're right. That did feel good!" Roxanne said, before storming over to the passenger side and kicking out that headlight as well. For the first time since they had left the house, Roxanne had a look of pleasure on her face.

I must be losing my mind, Trevor told himself. *Deep down, I know this isn't funny. We're being stupid. But the van is trashed anyway and all we have is liability on it.*

Dalton and Derrick hesitantly joined the fun. Each of them picked up large branches from off the ground and started beating up the van as if it had been their archenemy. They broke the mirrors and taillights and put scratches all down the sides of the van.

After a few moments of observing the destruction from his place on the ground, Brady yelled, "Stop it! What are you doing?"

Roxanne, noticing for the first time that her eldest son was barely clothed, screamed "Brady Allen Clark, where are your breeches?"

Brady slowly stood to his feet. "They're in the back of the van," he said with a grin. "I'll get 'em right now."

With that, Brady picked up the largest rock he could find and completely shattered the back glass. "That felt awesome!"

Roxanne laughed out loud at the sight of the van and at the amount of fun everyone seemed to be having destroying the only means of transportation they had. "Are we crazy?" she asked, while laughing like she had not laughed since she was a teenager.

[31]

"No, we're not crazy. We're just a great big happy family!" Trevor chuckled.

Maybe this isn't going to be such a bad camping trip after all, Trevor thought. Even though he knew he and his family had acted completely irrationally and had stepped way out of their natural character, it was nice to see such bright, shining faces and to hear the sound of laughter in the air again.

Brady, on the other hand, was still eager to cover himself up. "Dad, what are we gonna do? We need the food and stuff out of the van and we still can't get the doors open. Even though the windows are busted out, the seats are all full of glass now. If we climb in we're gonna get cut to pieces."

"Brady's not hungry, Dad. He just wants to put some pants on before Cindy comes back," Derrick teased.

"Let's not start that again," their father scolded. "Let's try to be nice to each other for a little while."

"Sorry, Dad."

"It's not me you need to apologize to."

"Sorry, Mom," Derrick said sarcastically, letting out a soft giggle.

"He means you need to apologize to me, you little dork!" Brady said.

"Okay, sorry you little dork!"

"Oh, you're dead now!" Brady laughed as he ran toward Derrick, still half naked.

4
THE SPIRIT OF REVENGE

DERRICK SQUEALED like a little girl who had just witnessed a black snake swallowing a beady-eyed mouse. "No! I didn't mean it!"

"Help me, Dalton!" Brady chuckled, nodding toward the lake. "You get his feet and I'll get his hands."

For once, Roxanne did not intervene; she let the boys be boys. Trevor just watched and laughed as well. The only one not laughing was Derrick. He was too busy screaming, "Help! Put me down! Let me go! Mommy! Daddy! Somebody! Anybody! Help!"

The older boys dragged him toward the lake while Derrick squirmed around like a fishing worm being run through with a hook. He wasn't sure what they were up to, but one thing was for sure—he didn't like it. He tried kicking his way loose, but Dalton was determined to not let go. The boy's legs moved faster than they would have if he had been trying to outrun a mountain lion. He tried jerking his arms around just as fiercely, but to no avail. "Let me go!" he whined.

By the time they reached the lake, Derrick calmed down. *I get it,* he told himself. *They're just trying to make me scream. They're just going to do that stupid one, two, three thing and then they'll set me down. Why did I fall for that?*

Right he was. "One!" Dalton yelled as they swung him out toward the water.

"Two!" Brady called, swinging him out again.

Together, the bullies hollered, "THREE" while swinging him out a third time, but to Derrick's surprise, they let him go. He went under the water with such force that his back connected with the bottom of the lake. The boy hadn't held his breath or pinched his nose. He really didn't think they would do it. After all, he still had all of his clothes on.

As soon as Derrick's head popped back out of the water, it was obvious to Brady and Dalton that the boy was outraged. He was not laughing. His bottom lip jutted out so far it nearly rested on his chest. His normally bright brown eyes were now filled with an indescribable coldness.

"I'm going to pay you back. You just wait and see," Derrick told them. His words were as sharp as a razor blade. He was going to get the last laugh one way or another.

"You have to catch us first," Brady teased.

Brady nor Dalton were afraid of the eleven year old, but running was the normal thing to do after a mean stunt like the one they had just pulled. Brady just hoped his mom would think it was funny too. The last time he had played a joke like that one, she had grounded him for three weeks. Most of the time, his mother did not approve of anything he considered to be fun.

Derrick dogpaddled his way back to the shore, with his blood boiling even more rapidly than before. *When I get finished with them, they'll be begging for mercy. The guys would have been better off stealing honey from a hungry bear than to have picked on me.*

As he got closer to shore, the boy stood to his feet. Water poured from his t-shirt and clingy jeans. The water weighted his pants down so much he had trouble keeping them on his waist. To prevent them from falling down, Derrick had to hold onto the waistband of his jeans with both hands as he ran. His shoes made a sloshing sound with each and every step he took. "Come out you cowards!" he yelled.

From their view from the top of an apple tree approximately thirty yards in front of him, Brady and Dalton looked at each other and laughed. "Cowards? Isn't he the one that was screaming like a sissy just a few minutes ago?" Dalton asked.

"Shhh... He'll hear us," Brady whispered.

"What's he gonna do if he does hear us? It's not like the little nerd can climb a tree anyway."

"Good point. Still though, let's be quiet and see what he does when he can't find us."

All of the sudden, Derrick stopped in his tracks. He looked behind him, squatted close to the ground, and examined the soil for footprints. *Aha!* he thought. *I see tracks! One set of shoe prints and one set made by bare feet.*

Picking up some dirt with his fingers, he sniffed it, pretending to be an experienced tracker. Then he stood back up, licked his pointer finger, and held it up to the wind.

Oh yeah, these guys are toast!

"Aha! I see you!" Derrick yelled, looking right at them. He was as proud as a new mother hen. *Brady and Dalton might be older, but I'm smarter!*

In less than two minutes, he managed to catch up to his assailants. "At last, revenge is mine!"

Derrick's jeans had been drying out while he was running so he no longer had to hold onto the waistband. He ran up to the tree and tried to climb, but his arms were so scrawny he was unable to pull himself up like the other two boys had done.

"Whatcha gonna do now, little sissy?" Brady teased.

Derrick stood and thought for a moment while examining his surroundings. *There's more than one way to skin roadkill.*

The apple tree the boys had climbed was not very stout. Derrick grabbed a hold with both hands and started shaking it violently. "I'm gonna knock two apples out of this tree!"

"Stop it Derrick. That isn't funny!" Brady yelled, clinging to a limb for dear life.

This is awesome, Derrick thought. *Look at the fear in his eyes. He's not so tough anymore now, is he?*

"What's the matter, Brady? I thought you liked picking on

[35]

people?"

Dalton suddenly came up with a plan of his own. Grabbing an apple from a nearby branch, he dropped it right on Derrick's head.

"Hey, that hurt!"

"How about this then?" Dalton teased, before dropping another one.

Just as it was about to hit, Derrick looked up and the apple caught him right on the nose; he started to cry. That is, until he heard Dalton say, "Go ahead and cry, you little baby. That's what you do best."

"Or you could just suck your little thumb," Brady added.

Now you've done it, Derrick thought. He had been trying to break the habit of sucking his thumb since he was a baby. Until now, he had managed to keep his bad habit a well-kept secret. *He'll pay for this if it's the last thing I do.*

The thumb-sucking insult wasn't all he was upset about. *Who does Dalton think he is dropping apples on my head?* After a little more thought, he backed up a few steps and grabbed a handful of apples from the ground.

Two can play this game. He hurled the first one directly toward Dalton's nose, but missed his target. *It's only one strike. There's plenty more where that one came from.*

Taking better aim, he threw a second one toward his brother's forehead. Brady tried to block it with his right hand, but almost lost his balance. The apple struck him on the chin.

"Quit, you little creep. You're gonna make me fall," Brady demanded.

"Creep?" Derrick repeated. "Surely you didn't just call me a creep?"

With the third apple, he managed to hit Brady right in the eye—the same eye Cindy had blacked for him earlier that morning. Brady's legs lost their grip from the tree. He was suspended in the air with only his arms to keep him from falling. "Help, Dalton! Pull me up!" he screamed.

Dalton was a better climber than Brady. He managed to hold onto the tree with one hand while reaching another down to his friend. In no time, both boys were back in place on the apple tree.

"Derrick, you better stop. If Dad finds out about this, he'll tan your hide," Brady warned.

"I don't care. Taking a whippin' would be worth it to see you fall out of that tree." Picking up another apple, he said, "Open wide; maybe you can catch this one in that big mouth of yours."

"No, Derrick. Don't!"

It was too late. Derrick had already launched the largest apple he could find. It hit his brother's stomach with so much force that it knocked the wind out of him. Brady groaned and appeared as if he might actually cry at any moment.

Derrick wasn't finished yet. While Brady was holding his stomach and whining, he threw another one at Dalton. With his foot, Dalton tried to kick the apple back toward Derrick. Unfortunately, Brady rose up at the exact same moment and Dalton's foot struck Brady in the back of the head, causing him to slip off of the limb. Fortunately, Dalton grabbed a firm hold on his ankle as he went down. Brady's face smashed against the trunk of the tree as Dalton held him upside down.

Derrick was scared to death. Blood was pouring from Brady's face. *I wonder how much longer Dalton can hold him up? If Brady falls, he might break his neck. If he lives to tell Dad what happened, I'm dead. And if the police get involved—what then?*

Derrick started to run away and pretend nothing happened, but he wasn't that kind of a person. He knew he could never live with himself if he ran away and something tragic happened to his brother.

"Hold onto him, Dalton," Derrick ordered.

"I'm trying."

Brady's whole life flashed before him as he imagined hitting the ground head first. He was helpless. One hundred percent at the mercy of Dalton and Derrick. If they failed to help him, he was as good as dead.

Brady started remembering every harsh word he had ever spoken: telling Derrick he was a sissy, making fun of Dalton's weight, relentlessly picking on the nerds at school. He thought about every cruel trick he had ever played: convincing his little cousin her sunburn was going to cause all of her skin to fall off, replacing Derrick's shampoo with maple syrup, ringing the neighbor's doorbell just to run off before she could answer it. He thought about all of the times he had violated his conscience: telling his parents he was too sick to go to church just so he could stay home and play video games, shoplifting those baseball cards, letting Derrick take the blame for things he and Dalton had done wrong. The number of thoughts able to race through his mind in those brief moments was astounding. Now, without another breath, his life could be taken from him.

Derrick ran to the tree as quickly as possible. Putting both hands on the lowest branch he could grab, he managed to pull himself up into the tree. He got both feet on that branch and was able to climb to the next one.

"I can't hold him up much longer," Dalton complained. "He's gonna fall!"

"Seriously man, don't let go of me," Brady whimpered in a voice filled with terror.

Derrick wrapped his right arm around Brady's waist while holding onto the tree with his left arm. Just as Derrick's arm was securely around his brother, Dalton lost his grip. Brady's legs started falling and his whole body twisted sideways. Derrick wasn't strong enough to hold him up, but he managed to help him get twisted around so that when Brady fell, he landed on his feet. Brady couldn't keep his balance of course so he dropped to his hands and knees.

I'm alive, he thought. *Praise the Lord God Almighty. I survived!*

"Are you okay?" Dalton hollered from the top of the tree. His voice cracked from where he had been crying.

"I'm still breathing, so I guess that means I'm okay," Brady called back. He didn't sound okay though. He sounded like he was in agony.

Derrick jumped down and knelt by his brother's side. "I'm sorry for throwin' apples at you and for tryin' to shake you out of the tree."

Brady shocked his little brother by thanking him for saving his life. He knew Derrick had caused his fall to begin with, but he could have just chickened out and left the scene; it took some guts to stick around and help.

Derrick took his shirt off and used it to wipe some of the blood off of his brother's face. He wasn't bleeding profusely, but the tree had done a number on him.

Brady was shocked that Derrick wasn't passing out from the sight of blood. He remembered one time before when his dad had driven a nail through his thumb. Blood had squirted everywhere. Derrick passed out as cold as a cucumber! Somehow, this time was different. Derrick was growing up.

As the blood was cleared from Brady's skin, it became obvious that all of it was coming from two sources: a busted nose and a cut lip. It could have been a lot worse; he was very fortunate.

Just as Derrick wiped the last streak of blood from his face, Roxanne and Trevor walked up behind them. "What's going on, guys?" Roxanne asked.

"I climbed up in the tree trying to get an apple and I fell," Brady lied.

"And when he fell," Dalton added, "he busted his nose and lip. Derrick took off his shirt and started helping him clean up the blood."

Trevor and Roxanne looked at each other and then at the boys. They had never known Brady to be clumsy enough to fall out of a tree. They had never seen Derrick help Brady when he was hurt. They had never seen Dalton be so polite when speaking of Derrick.

Roxanne said, "Wow, I'm impressed. You boys are actually being nice to each other. How unusual."

[39]

"I'm proud of all three of you," Trevor hesitantly agreed, as he and Roxanne helped Brady up to his feet. Brady wrapped one arm around each of them and they helped him limp back to the tent.

Along the way, Brady told them how Jordan and Cindy had managed to steal his pajama bottoms and run off with them, about how they were planning on showing all of his friends what he was wearing, and about how humiliated he had been. Now though, after nearly losing his life, something as silly as teddy bear pajamas no longer seemed important.

Upon arriving back at camp, they were shocked to find Dalton Ryan's mother there to pick him up. She had driven out to the campsite after rumors had circulated throughout the town about how Mrs. Clark had been missing and then was found sleeping out away from everyone else.

"I don't know what's going on here," Mrs. Ryan snapped. "Your van is smashed to pieces. Your oldest son is walking around in his boxer shorts. Your youngest son has no shirt on and he's holding a bloody rag in his hands. All of you are filthy dirty." Mrs. Ryan was livid. "Dalton, come with me. We're going home."

"Mom, don't do this. Please let me stay. We're having a good time."

Really? What did they do, brainwash my son? Mrs. Ryan thought. "It looks like you're having a good time! If I let you stay here any longer, you'll end up dying at the hands of these people. They're outta their minds."

"Mrs. Ryan, can I please explain what's going on?" Roxanne asked.

Mrs. Ryan wasn't having any of it. She refused to listen to anything Roxanne had to say and threatened to contact Child Protective Services to report the endangerment of her own son as well as the Clark boys.

Dalton begged his mother to stop meddling. He reminded her that books should never be judged by their covers. She

[40]

hadn't been there. She hadn't seen what had taken place. He told her the Clarks had invited him along on their trip, they had made him feel like a member of their family, and now she was ruining everything.

Instead of absorbing anything her son said, Mrs. Ryan lectured him for back talking and demanded Dalton get in the car with her so they could leave. She was doing everything in her power not to explode.

First, I see those pants hanging on the flagpole in front of the school. Everybody says they're Brady Clark's. I get here and find him running around in filthy underwear, with a black eye, and a busted lip. My boy tells me they're all having a great time.

Even though she was ready to speed off, she had to ask about the pants. "Brady, there are some rumors circulating through town. Are those really your pajamas flying on the pole outside of Washington High?"

Brady didn't miss a beat. He said, "If you're not willing to give your son a chance to have a good weekend with us, then why should I bother answering your question."

"Brady Allen Clark," Trevor interrupted. "That is not any way to talk to another adult. You are to respect your elders. You know better than that."

Brady was just about to apologize when Mrs. Ryan started mouthing off again. "His elders? What do you mean by elder? Are you calling me a grouchy old woman?"

"No one said that to you ma'am," Roxanne spoke up. "But if the shoe fits, wear it!"

Roxanne never spoke harshly to anyone. Trevor and the boys were shocked.

"Fine. We're outta here. Don't be surprised if you hear from my attorney," Mrs. Ryan threatened as she and Dalton got into their car.

She had never been friends of the Clarks. She didn't really even know them. Sure, their kids went to school together. Sure, she had allowed Dalton to spend time with the Clarks on a regular basis. *But there's no excuse for this type of insane behavior.*

[41]

Mrs. Ryan spun her tires just to show how angry she was.

Trevor clapped his hands and the rest of the family joined him in giving her the applause she deserved.

Mrs. Ryan was furious. *Never in my life have I been spoken to that way before. Never have I seen such a chaotic mess that anyone dared to call fun. I don't know what it is about those people, but there's something about the Clark family that I just can't stand. I never have and never will. It was foolish of me to allow my son to befriend such lunatics. This friendship stops right now.*

5

LOSING CONTROL

ROXANNE SOUNDED WORRIED as she asked, "Do you really believe Mrs. Ryan will contact an attorney or Child Protective Services?"

Trevor said he wouldn't be surprised.

Child Protective Services, Derrick thought. *Sounds like a nice place.* "What does that mean?"

"It means Mrs. Ryan is putting her nose where it doesn't belong," Brady grumped.

Trevor said Mrs. Ryan had a right to be upset. She had trusted the Clarks to take care of her son and they had obviously let her down. Without seeing what had happened firsthand, it was perfectly understandable that she would sense the children had been placed in danger. Trevor admitted that more than likely he would have been frustrated too if he had been in her shoes.

"You mean because her feet stink?" Brady asked with a smirk on his face.

Raising his voice, Trevor told Brady that was enough. He reminded the fourteen year old that reaching his teenage years did not mean he had graduated from boyhood. He insisted boys not talk about women, or men for that matter, in such a disrespectful fashion.

He's going to get it now, Derrick thought. *I think I'll keep out of this.*

It was far from the first time Derrick had heard such a

[43]

lecture. From the time he was knee-high he and his brother had been taught to show reverence to adults—especially to adults who were in authority over them.

"Dad, I'm not trying to be disrespectful. I was just joking around. Besides, Mrs. Ryan isn't even here right now. She didn't hear me say a thing," Brady complained.

Derrick could relate. *What's the big deal? Mom and Dad hate Mrs. Ryan just as much as we do.* He wisely chose to keep those thoughts locked deep within the confines of his heart.

As he suspected, the conversation was far from over. Trevor's voice rose to the next level as he ordered his eldest son to close his mouth immediately. He demanded Brady not made another sound for the next thirty minutes.

"Did I make myself clear, Brady?"

The boy nodded his head, but didn't utter a word.

"Answer me, boy! Do you understand me?"

Brady again nodded his head quietly.

"I don't hear you, Brady. What's going on in that noggin of yours? I asked you a question and you better answer it now!"

"You told me not to make another sound for thirty minutes. Now you're mad at me for doin' what you said and not talking. What do you want me to do, Dad? Not make another sound or answer you?"

With his eyes switching back and forth from Trevor to Brady, Derrick was beginning to get annoyed. *Do we have to go through all of this again? Why does this have to go on and on and on?*

He was thankful when Roxanne attempted to intervene. "Brady, I think your father—"

"Roxi, stay out of this," Trevor snapped.

Ut-oh, Derrick thought. *Now Dad's gonna tell Mom he's sick and tired of her always babying us. Brady and I need a firm hand and it's his place to train us to be men.* Not only that, but Derrick knew Roxanne would simply bow out of the conversation and then things were really going to get heated.

To his surprise, Roxanne didn't give Trevor the opportunity to go any further. She insisted she would not stay out of it. Brady and Derrick were her sons just as much as they were his. She refused to sit there like a tree stump sticking up out of the ground and idly watch her husband and son argue like that. Yes, Trevor knew how to speak in a loud voice. That didn't mean she didn't have a tongue. It didn't mean she didn't have opinions or that she couldn't or wouldn't share them.

Trevor politely, yet firmly told his angry bride to back off and let him handle the matter.

Derrick wanted to walk away; it seemed like everyone was turning on everyone. It was bad enough for his dad and Brady to be going at it, but he hated it when his mom got in the middle.

"Don't talk to her like that," Brady said. "She didn't do anything to you." Brady glared at his dad as if to tell him he had better take it easy or else.

Unbuckling his belt and quickly sliding it out of his belt loops, Trevor told Brady he would not be spoken to in that tone of voice again. He did not enjoy disciplining the kids at their ages and tried his best not to, but he could not allow Brady to continue on in his defiance.

Brady glared at him; his eyes shifted back and forth from the doubled over belt in his father's hand to the angry look on his face. After a brief moment of silence, he offered an insincere apology.

Derrick couldn't believe his ears. *Surely Dad knows he doesn't mean that! After all of this arguing, it can't all simply be forgiven and forgotten.*

Derrick had kept his mouth closed as long as he could. "I think you should whoop him anyway, Dad. You shouldn't put up with him talkin' to you that way or runnin' his mouth about Mrs. Ryan. I think he should be punished."

He didn't care if Brady got grounded, had to stand in the corner, lost privileges, had to write repetitive sentences, or had to run in place for twenty minutes. There was something funny about his big brother being forced to submit to authority.

"You need to—" Brady started to say before Trevor cut him off and told him to shut his trap.

Trevor didn't stop there. He also warned Derrick to mind

[45]

his own business before he became the one rubbing his own red behind.

Roxanne was not about to stand for that. "What has gotten into you Trevor?" she shouted. "A few minutes ago we were all talking and laughing and enjoying each other's company. Now, all of the sudden, you're acting like a wild man."

"Me? Sixteen years ago you made a vow to obey me. You used to stand by that vow."

"Here we go again. You're the man of the house. Me and the boys are supposed to bow down to you like you're our king. I'm sorry Your Royal Highness; we must have temporarily forgotten how much better you are than us."

Derrick hated it when his parents argued. He hated it when he was getting lectured, when Trevor removed his belt, when Brady was being a smart aleck, and when his Mom was upset. He thought about clicking his heels together to see if they would magically transport him home.

Trevor blamed Roxanne for their children becoming so ill-mannered. It was never appropriate for a woman to backtalk her husband—especially not in front of her children. He reminded her that according to the Bible, she was supposed to be in submission to her husband.

"It also says husbands are supposed to love their wives, Trevor!" Roxanne shouted back at him.

Derrick wanted to tell them that in Sunday School he had been learning about forgiveness. He thought better of it though and decided maybe he would wait until later to discuss that. In silence, he watched as his mom and dad argued like school kids out on the playground.

Seeing his brother was clearly off the hook, Derrick quietly asked him if the two of them could take a walk.

Brady was quick to remind him that only moments ago, he had practically begged Trevor to give him a whoopin'. There was no way he planned on going anywhere to do anything with him. The only person he wanted to be around was Dalton and Mrs. Ryan had already taken him away.

That did it! Derrick's being the only family member to stay

out of the fighting was over. He told Brady the whole mess was one hundred percent his fault. If Brady hadn't been running his mouth about Mrs. Ryan, no one would have been arguing whatsoever and the idea of a whipping would not have come up at all.

A lump rose in Brady's throat and his voice cracked a little as he warned his little brother not to mess with someone bigger than he was.

"Ewww—I'm so scared, I'm shaking."

"That's it!" Brady yelled, just before punching his little brother right in the mouth.

Derrick didn't even try to fight back. Instead, he grabbed his lip and began to blubber like a baby as Roxanne immediately came to his defense.

"Brady Allen Clark! I can't believe you did that. Just a minute ago I was trying to defend you and look what you've done now!"

"Why do you always side with him?" Trevor yelled. "Are you blind and deaf or just stupid? Surely you saw Derrick provoking that?"

Roxanne said it would have been impossible for her to hear anything over top of all of her husband's shouting.

He turned the tables and told her she was the one screaming like a drunken piece of trash.

"Stop it. Please stop!" Derrick begged. "My lip's bleeding and I'm scared."

He had tears running down both cheeks as he held his mouth with both hands. He needed someone to show him a little bit of sympathy.

With too much on his mind and too much anger building up inside, Trevor told him it was just a little bit of blood and he needed to get over it.

After telling her husband he should be ashamed of himself for being so cold hearted, Roxanne motioned for Derrick to come to her so she could have a look at his face.

Derrick's crying intensified as he got closer to his mom.

[47]

Trevor didn't say another word to Roxanne or Derrick. He decided to shift his focus back to Brady. He looked his oldest son in the eye and said, "You come with me young man."

Ah, man, Brady thought. *I was hoping he'd keep being mad at Mom and forget all about me.* Reluctantly, he followed Trevor, but didn't speak a word. With each step, he wondered what Trevor was going to do to him. *There has to be a way to wiggle out of this.*

Brady knew it was wrong to hit his little brother, but he wouldn't admit that to anyone, especially not to dear ole Dad.

The two walked in silence until they were out of sight and earshot of the other two.

"Brady, you know what you did to your brother was wrong," Trevor began.

Brady mumbled the answer was both yes and no. Yes, he had always been taught better than to express his feelings with his fists. Of course he could have talked things out. The truth of the matter—he just didn't want to. Using his fists was easier. The reason the answer was partially no was because by punching Derrick, he had gotten his Mom and Dad to stop fighting. That, he said, had been driving him crazy.

Trevor saw right through that. He asked Brady why he was trying to place the blame on him and his mother. He asked how it was possibly his fault that Brady had lost his temper.

Like most teenagers would have done, Brady refused to back down. Hoping to lay a guilt trip on Dad, Brady told him it was his fault. The whole campout was his father's idea. It was he who had pointed out Roxanne drooling. It was he who refused to go home before the tree fell on the van.

Brady quickly realized his plan was not having its intended effect.

Trevor took a few steps closer to him and wore a look so fierce that most boys would have trembled just as the sight of him. He told his son that hitting his brother was an act he had performed of his own free will and that it takes a real coward to hit someone that much smaller than he was.

Temporarily, Brady forgot about his scheme of escaping Dad's wrath. He reminded him that it had been only minutes before when he had admitted to Roxanne that he had heard Derrick provoking the fight. It wasn't fair that he was the one to get punished when he was just defending himself. That's when he took things one step too far—asking Trevor if he had suddenly become bipolar or something, while taking a step closer to his dad.

The two were now face to face and their eyes glared at each other. Trevor admitted hearing Brady and his brother arguing. However, he said he had been mad at Roxanne and didn't mean everything he had said to her. He said Brady was just as much at fault as his brother was.

"Oh, so now you're a liar too? I see. When you get mad, it's okay for you to lie to Mom but when I'm upset, I'm not even allowed to express it. That's real fair, Dad. Don't ya think?"

"Didn't I tell you about that tone of voice?" Trevor asked.

I heard you loud and clear, Brady thought, without saying a word. *Surely you didn't expect me to stand there and let someone yell at me without saying anything back?*

"Do I need to take my belt off and use it?"

"I don't know what you need to do, Dad. Wasn't it you who just said it takes a real coward to hit somebody that much smaller than they are? I'm just a little bit bigger than Derrick is. You're twice my size, Dad. How big of a coward does that make you?" As soon as he stopped mouthing off, he realized he had made a big mistake; he had pushed Trevor over the edge.

"Have it your way," he replied, while fumbling with his belt buckle.

"You aren't going to touch me!" Brady said, simultaneously shoving his father backward.

Trevor tripped over a rock behind him and fell to the ground; Brady took off running as if someone was going to kill him.

"Brady, get your butt back here NOW!"

Ignoring his dad, he continued running without even

[49]

looking back. It was the first time he had ever laid hands on an adult. He was scared—like a tiny mouse who had just bitten a cat's paw. At the same time he was excited—like David must have been after killing Goliath.

Trevor didn't chase him. *He'll be back sooner or later. He doesn't like the dark, nor does he like being alone.*

With his blood boiling, Trevor walked back toward his wife and younger son. He wasn't sure what was happening to his family, but somehow he had to get things pulled back together.

Approaching the camp, he heard loud voices. It sounded like Roxanne and Derrick were arguing. "Let go of me now!" he heard Roxanne say.

"No, you let me go!"

Trevor ran toward the sound of their voices. When he got there, he was shocked to find both of them on the ground. Roxanne was lying on her back with Derrick sitting on top of her with his hands around her neck. Roxanne was grabbing a handful of Derrick's hair, trying to pull him off of her and with the other hand she was digging her fingernails into one of his arms.

Trevor ran over, gave Derrick a hard smack on the behind, and hollered, "Get off of her now!" Never before had Brady or Derrick struck their parents. Never had he seen the children he and his wife had brought into the world act so violently. He couldn't believe how badly their behavior had changed in one day.

Letting go of his mom, Derrick practically fell on the ground next to her. His face was blood red, his hair was a mess, and he was crying hysterically.

Roxanne was completely out of breath. She too had a face covered with tears, yet a look of relief that Derrick was finally off of her. Trevor helped his wife to her feet and Derrick stood up on his own. "What happened here?"

"Your son called me a stupid idiot and told me he hated me."

[50]

"Because she started squeezing on my lip where Brady punched me. She pushed in one spot and said, 'Does this hurt?' and I cried and told her it did and she said, 'What about this?' It hurt!"

"So you called your mother names and choked her because of that?"

"No, I choked her because after she hurt my lip and I told her she was a stupid idiot, she said she was gonna snitch on me when you got back. I told her I hated her and she covered my mouth. I grabbed her arm and tried to pull it off of me, but she covered my mouth so hard I couldn't breathe. I kicked her, trying to get loose, and she started wrestling with me. When we fell down, I tried to get away and she wouldn't let me. I don't know how my hands got on her neck, but she made me do it!"

What has gotten into my family? Trevor thought. *Before this trip, we hardly ever argued. The boys know better than to take part in this kind of behavior. How can one night under the stars transform everyone into monsters?*

"That is not how it happened," Roxanne snapped, still crying and obviously very upset.

Trevor, knowing his wife was at her rope's end, told her to allow him to handle the situation.

This time, Roxanne knew she was not in any position to deal with a rebellious child. She gladly handed over the reins.

Trevor told Derrick he was never to call his mother names and that he was never to say he hated her.

He was shocked when Derrick asked why he couldn't speak the truth. He said he really did hate his mother. After all, she had hurt his lip, covered his mouth, threatened to get him in trouble, and even wrestled with him. What was to like?

"You don't really hate your mother. Stop saying that," Trevor lectured, with a stern look on his face.

"I do hate her and for that matter I hate you too," Derrick argued.

Roxanne didn't speak; she didn't know what to do. She didn't know what to say—what she did know is her sons were out of control. She didn't like it one bit.

Trevor had seen and heard enough as well. He told Derrick he was acting like a spoiled brat. He was an extremely loved and well taken care of little boy. Not only did he have clothes to wear and food to eat, but he got tucked into bed every night and he was taken care of when he was sick. There was absolutely no excuse for his talking to his parents in that fashion.

Derrick, however, argued that he had an excellent reason for talking that way. He was always being accused of being a tattle tale. His dad always took Brady's side of every argument. It was obvious that his father didn't like him. Not only that, but his mom allowed his dad to talk down to him. Now, on top of everything, she was starting to treat him horribly as well and no one seemed to care.

"So I hate both of you!" he yelled.

"Don't say it again," Trevor ordered.

"IT!" Derrick shouted. "IT! IT! IT! IT! You told me not to say 'it' and I can say 'it' all I want to. IT! IT! IT! IT!"

6

DEVASTATING LIES

ROXANNE was beside herself. She watched silently as her husband wrapped his strong arms around Derrick, pulled him down on his lap, and covered his mouth as she had before.

"Now you listen here—"

Before his father could continue, Derrick opened his mouth and took a bite out of his pointer finger. Trevor shoved Derrick off of his lap, knocking him to the ground. Before Trevor had the chance to figure out what to do next, Derrick sprung to his feet and ran as quick as lightning just like Brady had done moments before.

Even through all of the commotion, Roxanne did not make a sound. She sat like a statue which had no feelings, no emotions, and no ability to move. Her cold eyes focused on nothing, yet seemed to be gazing into another world.

"I'm sorry honey," Trevor told her.

"Sorry for what? Marrying me?"

"What does that mean?"

"Are you sorry you married me? Do you wish you had gotten hitched to someone else instead or just stayed single?" Roxanne's lower lip quivered as if she was going to cry.

Trevor assured her that slipping that ring on her finger was the best thing he had ever done. He had been an idiot to push her to join him on the camping trip. She had been right to want to leave when it was inevitable that a storm was about to hit.

Roxanne wasn't so sure. *Have I ruined Trevor's life? He's a country boy. An adventurer. I'm a city girl. I don't enjoy the outdoors at all. Have I been holding him back?*

Even when they had been dating, Roxanne remembered her parents cautioning her that there were huge differences between her and Trevor. She had been raised in a rather well-to-do family whereas he had grown up a poor farm boy. When they were younger, her idea of fun had been to hang out at the mall, where his idea of fun was putting firecrackers in the mouths of toads and blowing them to smithereens.

They had talked about that long before they got engaged. Their friends told them it was normal for opposites to attract and they would have nothing to worry about. Their marriage had lasted sixteen years, but looking back, Roxanne wondered if it had all been a huge mistake.

"Are you sure you don't wish you had married someone more like you?" she asked.

"Yes I'm sure. Why do you keep asking me that? Do you wish you had married someone else?"

"No. Yes. I don't know. Maybe. Sometimes I wonder what would have happened if—" Roxanne paused.

"If what?"

Roxanne gulped so hard Trevor thought she had swallowed her tongue. "If we hadn't gotten married," she whispered.

"Why would you think about that? Are you considering divorcing me?"

"No, Trevor. It's just that we have drifted so far apart that I don't know how long our relationship can last. I feel like we're strangers—like we don't even know each other.

Roxanne could see the surprise on her husband's face. *Surely he has been thinking about this too,* she thought. *I'm sure by now the thought has at least crossed his mind. I refuse to feel guilty for voicing what we both know to be true.*

Trevor told her she was crazy. They had been married for nearly two decades and had dated for more than two years before that. He claimed he knew her better than she even knew herself.

[54]

That kind of talk can get a guy in trouble pretty quickly. Roxanne asked for proof. She said there was one thing she had wanted to do. Something she had dreamed of since they had gone out on their first date. It was a dream she had never let go of. Now, she wanted Trevor to prove he knew her better than she knew herself. Putting him on the hot seat, she asked him what she had longed for all of those years.

Trevor sat quietly for a minute, trying his best to remember what on earth she had been talking about.

"Well—?" Roxanne asked impatiently.

"You wanted to have a big white house with a white picket fence in front of it and walk-in closets, right?" Trevor replied.

"My point exactly."

"What do you mean?"

"Trevor, since the first time I met you, I always wanted to slow dance with you. I wanted you to hold me in your muscular arms and dance the night away. I don't even know how to dance. I always dreamed of standing on your feet. You know, the way a daddy teaches his daughter to dance. I have hinted to you for years that I wanted that and you haven't even noticed."

Trevor lied through his teeth and told her he knew all about her desire to dance. Somehow he thought she was talking about something more complicated. Something expensive perhaps.

Right, Roxanne thought. *You must think I was born yesterday. How gullible do you think I am?*

Trevor went on to tell her the reason he had never asked her to dance is because he had two left feet. He didn't think he was capable of dancing all by himself, let alone with his wife stomping on his toes. Chuckling, he said he would probably fall down and take her down right along with him.

Roxanne giggled. "Oh really? How romantic."

Trevor chuckled again. "May I have this dance, Miss?"

"Hmmm…, let me think."

"Roxi—,"

"Hmmm. I don't know. My husband might not approve."

"He won't mind at all. What he doesn't know won't hurt

him, right?"

"Good point. Let's dance," Roxanne said, grinning from ear to ear.

Through trial and error, the two of them discovered how to lock their hands and arms together and how to glide across their forest dance floor at the pace of a crippled snail. Looking deep into each other's eyes, they giggled like a couple of high school sweethearts. It was the first time in years Roxanne had felt such compassion toward the man she had made a commitment to so long ago.

They danced for quite some time before being startled by the sound of an approaching vehicle. They stopped dancing and turned around to see a police cruiser pulling up behind their van.

The officer couldn't believe his eyes. *Wow*, he thought. *These guys are a couple of deadbeats.*

"Are you the parents of Brady and Derrick Clark?"

"I'm afraid so," Trevor said. "What have they done, officer?"

"What have *they* done?" the officer repeated. "It's not the boys who have done anything."

"Oh, no!" Roxanne shrieked. "What happened to the boys? Are they okay?"

Furious, the officer told Trevor and Roxanne to cut the innocent routine. Their boys had been both neglected and abused. He informed them that Brady and Derrick were in the care of the State of North Carolina until further notice. He had come to the campsite for the sole purpose of taking Trevor and Roxanne to the station for questioning.

"Officer, please let me explain," Trevor replied.

Oh this is a story I wanna hear, the officer told himself. *I'm sure things aren't really what they appear.*

He dared them to explain why their fourteen year old son was running around the woods in his underwear. Why he had no shoes or socks on. Why he had sores and cuts all over his feet from walking around the woods that way. He demanded an explanation as to how their eleven year old had gotten fingernail marks all down his arm and a busted lip. Not only that, but he dared them to explain why their boys looked like they hadn't bathed in days.

"Officer, did you ask the boys what happened?" Trevor asked.

Seriously? These people never give up, do they? If they want to play this game, we'll play!

The officer told them he had indeed questioned the boys. He said Brady told him Trevor had gotten in his face and threatened him with violence. About his little temper tantrum. About he and his wife fighting in front of him. Supposedly, Brady had said he was so afraid of his dad that he ran for his life.

Brady had reported hearing his brother being tormented by his mom as his own feet and legs were being pricked by briars and cut by tree branches as he ran. Derrick confirmed the entire account. He had gone so far as to report that his folks were so busy fighting with one another that they hadn't even attempted to break up their argument, which would have prevented him from getting a busted lip.

"I know how this sounds, officer," Trevor said.

"I know. I've heard it before. You're good parents, right?"

"Please, sir. This is just a big misunderstanding."

"I guess Derrick was making up a tall tale about you beating him when he and his mother were arguing? Did he fib about your wife digging her fingernails into his arm? I suppose Brady was lying about you getting ready to thrash him with your belt before he ran off? I suppose he just decided to walk around with no shoes and socks and tear up his feet that way all by himself? I guess when I pulled up, I didn't see you two dancing around with each other while your children were lost in the wilderness? Please, people. Don't expect me to believe anything you have to say."

Walking to the back of his squad car and opening the door, the officer asked the Clarks to take a seat. He explained that they weren't necessarily being placed under arrest—yet.

[57]

Roxanne looked at Trevor as if she expected him to get her out of this. Or to tell her everything was going to be okay.

Instead, he hung his head, walked silently to the cruiser, and got in.

Roxane followed her husband's lead and got in the car without making the situation any worse than it already was.

While their parents were being taken to the police station, Brady and Derrick were being questioned by Ms. Simms, a social worker with Child Protective Services. She told the boys their department had received a telephone call earlier that day from a lady who claimed her son, Dalton Ryan, had been with them for the majority of the camping trip.

She said Mrs. Ryan told her she had saw Brady outside in his boxers when she arrived to pick up her son and that the shirtless Derrick had been holding a bloody rag in his hand.

Enjoying the attention, Derrick began to explain about his bloody shirt, but Brady cut him off before he got far into the story at all.

Brady had been giving things a lot of thought. *Dad's gonna wear me out if I go back home. I disrespected both him and Mrs. Ryan, I punched Derrick, and I knocked Dad down and ran away. There's no way Dad's going to show me any mercy on this one.*

Before this whole episode, the worst thing he had ever done was steal that stupid pack of baseball cards. He had learned his lesson and would never do that again. But still, if Trevor had been that hard on him over shoplifting, he didn't want to know what he would do about this kind of behavior. *If I can stall things for a while, maybe he'll cool off a bit.*

"Yeah, I was up in a tree," Brady said, winking at his brother. "Dad had told me not to climb it. When he saw me up there, he said he was gonna beat me black and blue. I was scared. I begged him to forgive me and told him I was sorry. Dad started shaking that tree as hard as he could until I fell to the ground. He jerked me up to my feet and backhanded me. The bottom part of his hand hit my nose and I started bleeding.

[58]

Derrick let me use his shirt to get myself cleaned up."

Derrick had a look of shock on his face.

"Is that what happened, Derrick?" Ms. Simms asked.

Derrick glanced over at Brady. Brady was glaring at him and nodding his head. *Go along with the story. Come on, you can do it.*

After a brief pause, it appeared Derrick had read his mind. "Yes, ma'am. That's exactly how it happened."

Moving on, Ms. Simms told the boys they looked like they were starving half to death. She asked them what they had eaten that day and seemed annoyed at hearing about the cookies and brownies they had for breakfast.

When Brady told her they hadn't had any lunch, Ms. Simms looked like she was getting downright angry.

She changed the subject and asked how long it had been since the boys had bathed.

Before Derrick had a chance to answer, Brady decided to spoon some icing on the cake. "About two weeks or so. Mom doesn't like people wasting things and she says it wastes water to bathe too often. Usually every two weeks or so I take a bath and then when I get out of the tub, Derrick gets in. Even then we share the same tub of water to make sure we don't harm the environment too much."

Again, Derrick looked surprised. Still though, he was getting Brady's drift. Playing along, he said, "We don't wash clothes too often either. Mom says we don't need to wash 'em unless they're getting kind of hard. You know, when that green stuff starts growing on 'em."

Ms. Simms looked absolutely disgusted. Derrick winked at Brady as if to say, "See, you're not the only one who knows how to play this game."

"Boys, how are you normally disciplined at home? Like when you do something wrong, how is that handled?"

Brady didn't have to be the one to lie this time. Derrick had figured it out. He told her he would get smacked in his mouth if he told a lie. He said sometimes his mom would smack him, sometimes his dad would, and sometimes they both did it, one right after the other.

"What about the belt? Brady, you said you were afraid your dad was going to hurt you with the belt and that's why you ran away. Has he ever used a belt on you before?"

Brady thought for a moment. *Dad has definitely used the belt on me. He's given me three, four, and sometimes even five licks at a time.* It had been a while, but a belt had been applied to his derriere quite a few times in the past.

If I tell it like that though, Ms. Simms might not think it's such a big deal. There was no way Brady wanted to face his dad this soon. He had to change a few details.

"Yes, ma'am, he has. He uses the belt on me a lot. Like if I come home from school and he finds out I missed a word on my spelling test, he'll give me a whoopin'," Brady said.

Ms. Simms, as hard as she tried to show no emotion, looked highly upset. "For misspelling one word? How many words are normally on your test?"

"Twenty-five."

"So what happens if you miss more than one word?"

"Then Dad will give me more licks and harder."

"How many licks would you get and where would he hit you with the belt?" Ms. Simms asked.

"It just depends on what kind of mood he's in. If he has a good day, I might just get five or ten for each word I get wrong. But if he and Mom have been fighting or if he has had a bad day at work, I might get twenty or thirty for missing one word. One time, I completely bombed a test. I think he gave me somewhere around one hundred and fifty or two hundred licks. He told me I better not let anybody at school find out about the marks he left on me or he'd do it all over again."

The questioning went on for hours. Every question was answered with a tall tale. Brady and Derrick were determined their parents were going to learn not to ever tell them what to do again. Respect was a two way street. If they wanted respect, they had to give respect. Never again were they going to be ordered around like robots.

7

EMPTY NEST SYNDROME

FALLING APART, Roxanne stretched herself out on Derrick's bed, saturating his blankets with tears. *I can't believe this is happening. Only bad parents are supposed to have their children taken from them. We aren't bad people! This is not fair!*

Roxanne thought back to a conversation she once had with a distant cousin. Crystal had posted something on Facebook about Child Protective Services stealing her children. Roxanne sent her a private message and asked what had happened.

When Crystal told her their pediatrician had reported them because of an unexplained bruise on her toddler's back, Roxanne had asked where the bruise came from. She didn't believe Crystal when she said her kids were always playing around and she wasn't sure where that particular bruise came from.

I was so judgmental. I even told her the state would not have removed her children if they were not one hundred percent certain that abuse had occurred.

She wanted to crawl in the deepest cave she could find, bury her face, and never come out again.

Trevor came in and sat on the bed next to her, without speaking a word. He gently rubbed her back, while trying not to let his own emotions get the best of him.

"It's just not fair!" Roxanne said. "How can they just take our babies like that?"

She and Trevor had already discussed the topic at least a dozen times. Deep inside, she understood that the children she had carried for nine months, whose dirty diapers she had changed, whose spit-up she had cleaned, had made up lies about her and Trevor. She knew how Mrs. Ryan had gotten the wrong impression and about how bad things looked. *But still, what ever happened to being innocent until proven guilty? We didn't do anything wrong!*

The phone rang.

Knowing his wife was in no condition to answer, Trevor got it.

"Trevor, this is Pastor Franklin."

"Hi, Pastor. I'm assuming you've heard the news."

"We did. I just wanted to let you know we love you and your family and we're praying for you."

Trevor tried to reply, but he got choked up. He could no longer hold back his tears.

Roxanne rolled over and asked him what was wrong, but he found himself speechless.

A few hours later, Roxanne called her mother to cry on her shoulder about everything that had taken place. Even though it was obvious Mrs. Smith was disheartened at the news, she was a strong woman. A woman of faith. A prayer warrior.

"Baby, it's going to be okay," she said. "Our God can do anything! Do you remember that time when your daddy lost his job when you were just a wee little thing?"

Roxanne remembered alright. She was in sixth grade and it was exactly one month before her class trip to Washington D.C. She could still picture her dad walking in the door that night. He had tears rolling down his cheeks. Her mom asked what was wrong and he told her his company had reduced its workforce by twenty percent and he had been let go.

She remembered watching as her father, who had always been the breadwinner in the home, crumbled. He said he didn't know how they were going to make ends meet. There was enough money in savings to last them for a couple of weeks, but that was it.

[62]

Seeing her father in such a condition had broken Roxanne's heart. She volunteered to back out of her sixth grade trip, knowing her family could no longer afford it.

Her praying momma wasn't about to see her daughter miss out on a once-in-a-lifetime opportunity like a sixth grade trip.

She could still see her mom kneeling there in the middle of their living room floor. She clutched her Bible in her left hand and raised her right one high in the air.

"Dear God Almighty! You didn't bring us this far to let that nasty ole devil get his way and ruin this family. Lord, we know you don't want this dear, sweet child to miss out on her D.C. trip. We know you aren't going to let us go hungry. We have seen you work miracles in the past and Lord, we're asking you to do it again!"

Chills had crept all up and down Roxi's spine as she listened to her momma pray that evening. That prayer was only the beginning.

In the mailbox, the very next morning, was a check for $1,000 from the company that held the family's mortgage. Roxanne struggled to remember the details, but it seemed like it had something to do with some escrow that had been accumulating with their payments. Two days later, her father's former employer called; a friend of his was looking to hire a few good men at a lumber yard.

Sure enough, her dad got the job and she was able to go on her trip after all. No one dared say it was a coincidence. Momma would have strung them up by their ears and beat them like piñatas.

"I remember, Mom. Will you pray about this situation?"

"Honey, you know I will. But what about you? Have you been praying? You are the woman of that house! You are Trevor's helpmeet. Brady and Derrick's mother. God put you in that place for a reason. You have an important role. Have you been talking to the Lord?"

Roxanne's heart sank. Honestly, she hadn't even thought about bringing her problems to God. Somehow, over the years

[63]

her faith had dwindled. Sure, she was a Christian, but somehow she had come to rely on herself and on her husband for providing for their needs—not God.

Maybe that's why we're going through this. Maybe God brought this trial into our lives just to bring us back to him, she thought.

Roxanne thanked her mom for the wonderful advice, got off the phone, and dropped to her knees.

"It's been a long time since I've called out to you, God. I need your help! My babies are gone. I know Trevor and I are somewhat at fault. Okay, maybe we're a lot at fault. We messed up. Not only did we make some stupid decisions while we were camping, but we've failed as parents. We've become somewhat of a dysfunctional family. God, I'm sorry for drifting so far from you. You provided me with a husband who loves me dearly, a wonderful marriage, beautiful children, and blessings I've never been worthy of."

Following her momma's example, she lifted both hands up toward Heaven. "God, please forgive us. Even though I realize I'm not in any position to ask you for anything, I'm going to ask anyway because I know you're a merciful God. Lord, please. I'm begging with everything in me. Please, please, please give us our family back. We will come back to you. We will serve you. We will train those children up the right way. Please, God! You know I would never lie to you. Please help us!"

After wrapping up her prayer, Roxanne wiped the tears from her face and walked downstairs to find Trevor. As soon as they made eye contact, Trevor set an old family photo back down on the mantle.

"What were you doing?" Roxanne asked.

"Just dusting off the mantle."

"You? Dusting?"

"Okay, you caught me," Trevor said. "I was just looking at some old pictures and thinking about how much I miss the boys already. I can't help myself."

8
WARDS OF THE STATE

BACK AT her office, Ms. Simms told the boys she had found a temporary foster home for them to go into for a few days until a more suitable long-term arrangement could be made.

They would be staying with a single foster mother by the name of Samantha Hilton. Ms. Simms said Samantha had been a foster parent for the agency for several years and already had one other foster child in the home.

A foster home? Brady had heard horror stories about foster homes. *So we're going to move in with some rich snob that gets paid for watching us. Probably doesn't even like kids.*

Ms. Simms put the boys in her Mercedes and drove them to toward Ms. Hilton's place. On the way, she stopped at a used clothing store and bought each of them a new outfit so Brady would not have to meet his first foster family in only his boxers and so Derrick wouldn't show up wearing filthy rags.

As they pulled into the driveway, the boys were disappointed to learn that Ms. Hilton lived in an older, single-wide trailer. It was located inside of a mobile home park with no yard to play in and broken down cars were parked along the street. It was nothing like the home they had just came from.

"I don't want to go in," Brady argued.

"I'm sorry, Brady, but you have to stay somewhere," Ms.

[65]

Simms replied.

As they were stepping out of Ms. Simms's car, Samantha walked out onto the porch. She was an older lady who had already put her hair up in curlers for the evening.

I bet she's been wearing that same dress since the sixties, Brady thought. *I know Derrick and I wear hand-me-downs and stuff Mom gets at the thrift store, but there are times when wardrobes need a makeover and I think it's about time somebody let this old woman know her clothes are way out of style.*

With a smile adorning her face, Samantha said, "Hello there. Look at these fine looking young lads."

As she finished her sentence, Daniel, her other foster child, stepped out on the porch behind her. He looked rough. His blue jeans were sagging down to his knees. A thick gold chain hugged his neck. He had a bandanna wrapped around his head. "Wassup guys?"

"Nothing. What's up with you?" Derrick replied.

Brady glared at him without uttering a word.

"Brady and Derrick, I'd like to introduce you to your new temporary foster family," Ms. Simms announced, as if it was the best day of their lives.

Brady gave her a dirty look and then glared at Daniel. *I don't like him already. The guy looks like a gangster.* He didn't like Samantha either. *Looks like she could keel over at any minute. That pasty white body of hers. That nasty, flabby skin bouncing under her arms every time she moves.*

Ms. Simms walked the boys inside and talked to Samantha for several minutes. She assured her the boys would be there for a maximum of one week and that if she had any problems, not to hesitate to call the agency's crisis line.

"Until you hear otherwise from us, the Clark children are not allowed to have contact with any of their friends or relatives," Ms. Simms told her, before leaving the trailer a few minutes later.

No contact? With our parents? Is that legal? Brady thought.

There wasn't much time to think.

Ms. Simms asked Daniel to show them to their sleeping

quarters.

Brady almost laughed as he watched the style with which Daniel carried himself. He walked like a penguin, more than likely to keep his pants from falling down around his ankles. Brady couldn't help but wonder if his pants were sagging that low because he had pooped in them and all that weight was pulling them down. He decided his first day there was probably not the best time to bring this up.

"Your room is right here next to the bathroom," Daniel informed them as he opened their bedroom door.

Not much to look at, Brady thought. It was every bit as luxurious as he assumed it was going to be. An old set of wooden bunkbeds, a small built-in two drawer dresser, and a closet too small for a skeleton to be hanging in. The walls were an off-white color and had no decorations on them—no shelves, pictures, or designs of any kind. The room was boring to say the least. Worst of all, he had no privacy. He had to share the room with his bratty little brother.

"Why do you get your own room?" Brady asked.

"Cause I'm older than you, Dawg."

"I doubt that. How old are you?"

"How old are you?" Daniel asked.

"I'm fourteen, but I asked you first."

"Take it easy big guy. I'm fifteen."

"Look Droopy Drawers, my name's not Dawg and my name's not Big Guy. It's Brady. Got that?"

"What's your deal, punk? How you gonna creep up in my crib and start talkin' smack?"

"Your crib? That'd explain the sagging breeches. You need me to have Samantha come change your diapers?"

"You better watch your mouth, kid. I'm tryin' to play it cool with you, but if you keep it up, you're gonna get a beat down."

"From who?"

"Stop, Brady! Don't do this," Derrick whined.

"Yeah, listen to your lil bro. He's obviously smarter than you so why don't you follow his advice and quit torturing me

[67]

with that funky breath!" Daniel said.

"Boys, what's going on back there?" Samantha called from the living room.

"Nothing, Samantha," Daniel lied. "I was just helpin' these guys get used to their new place."

"Good. Just making sure everything's okay."

"Peace out BRADY. See ya around, Derrick. Keep your smelly brother in line for me, will ya?" Daniel said.

"I'll try."

With that, Daniel left the room and closed their door behind them.

What a punk, Brady thought. *I can't stand the way he looks, the way he talks, or the way he walks for that matter. Does he think he owns the place?* Even if he did own it, which he didn't, it was nothing but a dump. As far as Brady was concerned, this foster home was not going to cut it. He didn't even know if he could make it work for a week.

"What do we do now, Brady?" Derrick asked after Daniel left the room.

"What do we do about what?"

"I mean, what do we do? Do we have to stay in here? Should we go back to the living room? Should we go take a bath? Should we watch television? I don't know what to do."

"I don't care what *you* do. I'm going to bed."

"Without dinner? Aren't you hungry, Brady?"

"No. I'm not."

"I am. Come in here with me so I can get something to eat," Derrick pleaded.

"Go get it yourself. I'm goin' to bed."

Derrick continued to plead, saying he was scared and he didn't know those people.

Brady didn't know them either, nor did he care to. He told Derrick if he was hungry enough, he would go eat on his own. He just wanted to be left alone.

Derrick told him that was fine. He could just go to sleep. As a matter of fact, he didn't care if Brady ever woke back up. Before leaving, he made sure to let Brady know he was not a very good big brother.

Without saying a word, Brady hopped up onto the top bunk and laid down.

"Hey, that's my bed!" Derrick complained.

"Think again, ya little shrimp."

"I'm telling Mom!"

"Mom's not here!"

"Fine! I'll tell Samantha," Derrick replied, stomping out of the room.

Brady couldn't decide if he was hungry or not. He wasn't accustomed to losing his appetite. He wasn't sure what was going on with his body, but he didn't feel like himself anymore. He didn't like being a foster child. He didn't like living in a trailer park. He didn't like life in general for that matter.

While Brady was trying to fall asleep, Derrick found Samantha sitting on the sofa, intrigued by a movie she was glued to. Plopping down beside of her, he said, "Brady took my bed."

"Excuse me, young man. Did I give you permission to talk to me?" Samantha asked hatefully.

Derrick gave her a confused look. *Is she joking?* It sure didn't look like it. "I'm sorry, ma'am. Do I have to get permission first?"

"Of course you do. Show a little bit of respect."

"Yes, ma'am."

"Now what was it you were saying about Brady? Did you say he is making his bed?"

"No, I said he took my bed!"

"Oh, I see. Let me guess, he's on the top bunk and that's where you wanted to crash. Am I right?"

Smart lady, Derrick thought, before admitting that was the problem and insisting Samantha make him get up.

To his surprise, Samantha told him to grow up and leave Brady alone.

Great, she's just like Dad! Always gonna take Brady's side.

[69]

Derrick wondered why his mom was the only one who always sided with him. *I miss Mommy*, he thought.

Samantha, not even noticing the boy was beginning to feel homesick, told him to tell Daniel it was time for his shower.

Derrick was starting to not like this place any more than Brady did. Still though, he did what he was told. Slowly, he walked down the hall to Daniel's room. The door was closed; Derrick barged right in. "Time to take—"

"Get outta my room!"

"Samantha said—" Derrick tried again before being told off.

"I don't care what Samantha said. I said to get outta my space and I suggest you get to steppin'!"

"Fine. Whatever," Derrick mumbled before going back to the living room.

"Did you tell him?" Samantha asked.

"I tried, but—"

"I don't want to hear any excuses. Did you tell him or not?"

"No, ma'am, but—"

"Did I not just tell you that I do not want to hear any excuses? Have your parents not taught you any better manners than that? When I tell you to do something, I mean for you to do it. Now go back in there and tell Daniel to take his shower, NOW!"

Derrick started to cry again. *Nobody listens to me. Not my brother, not Daniel, not Samantha. No one cares what I think. No one even wants to talk to me. Why does everybody just want me to go away?*

Slowly, he moseyed back to Daniel's room and barged in again. "Samantha said—"

Jumping up, Daniel charged toward him, shoving Derrick out of the room and causing the boy to hit the back of his head against the wall.

Derrick allowed himself to slide down into the floor where he cried like a baby.

"Awww... Poor little fellow," Daniel teased. "Maybe that'll teach you to stay off my turf like I told you."

I hate my life. I wanna go home. I hate it here! Derrick thought.

Samantha hollered again. "Daniel! Did that boy tell you it's time for your shower?"

"Nope. Didn't tell me anything!"

"What? You have to be kidding me!" Samantha yelled. "Derrick, get in here!"

Derrick couldn't believe this. Walking toward the living room, his pity party continued to grow. *No matter what I do, somebody's mad at me. Here I go again—just like at home. I'm about to be punished when I didn't do anything wrong. I tried to do what she told me. It's not my fault Daniel wouldn't listen.*

As soon as he arrived in the living room, Samantha chewed him out. "I told you to tell Daniel to take his shower. I'm tired of you not listening to me. I'll cut you some slack tonight, but this had better not happen again. We're going to get you something to eat. After that, you're going to take your shower. After that, it's off to bed. Understand?"

9

A LESSON IN REBELLION

Since it was getting late in the evening, Samantha did not cook a big meal. Instead, she made him a grilled cheese sandwich and threw in some potato chips for a side and a glass of ice water.

"Can I have some pop?" Derrick asked.

"Now Derrick, if you could have some soda, which is what it is rightfully called, do you think I would have just poured you some water?"

"Sorry." *I wonder how many years of practice it took her to become such an old scrooge,* he thought.

As soon as Derrick finished his meal, he and Samantha heard the water turning off in the restroom.

Samantha told him to empty his plate and get in the shower.

That's not fair. Brady didn't have to take a shower. Why do I have to? Knowing he was already wearing thin on Samantha's nerves, he decided not to make a big deal out of it.

Instead of talking back, he took his time walking to the restroom. It was actually quite a relief to go in there and close the door. It felt wonderful to isolate himself from all of the hateful people in the household. *Finally, peace at last!*

At his house, Derrick had always taken baths, but since Samantha was so picky and had specifically told him to take a shower, the youngster decided he had better do just that. He took his new clothes off, stepped into the tub, and jerked the shower curtain closed. He had never used a shower curtain before so he wasn't sure if he should put it on the inside of the tub or on the outside. To give him more space, he decided to put it on the outside. And so it wouldn't be quite so dark in there, he left one end partially open.

To his unpleasant surprise, Daniel had used every drop of hot water. It was bad enough that he didn't get to soak in the tub, but taking a cold shower was not his idea of bathing. Still though, Derrick knew he was filthy so he washed the best he could. Using the shampoo lying on the side of the tub, he washed his hair and made sure to use plenty of soap like Mom had always told him.

He could hear her voice rattling through his head. If she was at Samantha's, she would be undoubtedly be saying, "Make sure to scrub your armpits. Don't forget to get your back or in between your toes. Don't worry about using too much soap. You need to be squeaky clean. I'm sure you don't want to smell like Uncle Lester."

Right she would be too. Nobody in his right mind would want to smell like Uncle Lester. He worked at a fish hatchery and always reeked of trout. For whatever reason, he smelled like dead ones. He remembered hearing his grandma tell Uncle Lester on numerous occasions that he needed to shower, put on deodorant, and half a bottle of cologne before attending family functions. No, sir. He did not want to smell like Uncle Lester.

After giving himself a good scrubbing, Derrick turned the water off and opened the curtain. He stepped onto the floor and *whoosh!* It was soaked. Derrick slid and fell right on his tushie. He fell so hard a thud could be heard throughout the trailer.

"What's going on in there?" Samantha yelled.

Too embarrassed to tell her about the fall, Derrick hollered back that everything was okay and she had nothing to worry about.

"It didn't sound like 'nothing' to me. What happened?"

"I fell. Okay, I fell!"

"You didn't tear up anything, did you?"

How rude. She didn't even ask if I'm okay. All she's worried about is her stuff. "No, ma'am," he told her.

Slowly, Derrick got back to his feet before looking around for a towel. As luck would have it, he didn't see one anywhere. He looked under the sink; it was empty. There was no feeling quite like being in an unfamiliar house with unfamiliar people more naked than a shaved kangaroo and having nothing to cover up with.

Maybe I should just put my clothes back on without drying off, he thought, while reaching down to pick them up. *Great! They're soaked! Now what do I do?*

What a mess he had on his hands! He could tell Samantha despised him. How could he tell her he had no dry clothes to wear and no towel? Brady had already told him to stop bothering him. Daniel had already hurt him once.

"Samantha! Can you bring me a towel?" he finally yelled.

"Not right now. I'm in the middle of a movie. If I get up, I might miss something."

Shivering, Derrick hollered that his clothes were all wet. He had nothing to put on and no way to dry off.

Samantha told him he was a big boy and he could figure out something on his own.

"Keep it down in there, Derrick," Brady fussed. "I'm tryin' to sleep."

Derrick couldn't believe it. His own brother couldn't have cared less that he was stuck in the bathroom wet and cold, not to mention nude. He thought about coming out of the bathroom in his birthday suit, but that would be way too humiliating.

All of the sudden, the bathroom door burst open—it was Daniel. "So how do you like it when people just barge in without knocking? Kind of rude, huh?"

Derrick held his sopping wet clothes in front of him, trying to hide as much of his body as possible. "At least you were

[74]

dressed!"

"But I could've been changing clothes or something. You didn't even consider that, now did you, little man?"

"No I didn't and I'm sorry. Now please get out of here."

"Get out? Oh, you mean you don't want the towel I brought ya?" Daniel chuckled, turning to leave the room.

"Yes, I mean, no. I mean, I want the towel. Please." Derrick whined.

Daniel did the right thing, but told Derrick he owed him big time.

Derrick promised to return to the favor.

After getting himself dried off, Derrick wrapped the large red bath towel around him and walked back to Daniel's room. He put his hand on the doorknob, before thinking better of it and knocking. "Can I come in?"

"What do you want?" Daniel barked.

"Just to talk."

Derrick was surprised when Daniel actually told him he could come inside. He was even more surprised to check out the nice setup he had in there—his own television, a telephone, a stereo, a miniature pinball machine. You name it, he had it.

"What are you listening to?" Derrick asked.

"A new album called 'None of Your Business.' What, are you writin' a book or something, little man?"

"None of Your Business'? Who sings that?" Derrick asked.

"No, idiot. I mean it's none of your business what I'm listening' to. What'd you wanna talk about?"

"I don't know. Why'd you bring me that towel? You were mean to my brother earlier so why are you being nice to me?"

"I felt bad cause I knocked you into the wall earlier," Daniel told him. "Just thought I'd do something to make that up to ya."

"Where does she keep the towels anyway?"

"Normally, the old battle-axe keeps them in the hall closet. However, I got the one I gave you from Samantha's dirty laundry basket," Daniel laughed.

"What? You mean I have a towel wrapped around me that

[75]

Samantha used the last time she was in the tub? That's gross! Well, just remember that while ago I promised I'd pay you back. I meant that too," Derrick said, with an evil grin on his face.

Derrick had a lot of thinking and planning to do. Daniel had played a pretty dirty trick on him and somehow he had to return the favor. He wasn't much of a practical joker, but Brady was. *Maybe he'll help me come up with a plan.* Derrick decided to ask him about it in the morning.

While the gears of his brain were turning once more, a loud bang followed immediately by a scream suddenly filled his ears. "Owww," Samantha screeched. "Who got this floor all wet and didn't dry it up? I just slipped and fell."

"Sorry, ma'am," Derrick apologized.

"I hurt my back. I don't think I can get up. Get in here and help me, boy."

What goes around comes around, Derrick thought. *Dad always said respect is a two way street. She didn't respect me, so I'm not about to respect her.* It wasn't quite what his dad had meant, but that didn't matter. That was how he planned to apply it.

"I can't," he replied.

"Why can't you?"

"Remember earlier when you couldn't get me a towel because your movie was on? Well now I'm in the middle of a conversation with my new friend, Daniel, so I'm too busy to help you."

"Why never in my life have I met such a rude little boy," Samantha yelled. "You get in here right now and help me up since you made this mess."

"Why don't you come in here and make him?" Daniel laughed.

"Daniel! You know better than to talk to me like that," Samantha yelled.

Daniel ignored her. He was not always as compliant with her as she wanted the boys to think. Daniel was somewhat of a rebel. He didn't take kindly to adults telling him what to do or what not to do.

He had been in foster care for four years. His biological father left him when he was two. His biological mom was a drug dealer. She taught him street smarts. Part of what he learned from her was not to take anything from anybody.

His mom had been a fireball. On more than one occasion, he witnessed her brawling with other women and at least once, with a man.

That's how he ended up in foster care. His mom was doing her nails while sitting at a stoplight when a guy behind her started laying on the horn. She threw her car in park, jumped out, and stormed back to his vehicle. She jerked his door open and popped him right in the mouth.

The next thing they knew, the police were on the scene. They found drugs in her car. Ever since then, she had been trying to get him back into her care. She had gotten clean, maintained steady employment, and had a house. However, she could not seem to get along with the social worker overseeing the case and the lady had always come up with another loophole she demanded his mom jump through.

Daniel had no respect for that social worker, for Samantha Hilton, or for anyone else who aided those who were keeping him away from his mother.

"Guys please, I need some help in here!" Samantha yelled.

"Did you tear up anything when you fell?" Daniel asked.

"No, I did not. Now come help me up!"

"Would you all quiet down? Some of us are trying to sleep," Brady fussed.

"Hold your horses Samantha, I'll be there in a minute," Daniel said.

"Never mind. I'll get up on my own."

"Is she always so mean and hateful?" Derrick asked.

"Most of the time."

"I heard that!" Samantha yelled. "If you think you've seen me be mean and hateful, you just wait! After the way you all have just treated me, you'll see."

"What'd she mean by that?" Derrick asked. "Is she going to beat us?"

"No, she wouldn't do anything like that," Daniel replied.

[77]

"She won't? How about spank us?"

"Look kid, you're in foster care now. No one's allowed to lay a hand on you when you misbehave."

Daniel gave him the low down on what "system life," as he liked to call it, was all about. If Samantha told him to stay in his room and he didn't want to, there wasn't a thing she could do about it. She could tell him to stand in a corner, but he could refuse and she wasn't allowed to touch him. If she told him to stay in the house and he went outside, oh well.

With some prodding from Derrick, Daniel told him every foster home was that way. Adults couldn't push him around anymore. He could do whatever he wanted, whenever he wanted, and nobody could stop him.

Derrick had never been the type of child to challenge authority; he was an intelligent child. Under normal circumstances he knew that if he misbehaved, he would have to suffer the consequences. Usually the consequences were severe enough that Derrick tried to avoid them at any cost. Now though, at least according to what Daniel was saying, he could do anything he wanted and not have to worry about any disciplinary action at all.

In no time, Samantha came out of the bathroom and knocked on the door to Daniel's room. "Boys, I want you to get ready for bed now."

"Yeah, whatever," Daniel mumbled.

Derrick didn't know what to do. He thought about just going to bed like he was told. That's what he would have done back at home. Then he thought about refusing to go to bed just to see if Daniel was right. He was half afraid to though. *What if Daniel is lying to me, just trying to get me in trouble?*

"I'm serious, Daniel. It's time for bed," Samantha ordered. "You two were so inconsiderate to me that I am not going to allow you to stay up any longer. Derrick, you need to go back to your room and put some clothes on and then get into bed."

"I don't have—"

"Don't backtalk me young man. I said to do it, now go!" Samantha snapped.

Derrick, frustrated by the fact that he had no clothes to

[78]

change into, temporarily forgot what he had been told by Daniel. He stood to his feet and started toward the door.

He was planning to go to his room and just go to bed, but Daniel had something else in mind. "Don't listen to that old hag. Hang in here with me. She can't stop you."

Derrick didn't know what to do. Samantha was standing in the doorway with her arms crossed across her chest. She looked pretty mad. Daniel plopped down on his bean bag chair, pretending she hadn't said a word.

"I'm sorry Daniel, but I have to go now," Derrick whispered.

He was ashamed of himself. *The whole point of getting Mom and Dad in trouble was so they couldn't push us around anymore. Daniel just told me how things are supposed to work in foster care. I'm supposed to be able to tell the adults what to do—not be ordered around.* Still, he was scared.

Derrick walked slowly past Samantha, half expecting her to spank him as he walked out of the room. She didn't lay a finger on him though—she didn't say a word.

"Are you gonna tuck me in?"

"Do you really think I'm going to tuck you in after the way you just talked to me?

Oh, how badly he missed being at home. *Mom always tucked me in, no matter what! Even if she was sick. Even if she was mad. I hate this place.*

"No. I guess not. It's just that—"

"It's just that you are going to go to bed just like I told you to young man. You have to the count of ten to be in that bed or else."

"Or else what?" Daniel asked. "What are you gonna do if he doesn't?"

"Daniel, you're not helping matters any. Why do you always have to do this when others are around?"

"Don't say things unless you can back 'em up. Don't threaten the kid when you know good and well you ain't gonna do anything to him if he doesn't listen to you."

[79]

"That will be enough, Daniel. Lights out in five minutes."

"You can turn your lights off in five minutes if you want to. My lights are staying on."

"Daniel, shut up! I'm leaving the room. You are to be in your bed in five minutes. I mean it," she demanded.

"How come I have to be in bed before you count to ten and he doesn't have to for five whole minutes? That's not fair," Derrick complained.

"Boy, get in that bed right now. Don't mess with me," Samantha ordered.

Hanging his head, Derrick walked to his room. He was disappointed to find Brady already asleep. He had gone to bed with his hair covered with sweat and dirt. His face was plastered with what looked like soot from a fireplace. He was snoring lightly, but seemed to be sleeping as if nothing had happened.

Derrick closed the door back and climbed onto the bottom bunk, still wearing only the dirty red towel. It felt good to lay down on a nice, soft bed as opposed to the tent floor he had slept on the night before. Still, it wasn't home. He didn't know if he could fall asleep without a bedtime story and without being tucked in. Still, he knew he had to try.

Lying there, he wondered what the next day would hold. *Maybe I'll get to talk to Mom and Dad. Maybe I can even go home and get out of this dump. Then again, maybe that's not such a good idea just yet.* He figured Trevor hadn't calmed down yet. After all, he had bitten him. Maybe they should wait a few more days before they went home and by that time his father would probably forget all about it anyway.

Sleep seemed impossible that night. He couldn't get home off of his mind. *I wonder if Mom and Dad know where we are. I hope they're okay and I hope they found a way out of the woods. I wonder if they'll go to church tomorrow morning? I wish I could take back everything that happened. If I could go back, I would do it a lot differently. I wouldn't have made mean comments to Mom. I wouldn't have back talked Dad. I wouldn't have thrown apples at Brady. I wouldn't have went along with Brady when he was telling lies. I hate myself.*

After giving himself a good mental thrashing, the boy finally managed to drift off to sleep. The one good thing about

[80]

tomorrow was that he planned on getting even with Daniel. Before falling asleep, he tried to come up with some ideas, but nothing really came to mind. Even though Brady was being grumpy that first night, he had a feeling his big brother would jump at the chance to do something mean to Daniel. There was only one way to find out.

10

THE BEGINNING OF A PRANK WAR

Brady whispered, "Derrick, wake up."

The little guy was dead to the world. It had been a long, exhausting couple of days and he had missed out on some much needed sleep.

"Derrick, come on. I need you to wake up," Brady whispered louder as he started shaking his little brother.

Brady kept shaking him and whispering to him until finally he saw the eleven year old's eyes open about half way. "What's going on?"

"We have to get outta here. Come on, let's run away. I sneaked into Daniel's room and got you some of his clothes to put on."

"Where are we gonna go?" Derrick asked.

"To find Mom and Dad," Brady answered. Brady had tossed and turned all night long. He would drift off to sleep, just to find himself waking back up every twenty minutes or so. He was worried. Ready to turn himself in. To admit his mistakes and accept whatever punishment Trevor saw fit.

He was somewhat disappointed to hear Derrick say he wasn't ready to leave yet. The weirdo said he kind of liked it there. Besides, he had promised Daniel a payback.

How can my baby brother possibly enjoy staying in this dump? There's nothing to do here. Samantha's old and boring. Daniel's not even worthy of being called a human being. The place was so small, Brady would have felt cramped even if he was the only one living there.

[82]

After giving the situation a whole fifteen seconds of thought, Brady told him stealing Daniel's clothes would have to suffice as his payback.

It was a nice try, but Derrick wasn't going for it. He hadn't stolen from Daniel; his brother had. Derrick said he wanted to do something a lot meaner than steal clothing. He wanted Daniel to know he couldn't get away with kicking them around like he had done the evening before.

Brady knew Derrick had a point. It wasn't like his little brother to be so vengeful though. *Then again, the little jerk is getting older. It was just yesterday he basically knocked me out of a tree.* The kid was definitely growing up. Maybe they could stay just one more day. Brady had recently heard of a prank he knew would make a great payback for Mr. Droopy Drawers.

While Daniel and Samantha were still asleep, it was time to put his plan into action. "Derrick, I need you to go into the kitchen and see if you can find a piece of candy—something that'll get really sticky when it gets wet. Got it?"

"Why?"

"Just do it. We don't have much time. You'll see what it's for in a few minutes. Meet me in the bathroom."

"In the bathroom?"

"Yeah. You know, the room that has the toilet and sink? The room where you fell on your butt last night?"

"I know where the bathroom is. I was just surprised that that's where you want to meet me. That's all," Derrick told him.

"Okay. Now, hurry up and go find me a piece of candy."

Derrick quickly put on the clothes Brady had stolen from Daniel's room and then tip-toed to the kitchen. *Where would they keep the candy?* There was nothing lying on the counter. He didn't see anything but real food in the refrigerator. *What if they don't have any? Brady'll kill me if I come back emptyhanded.*

Derrick searched and searched and finally found one Jolly Rancher still in its wrapper in one of the cabinets under the sink.

[83]

While he had been busy looking for a piece of candy, Brady had been disassembling the showerhead in the bathroom. He had just gotten everything ready when Derrick returned with the Jolly Rancher.

"Will this work?" he asked.

"It'll be perfect," Brady laughed. "Unwrap it and put it right here inside of this shower head."

"Why?"

"Just do it. You'll see."

As soon as he put the candy inside of it, Brady quickly hooked the showerhead back up. He couldn't help but chuckling as he imagined how this would work. A few days before their camping trip, a friend of his had told him about this prank. When Daniel turned on the shower, the Jolly Rancher would get wet. If it worked according to plan, Daniel wouldn't even notice that the water he was washing his entire body with was contaminated with stickiness from the candy. It would take a while for him to notice, but as the day went on, there was no way he could ignore it.

"Let's go back to bed now so they won't suspect anything," Brady said.

"Sounds good to me."

Two hours passed before Brady heard Daniel's bedroom door open. *Yes, he's up,* Brady said to himself. He started to wake Derrick, but decided there was no need. He would just listen to the water run and try his best to hold his laughter in.

In a matter of a minute or two, he could hear Daniel making his way to the restroom. He listened to the door close. Another minute or so passed and he heard the water turn on. A smile spread across Brady's face as he pictured what was about to happen. He wasn't sure why he didn't like Daniel, but even if he liked the guy, this prank was the best!

The sound of water running caused Derrick to wake up feeling the need to drain his bladder. Water always had that effect on him. "Brady, are you awake?" he whispered.

"Yeah, why?"

"I gotta go to the bathroom."

"You're just gonna have to wait. Our fun with Daniel is just beginning," Brady chuckled.

"What's gonna happen to him?"

"Just wait and see. You'll be impressed."

"Can't you tell me? Please?" Derrick whined.

"No, sir. I want you to be surprised. But listen, whatever happens in a little while, try not to laugh. Act like you don't even notice anything funny. Okay?"

After Daniel's shower, he put on his robe like he did every morning. Then he made his way to the kitchen for a bowl of cereal.

Brady and Derrick decided to join him. "Just remember to act like nothing's up," Brady said.

As soon as they entered the kitchen, Daniel asked Derrick why he was wearing his clothes.

Brady covered for him in a heartbeat, claiming Samantha had given them to him before they went to bed. He said Samantha had insisted Daniel wouldn't mind on account of Derrick's clothes being wet and all.

The boys were thrilled when Daniel bought it. He said it was okay, but just that once.

"You guys want some cereal?" Daniel asked.

"Sure!" Derrick replied excitedly.

"Good. Fix it yourself," Daniel chuckled.

Whatever, Derrick thought. He got a bowl out of the cabinet, opened the box, and filled his bowl to the top. After all, a growing boy needs lots of food—that's what Dad always told him. Then it was time for the milk. The gallon was pretty full, but Derrick could handle it. He was eleven years old, not a little baby. He opened the lid and started pouring. What a mess he made! *Ah, man. I forgot to leave enough room for the milk again.* Cereal and milk spilled out all over the counter and onto the floor.

[85]

"Look at you! Samantha's gonna kill you," Brady said.

Derrick thought back to his conversation with Daniel the night before. "No, she won't. She's not allowed to touch me. Isn't that right, Daniel?"

"Can't do a thing about it."

"Sure," Brady said. "We'll see about that."

Just then, Samantha entered the room wearing her nightgown; she still had curlers in her hair from the night before. "Good morning, gentlemen."

"Good morning," all three spoke in unison.

Samantha made her way toward the refrigerator and then she saw it. "Who made this mess?"

"Ditzy Derrick over there," Brady replied.

Glaring at Derrick, she snapped at him to clean it up at once.

Testing the waters, Derrick told her he would get it after he had finished eating.

Trying to be a good big brother for once in his life, Brady whispered and told him to clean it up immediately. He told him he didn't want to see him get in trouble and he knew their mom and dad had taught them better than that.

"What did he just say to you?" Samantha asked.

"It's a new joke called None of Your Business," Derrick said. He was really testing her now. He wanted to see just how right Daniel was.

"Boy, I can't wait until they find another place for you to go. I'm going to call the foster care agency and tell them it's time for you to move on. Your parents must have been a couple of deadbeats that just let you get away with anything."

"Don't talk about our parents," Brady spoke up.

"I don't take orders from teenagers. I'll talk about whoever I want to talk about. This is my home."

Brady let it go, realizing there was no point in bickering back and forth. It wasn't going to resolve anything.

Samantha cleaned up Derrick's mess without saying another word about it.

Daniel was right, Derrick thought. *I really can get away with anything. Maybe this whole foster care thing isn't such a bad program after all.*

Before long, Daniel finished his cereal and returned to his room to get dressed. Samantha had promised to take him to the recreation center down the street to play some basketball. He came out wearing a pair of gray sweatpants and a tight fitting muscle shirt, obviously hoping to intimidate his opponents as well as to impress Brady and Derrick.

He asked if either of his temporary brothers were interested in shooting some hoops with him.

Obviously excited about the opportunity, Derrick said he would love to play. He wasn't very good at basketball, but it was fun nonetheless.

Brady had no desire to go anywhere with Daniel. He almost said no—until he remembered the Jolly Rancher. "Sure, I'd love to play," he lied.

It didn't take long for everyone to get dressed and pile into Samantha's car. Daniel couldn't wait to get to the rec center. *I'm gonna wipe the floor with these sorry losers,* he told himself. Daniel knew he was the best player in the neighborhood and he was a showoff. What he didn't know was that Brady was also a big basketball fan. Brady was not only a good athlete, but a very cocky one as well. Daniel was not going to have an easy win— not if Brady could help it.

The rec center was packed. Brady couldn't believe how many guys were there. It must have been the only thing to do in town. Still though, he was impressed. The more people that were there, the more fun it would be when his little prank started taking effect! Not to mention how much fun it would be to beat Daniel at his own game in front of an audience!

"Wanna play a little game of one-on-one?" Daniel asked Brady as soon as they stepped onto the gym floor.

"Let's do it!"

"What about me?" Derrick whined.

[87]

"You can play the loser," Brady told him.

"No, I wanna play the winner."

"What, you don't want to play against your brother?" Daniel asked. "Cause you know I'm gonna mop the floor with his behind out here on the court, right?"

Derrick didn't say a word. He knew better than to answer that question. If he agreed, Brady would be mad at him. If he disagreed, Daniel would. For once in his life, Derrick's lips were sealed.

"I get ball first," Daniel said.

"Good idea," Brady told him. "That'll probably be the only way you get to touch it this game. Maybe if you get the ball first, you'll actually know what it feels like before the game's over."

"Ewww... You're such a funny guy. You should be a comedian. You almost sounded convincing with that one."

As soon as the game started, Brady covered Daniel like gravy on mashed potatoes. He was determined to keep him as far from the basket as possible. Daniel tried his best to get around him, but it was to no avail. Brady was quick. Daniel decided to try to shoot over his head. He jumped and attempted a shot, but Brady knocked the ball away with his right hand.

"Nice block," Daniel said.

"Thanks, man. Better luck next time."

While the two were playing, Derrick was busy observing. One thing he was beginning to notice was that Daniel's pants were starting to stick to his legs. *It looks like they're glued to his knees.* As he was running, Derrick saw Daniel tugging his pants away from his legs several times. As soon as he let go though, they started hugging his knees again.

Brady went toward the hoop. Daniel was pretty good at defense as well. He stole the ball and juked Brady, going straight toward the basket. He jumped up and actually slam-dunked the ball, scoring the first two points of the game.

"In your face!"

Brady was not happy. He didn't want Daniel to score at all. More importantly, he really didn't want him to make the first basket. It was okay though. It was just one basket. He just had to

[88]

make sure it didn't happen a second time.

As far as Daniel was concerned, that one basket was two points closer to a victory. He planned on beating Brady so badly that he would crawl home. The only problem was, something was going on with his clothes. He wasn't quite sure what, but it was almost like he had forgot to put fabric softener in when he did his laundry. His pants and shirt were both clinging to him. It seemed like the more he played, the worse it was getting.

Derrick was getting bored. The only thing that occupied his mind was wondering why Daniel's clothes were sticking to him. It was starting to look kind of funny. The bottom of his pant legs were beginning to ride up on him like a pair of high-waters. They weren't like that when they first left the trailer. *I wonder if it has something to with that Jolly Rancher?*

"Come on big boy, let's see you try that again," Brady said as soon as he got the ball.

"What? You think you can stop me?"

"I don't have to stop you. I have the ball. You have to stop me."

"As you wish," Daniel threatened, before stealing the ball again and driving toward the basket.

Somehow he had again managed to run right past his competition. As he jumped into the air, Brady noticed his pants for the first time. He almost laughed as he couldn't help but to notice what looked like an atomic wedgie that Daniel now had. His pants were sticking to him like flies stuck on those nasty yellow fly strips. It was hilarious. Brady had a very difficult time keeping himself from chuckling.

"Who's laughing now?" Daniel asked, referring to the basket he had just made.

"I am," Derrick called out from the bleachers.

"Why are you laughing? You're not even playin' the game."

"I'm laughing at you. Why are you prancing around like a reindeer?"

"I'm doing what?"

Brady could no longer keep his mouth shut. "You are

[89]

walking kind of weird, man. Like you got something stuck up your rear end."

"I don't know what you're talking about," he said. However, he did know, quite well actually. He wasn't sure what was going on, but he felt like the cheeks of his buttocks were sticking together. Every step he took felt icky. He didn't mind his shirt sticking to him because that just made him look stronger. His pants were a different story. They were sticking in all the wrong places and were starting to make him look like a geek.

"You know what guys? I'm not feeling so well. Maybe we should find Samantha and go home," Daniel said, after giving the situation some additional thought.

"No, we can't. I haven't even had a chance to play yet," Derrick whined.

"And I haven't had a chance to beat you," Brady added.

"Man, you couldn't beat me at a game of b-ball if I was a cockroach," Daniel told him, while trying to pry the back of his breeches out away from his body.

11
SAPPYBLOODITIS

Brady asked him why he was trying to quit the game then. He knew good and well why he wanted to quit, but he wasn't about to let Daniel go home and clean all that stickiness off of himself just yet. It was too much fun to watch him squirm.

"I ain't no quitter, dawg," Daniel said. "Let's do this then. I don't feel good. Let's say whoever makes the next shot wins the game. Deal?"

"Deal."

"Then I get to play the winner," Derrick insisted.

"That's right. That's what we agreed to when we first came in the door," Brady said.

Daniel didn't look too happy about the idea of playing another game. He thought about losing intentionally so he wouldn't have to play anymore. He hadn't lost a game on that court for nearly two years. What would that do to his reputation? He would have to start all over again and he wasn't prepared to do that. No way was he going to give in that easily.

"It's my ball," Brady said.

"Not for long."

"We'll see about that."

One thing Brady had noticed was that Daniel was good at stealing the ball. He didn't want to hold onto it any longer than possible, so from the three-point range he decided to take a shot.

Jumping as high as he could possibly jump, he released the ball into the air. It went straight toward the hoop, hit the backboard, rolled around and around the rim, and came down—without going into the net.

Brady couldn't believe it. He almost never missed that shot. He was not having a good day. Even worse, Daniel picked up the rebound, shot, and scored. The game was over. Brady had been skunked.

How did that happen? I can't believe that wedgie-toting punk actually beat me. I should never have agreed to that deal. If we had finished the whole game, I would have beat him and beat him good. Brady would have been absolutely ashamed of himself if he wasn't so amused by Daniel's appearance. He looked so miserable and embarrassed that it was still difficult to keep from laughing, even after losing a game.

"My turn!" Derrick said. "I get to play against Daniel now."

"No, little man. You're gonna have to play against your brother. I'm not feeling so well. We'll play next time," Daniel said.

"I see. So you're afraid of being beat by an eleven year old. Is that it?" Brady teased, determined to get him to play more.

"No, that's not it. When I play ball, I like some competition. I'm not into playing games with little boys."

"Whatever," Derrick said. "I don't care. Will you play me, Brady?"

"Yeah, I'll play you. Fair's only fair. You watched our game so now you should get some time too. I'm sorry Daniel LIED to you like that. That wasn't cool, was it?"

"I didn't lie to the kid. I just don't feel good. That's all," Daniel told them.

Brady rolled his eyes. "Sure. If you say so, DAWG."

Daniel still did not give in. There was no way he was going to go back out on that court with his sweatpants rising further

[92]

and further into the crack of his behind. *By now, I'm sure Brady and Derrick are not the only ones who've noticed. Maybe if I can just stay here on the bleachers, people will forget about it or at least nobody else will catch on.*

"Let's play Pig," Derrick suggested.

"Sounds good to me," Brady agreed. "You remember the rules?"

"I sure do. I shoot the ball from anywhere I want. If I make it, you have to shoot from the same place. If you miss it, you get a letter P. The next time that happens, you get an I, and then you get a G and I win!"

"You have the main idea down right. But you have it backward. I'm not the one who's going to be missing all of the shots."

Daniel sat on the bleachers, trying to figure out what was going on. Had someone put something sticky in his clothes before he put them on? *That's just not possible. The boys had no idea what I was going to wear; they couldn't have done it.* Samantha had said she was going to turn into a mean, grumpy woman after what they had done to her the night before. *But Samantha would never think to do something that evil. There has to be an explanation.*

Daniel, as he often did when he was thinking, ran his fingers through his hair. *Why doesn't it feel as soft as normal? It's kind of... sticky. Could my body be having a reaction to something here at the center?* Whatever was going on, he sure didn't like it.

"You missed," Daniel heard Brady say. "Now I get to shoot from anywhere on the court."

Brady stood right beside the basket, threw the ball up, and it swished into the net.

"I can do that." Derrick took the ball and stood exactly where he had watched his brother shoot from. He shot, the ball hit the backboard—and bounced right back to him.

"That's a P for little man," Brady laughed. "That also means I get to pick the next spot to shoot from. Still my call."

[93]

Daniel watched with disgust. He wanted to be out there playing too. *I can't though. Something's wrong. I just hope it's nothing serious.* He wanted to tell somebody about his concerns, but he was afraid to. What would they think of him?

Carlos, one of Daniel's buddies, approached the bleachers. "Wassup, Danny Boy?"

"Not much, man. Wassup with you?"

"Just chillin', man. Wanna shoot some hoops with me and the boys?"

"Nah, not today. Feelin' kinda lousy."

"Come on, dawg. We need you out there. We're gonna play some three-on-three and we only have five players. We need one more guy and you're him," Carlos pleaded.

Daniel didn't want to disappoint the guys. *Maybe they wouldn't notice my clothes. With six of us playing, there won't be time to pay much attention to such things,* Daniel told himself before standing to his feet.

As soon as he did though, Carlos cracked up. "Why are you wearing a twelve year old's pants?"

Daniel looked down. His pants were now fitting him like a glove. "I don't believe this," he mumbled.

While looking at his sweats, Daniel suddenly felt a weird sensation on his backside. Sitting on the bleachers for a few minutes had caused the seat of his pants to fasten themselves more securely to his rear end; he could feel it. Taking a step forward, he thought he wouldn't be able to move without his pants ripping in two.

"Brady, Derrick, we've gotta go," Daniel insisted.

Brady replied, "What's wrong? You gonna puke?"

"No. It's worse than that. Let's just get outta here."

"Oh, I know what it is," Carlos guessed. "You've got stuff coming out the other end. Diarrhea, man?"

"No, I don't have the runs," Daniel mumbled, tiring of everyone's questions. "Look guys, I'm serious. We have to go home. I can't stay here any longer."

[94]

"Our game ain't over yet," Derrick complained. "I wanna play.

"You're gonna have to play some other time. Come on, let's find Samantha," Daniel insisted.

"We're not gonna quit our game unless you tell us what's bothering you," Brady said as he and Derrick approached the bleachers.

Daniel begged him to not be like that. He was determined they had to leave and right at that instant—he said he wasn't comfortable telling them what was wrong.

Brady wasn't having any of it. He said he had to tell them within thirty seconds or they were heading back out on the court.

"I'm scared, man. Okay?" Daniel finally managed to spit out. "Something's seriously wrong with me."

"What is it? Do you have cancer?" Derrick asked. "Are you dying?"

"Shut up, you idiot," Brady insulted.

"No, I don't have cancer. No, I'm not dying. At least, I don't think I am. Everything's stickin' to me. Look at my shirt," Daniel said, trying to pull it off over his head. The shirt was sticking to him so badly it sounded like he was ripping duct tape from his flesh.

"Man, that sucks," Carlos said.

"It's not just my shirt; look at my sweats," Daniel complained.

"We noticed," Brady laughed. "What'd ya do? Glue your clothes on this morning?"

Derrick couldn't take much more of this. He knew he promised to not laugh and to pretend he didn't know anything, but he did know. Somehow that Jolly Rancher made Daniel's body so sticky he couldn't hardly move without his clothes getting tighter and tighter. Derrick turned his back so Daniel wouldn't see the grin on his face.

[95]

"I'm scared guys. What do you think this means? Have you ever heard of anything like this before?" Daniel asked.

"Yeah, man. Actually I have," Brady lied. "I was watching this movie once and a dude started having everything stick to him. He had some weird disease that turned all of his blood into this weird substance kind of like tree sap. When he sweat, it wasn't water that came out. It was sticky stuff, just like out of a tree that not todhad been cut on or something."

"No way. You messin' with me?"

"Yeah, I heard about that too," Carlos agreed. Carlos had no idea Brady was just pulling Daniel's leg. He didn't want anyone to think he didn't know about this disease. "Wasn't it called Sappyblooditis or something like that?"

"Something like that—I'm not sure," Brady said.

"What else does the disease do?" Daniel asked, with his face turning pale.

Derrick had regained his composure. He wanted to get in on the fun. "It made the guy lose control of his bodily functions. Like, for example, his nose started running when he least expected it and that gunk got all over everything. He sometimes started slobbering while he was wide awake for no reason. They said sometimes he even had 'accidents' like kids who are being potty-trained do."

I'm gonna puke! Daniel thought. *This can't be happening to me. I'm too young to have Sappyblooditis or whatever it's called.* "Guys, we have to tell Samantha. Maybe if we get to the doctor soon enough, they can make me better before it gets that bad."

Carlos looked like he was getting sick too. "I can't remember, Brady. Is that disease contagious?"

"I think so," Brady said.

"Look guys, sorry I can't stick around, but the guys are waiting on me over there," Carlos said before sprinting to the other side of the gym.

Derrick couldn't control himself anymore. He laughed so hard he literally fell in the floor and started rolling from side to side. Tears poured down his face.

"What's so funny?" Daniel shouted. "Do you think it's funny that I might be dying?"

"Told you I'd pay you back, didn't I?" Derrick said, laughing even harder.

"Pay me back? I don't get it." What'd you do to pay me back? Did you somehow pass a disease to me?"

Brady started laughing too. Poor Daniel. He was absolutely horrified. He really thought he was going to mess himself in front of everyone in the gym. He was scared to death of what might happen to him next. What he could not understand is why both Brady and Derrick seemed to think the situation was so funny. *If it's as contagious as they told Carlos it is, they should be scared too. After all, they've been living in the same house with me for the last twenty-four hours.*

"Do you really want to know what's so funny?" Brady asked.

"Humor me," Daniel agreed. "I need a good laugh about now.

"Well, we messed with the showerhead this morning. We put a Jolly Rancher in it and when you took a shower, the water melted it and got all that stickiness oozing all over you," Brady said.

"No way. You mean, I don't really have Sappyblooditis?"

"Nope. Just a case of a good payback," Derrick said.

"You dudes are dead. I'm gonna kill both of you. This is far from over. You just wait and see. If you punks chill at my crib much longer, you'll get what's coming to ya," Daniel said, again attempting to undo the wedgie their prank had caused.

[97]

12
FISTS OF FURY

Upon arriving back at Samantha's trailer, the boys discovered she had a bit of news to share. "Fellas, I wasn't bluffing about calling the agency. I made a phone call while we were at the rec center and they're going to find a new home for you both. I don't know if you'll be able to stay together or if they'll put you into two different homes. I just know that I cannot handle having all three of you in his household," she said.

Derrick and Brady just looked at each other. What did she mean, they might not get to stay together?

Daniel was glad to hear the news. He didn't take too kindly to having other kids in the home. He would much rather be there by himself. One thing he quickly realized, however, was that he had to think fast if he was going to pay Derrick and Brady back for the whole Jolly Rancher gag. He had seen kids get kicked out of foster homes before. Actually, he had been kicked out of several himself. It could take weeks or it could happen overnight. He needed a plan and fast!

Acting as if he needed some time alone, Daniel went to his room. He logged into his computer, went to a search engine, and typed in, "How to get revenge." He read listing after listing, but found nothing he wanted to do. He went back to the search engine and typed in "best pranks." Again, he clicked on link after link—finally, he found the perfect idea.

Over the years, Daniel had been collecting alarm clocks. He didn't know why. Some boys collected baseball cards, others collected coins; he chose to collect clocks. Now he had found the perfect way to use them. Going to his closet, he took the first one off of a shelf and set it to go off at midnight. That was the first alarm clock he ever had and its alarm sounded like a rooster crowing. It was sure to not only wake them up, but to give them a good scare in the middle of the night. He went back to the closet for a second clock—a black wind-up that blasted music as an alarm. He had stolen it from his first foster family when they kicked him out for stealing his foster dad's cigarettes. He set the alarm on this one to go off at 1:15 am.

Daniel was truly enjoying himself. This was the ultimate prank and the boys would never forget it; he was quite certain of that. He picked up a third alarm clock. This one actually had a person's voice that shouted, "WAKE UP, DIRT BAG! WAKE UP! GET UP OUT OF THAT BED! WAKE UP, DIRT BAG! WAKE UP!" It would continue hollering until it was eventually turned off. This alarm clock he set to go off at 2:45 am. *They'll be ready to strangle me by the time the night is over.*

He pulled out one more—he had saved the best for last. This one was in the shape of a rocket launcher; the launch pad was the actual clock. On it sat a rocket that would be shot into the air when the alarm went off. The alarm clock would screech until Brady or Derrick found the rocket and physically placed it back on the launch pad. He set this alarm to go off at 4:00 am. He couldn't wait.

While Daniel had been scheming, Derrick and Brady were sitting at the kitchen table with Samantha. They were trying to talk her into letting them stay—not because they liked her or Daniel or even the trailer, but because they wanted to stay together. Being separated scared them after everything they had already been through.

"I don't know, boys," Samantha said. "You guys have nasty manners. Daniel seems to be picking up some very bad habits from you two. I just don't think I can take much more of this."

As the boys continued trying to convince her to give them one more chance, Daniel sneaked into the their bedroom. He hid the first alarm clock in the bottom dresser drawer. He placed the second one behind the curtain by the window. The third one he wrapped up in the towel Derrick had thrown in their closet. He then took the rocket launcher alarm clock and gently laid it on top of one of the ceiling fan blades. He only wished he could see the expressions on their faces as they were woke up time and time again throughout the night.

"Good night, Samantha," Daniel heard Brady say.

"See you in the morning," Derrick told her.

Daniel gave the room one more quick look just to make sure he didn't leave any evidence. By the time he got to the door, Derrick was already at the end of the hall.

"What are you doing in our room?" he asked.

"I was... coming to tell you good night," Daniel lied.

"Oh, well we were in the living room. Good night."

Daniel made his way back to his room. When he closed the door, he left it cracked just a little so he could hear everything that happened. It was only 9:30 pm and the boys were already going to sleep. By midnight they should definitely have drifted off. Knowing he was going to be woken up several times himself, he went to bed as well.

As soon as he had gotten his night clothes on and gotten into bed, he could overhear Derrick and Brady talking. "Can you believe she's not gonna let us stay?" Brady asked.

"I can believe it. Daniel was right. Samantha is just an old hag."

"She is. I agree with you, but don't start talking like that. You know Dad would kill us both if he knew we were talking that way."

"But Dad isn't here, remember Brady?"

It was obvious both of the boys were really upset. They couldn't stand the thought of being separated. Daniel could relate to how they felt. He remembered the worry of having to move. He had been in nine different foster homes. Samantha had allowed him to stay with her for two years, which was the longest placement he had ever had.

Even though he felt sorry for the Clarks, he was glad they were leaving. With them there, Samantha might decide she liked them better and kick him out. This way, he wouldn't have anything to worry about.

Before long, the entire trailer was quiet. At least, no one inside was making any noise. Outside, however, was a different story. Barking dogs were everywhere. A man and woman across the street were having a screaming match about who should stay home with the kids so the other one could go out partying. Eventually, the whole area grew quiet and everyone was able to drift off to sleep.

At midnight the first alarm clock sounded. "Er, er, er, er, er, er errrrr," the rooster crowed. Again and again it repeated the call.

Daniel woke up laughing. He slipped into the hallway and tip-toed toward the boys' bedroom, where he placed his ear against the door to listen.

"Where is that awful racket coming from?" Brady asked.

"I don't know. It's echoing off of everything. It sounds like it's all around the room."

Daniel was giggling. *This is awesome!*

Luckily for him Samantha was a very sound sleeper and didn't hear a thing.

"I don't believe this," Brady grumbled.

"Me either," Derrick agreed.

After three whole minutes of searching, Brady found the alarm clock and shut it off.

"I thought you'd never find it," Derrick said. "That thing was givin' me a headache."

If only they knew what was ahead of them. One thing was for sure, they weren't going to be getting any beauty sleep that night.

Derrick and Brady went back to bed and angrily managed to fall asleep. Daniel decided to just lay down outside their door and go back to sleep himself. That way, he wouldn't have to go as far the next time everyone had to wake up.

An hour and fifteen minutes later, the sound of a trumpet blaring "The Star Bangled Banner" startled all three of them. *This is great,* Daniel laughed.

Derrick and Brady, on the other hand, were getting very annoyed. As if once wasn't bad enough, now they had to search their room for another clock.

Luckily, it didn't take quite as long this time. Derrick

[101]

managed to find it and together he and Brady quickly figured out how to turn it off. Daniel was disappointed that they found it so quickly, but still there was more to come.

An hour and a half passed before the next clock went off. Derrick was terrified by the sound of a deep, masculine voice shouting, "WAKE UP, DIRT BAG!" He literally screamed.

"I'm going to kill Daniel," Brady complained. "He is such a jerk. I know he's behind this."

Again, both boys got up and searched their bedroom. It was hard to keep their eyes open. They wished they had brought some earplugs. All of the racket combined with such a lack of sleep was giving both of them headaches.

Daniel couldn't wait for the final alarm. The rocket launcher was by far his favorite. He didn't even know if the boys would have a clue how to turn it off when the rocket shot into the air. Even if they did know, it would still be fun to listen to them scrambling around the room trying to find the rocket.

"Can you believe he's doing this to us?" Brady asked.

"I think it's kinda fun," Derrick said.

"I don't. He's dead come morning."

Daniel's whole body began to tremble from trying to hold back his laughter. Still, somehow he managed to keep it in.

A little while later, the rocket launched and the room was filled with an ear-piercing squeal so loud that even Daniel no longer enjoyed this. It was so loud, in fact, that Daniel couldn't even hear what the boys were saying. That was ruining the fun for him so he had to open the door and peek in.

As the door cracked open, Brady saw him. "You jerk!" he said.

Daniel laughed. "Payback's rough, huh?"

"Just wait til I get this turned off and you're gonna find out just how rough it can be."

Daniel didn't see the point of exchanging threats. He covered his ears, grinned as big as he knew how, and watched the fun. Brady and Derrick were scrambling around the room like chickens who had just had their heads chopped off. It took a while, but finally they managed to find the rocket and get it back on the launcher.

As soon as the alarm sound died down, Brady charged at Daniel full force. He punched him right in the gut.

"Oh no you didn't!" Daniel shouted.

With that, he swung around and gave Brady a severe blow to his left cheek, knocking him to the ground. "Yeah, now who's the tough guy?"

Brady was down, but he was far from out. Jumping back to his feet, he ran at Daniel again. This time, he plowed into him with his whole body and both of them fell to the floor. Brady started swinging and hit Daniel anywhere and everywhere he could possibly land a punch. Daniel had been in a lot of fights, but never with someone going as crazy as Brady was. He didn't have time to punch because he was too busy trying to block Brady from hitting him.

Derrick didn't know what to do. He had never been in a fight in his life. Brady and Daniel were both much bigger than him. The one thing Derrick did know how to do was tattle. He decided to run past them and get Samantha to come help. When he got right beside them though, Brady reached out and grabbed his ankle, causing him to fall flat on his freckled little nose.

"Stay in here," he demanded.

Brady had made a huge mistake. When he grabbed his brother's ankle, Daniel saw just the opening he needed. He reared back and head-butted Brady. He rolled on top of him and started pounding him in the face over and over again. Blood was everywhere.

Seeing enough, Derrick jumped on top of Daniel, wrapped his right arm around his neck, and attempted to knock him off of his brother. It was no use. Daniel was too big and Derrick couldn't wrestle him off; it was impossible. Derrick knew there was only one thing to do. He opened his mouth as wide as he could open it, lowered his head down, and bit Daniel right between his shoulder blades.

Daniel hollered and flipped off of Brady. Brady jumped up and punched Daniel between the legs so hard that Daniel dropped to his knees. Brady knew it was a dirty move, but he

[103]

had to do something to get even. With Daniel on his knees, Brady punched him in the nose and the prankster fell all the way down on the floor. Brady could have stopped, but he didn't want to. He sat on top of Daniel, grabbed a handful of his hair, and began slamming his head against the floor. Not once, not twice, not three times. He slammed it again and again until Daniel was no longer conscious.

"Oh my gosh, you killed him!" Derrick screamed.

Just about that time, Samantha came down the hallway. "What's goin' on in there?"

Before the boys had a chance to come up with a lie, she opened the door and saw the bloody mess and Daniel lying on the floor. "What have you done?" she screamed. "You guys are out of here, NOW! You will be leaving today, I guarantee it!"

Daniel wasn't dead. He had just temporarily passed out. To be on the safe side, Samantha called an ambulance to come out just to make sure he was okay. When the dispatcher heard what had happened to him, she notified Child Protective Services who sent Ms. Simms rushing to the scene as well.

Samantha was irate. "Can you believe how horrible these kids are? Look what they did!" she screamed when Ms. Simms arrived.

"Calm down, Ms. Hilton. Please calm down," Ms. Simms said. "Just tell me what happened."

"I don't know what happened. I just heard a lot of commotion and when I went to see what was going on I found Daniel in the floor covered with blood and Brady was sitting on top of him looking like a mad man. Derrick was just standing there watching like it was the funniest thing he had ever seen. I want these kids out of here now!"

Ms. Simms reminded Samantha that under normal circumstances she would have had to provide the agency with fourteen days' notice before the children would have to be removed from her home. However, since this was only a temporary emergency placement anyway, she would find another place for the boys to stay.

Telling the boys to come with her, Ms. Simms got back in her vehicle and headed back toward her office. "Okay Brady, I

[104]

want to know what happened in there," she said.

"I'm not tellin' you anything."

"Brady, come on. You have to tell me."

"What are you gonna do if I don't?"

"You know what? I guess it doesn't really matter what happened. Just listen to me for a minute," Ms. Simms lectured. "I know you boys came from a violent home where it was normal to fight with each other and to see your parents fight. I heard about how bad your van was beaten up when the officer showed up on the scene the other day. Violence is not the answer here. You're going to have to learn to talk things out."

"Talking's for sissies," Brady argued.

"Brady, have you ever been put on any kind of medication to help you deal with your aggression?"

"What kind of medicine?"

"There are many types of medicines available. I'm going to have a psychological evaluation scheduled for you. Maybe some medication will help calm you down," Ms. Simms said.

Medicine? Why was she going to give him medicine for fighting? At home, he would have got gotten his bottom busted and sent to his room for the evening.

Brady had been in a few fights, but only when he had been provoked. As far as he was concerned, all he did was defend himself. Daniel had started the whole thing by ruining all of his sleep. Maybe Daniel was the one who should have been on medicine. Then again, he was. Brady remembered seeing some medicine bottles with his name on them in the restroom.

13
STAY CALM

TO SAY ROXANNE was upset would have been the understatement of the millennium. *I can't believe that woman expects me to stay calm. Brady knocked a kid unconscious and got himself and Derrick kicked out of a foster home and I'm not supposed to be upset?*

She had no idea how she was going to break the news to Trevor when he got in from work. Last night had been the first night he had managed to get a decent amount of sleep since their camping trip had ended.

She plopped herself down on the couch. *I can't believe they won't even let me talk to my babies. I need to hear their side of this story. I need to know they're okay. A person would think the agency would at least have the decency to let us talk to each other.*

Roxanne could feel her blood pressure rising. Her face was getting tighter. Her palms were sweating. Her belly was beginning to ache. *I don't know if I want Trevor to be here with me right now so he can tell me everything's going to be okay or if I'm glad I'm here alone so I can sulk.*

After giving herself a few moments to calm down, Roxanne convinced herself she had to get up and do something to get her mind off of it. *I could start working on dinner. No, I don't have an appetite. That can wait for later! I guess I could always clean out the refrigerator. No. I'm just not in the mood for working right now. I just can't bring myself to do it.*

The struggle was real. After tossing out a few more ideas, she finally settled on what she had come to know as artistic prayer. Roxanne wasn't an artist per se, but as a little girl she had somehow created her own unique way of talking to God.

After getting a sheet of paper and a pencil, she walked out

on the porch and sat on the glider.

In a soft spoken voice, she barely whispered, "God, it's been a long time since I've came before you in the form of artistic prayer. Here goes."

She touched her pencil to the paper, but before she could begin her sketch, two little girls came trotting up her walkway. "Hi there," one of them said. "Our school is doing a fundraiser. Are you interested in ordering any popcorn tins?"

Frustrated, Roxane fought to maintain her composure while telling the girls she had too many things going on in her life at that moment to worry about a school fundraiser. She wished them luck and sent them on their merry way.

Okay, now where was I? Oh, that's right, I was getting ready to sketch this house God has blessed us with. "God, I'm sorry for that interruption. Lord, I really need to talk to you. My heart has been so heavy. Sometimes when I go to bed at night, I'm inwardly hoping I won't wake back up the next morning. The pain is unbearable."

Taking her time, Roxanne began drawing an outline of the house—beginning with the roof and working her way down.

"Lord Jesus, I remember the day when Trevor carried me across the threshold. We, or at least I, wanted a Godly home. Trevor and I were madly in love with each other. When those precious little boys were born, even Trevor recognized your handiwork in the miracle of life.

"God, I've been foolish. I've messed up in so many ways. My husband, the leader of our home, has messed up as well. God, please do something. We're falling apart. This is way too difficult for us. We can't get our boys back unless you make it happen."

Instead of drawing the windows or the doors of their house, Roxanne began to draw a tree in the front yard. Before she could dive further into her artistic prayer, she heard the phone ringing. *Why is it that every time I try to cry out to God for my babies, something gets in the way?*

Setting her pencil and paper down, she rushed into the

[107]

house and grabbed the phone; it was Trevor.

"Hon, do you have a minute?" he asked. "I just need to talk to someone."

"About what?" Roxanne asked.

Instead of telling her what he was calling about, Trevor asked his wife what was wrong. He could hear it in her voice.

Roxanne tried to stall. "Nothing's the matter, honey. What do you need to talk about?"

"Roxi, what's the matter? What are you not telling me? Does it have something to do with the boys?"

How does he always know? Sometimes I think that man sees right through me.

Seeing no choice in the matter, she spilled the peanuts about the fight and broke down into tears as she did so.

"Where are the boys now?" Trevor asked, after hearing about the fight.

"I don't know. Ms. Simms said they would have to find another placement for them."

"Are they staying together?"

"I don't know that either."

A customer came into the bank and Trevor had to get off of the phone.

Roxanne would just have to keep herself busy until her husband got home later that evening.

Trevor found it difficult to separate his family life from his job sometimes—this was one of those times. He had called his wife because he had already been struggling emotionally.

He couldn't talk to his coworkers about his broken heart. It was one of those things that no one could understand unless they had already taken a walk in his shoes. He had hoped he and Roxanne could vent to one another for a few minutes. The last thing he had expected was to hear the boys were being moved so soon. But there was no time for those types of thoughts.

"Hi, I would like to see about taking out a loan," a lady told him, entering his office.

"Okay, what type of loan are you looking for?"

"A mortgage. My husband is in the service and he's overseas or he would be here with me right now. We're looking to buy a larger home. Five children and one powder room doesn't cut it very well."

Children, oh how I miss my children, Trevor thought. Staring off into space, he thought back to the day Brady was born. Roxanne had been larger than a whale, but had such a radiant glow about her that she was absolutely gorgeous to look at. He remembered it like it was just yesterday. They were on their way to his nephew's birthday party when Roxanne told him she was having contractions.

He did a U-turn right there in the middle of the street. As luck would have it, a police officer saw him and there came the blue lights.

"Sir, are you okay?" the customer asked, interrupting his train of thought.

Trevor came back to his senses. *I can't believe I just drifted off like that.* "Yes. Yes, ma'am. I'm fine. So how much are you looking to borrow?"

"Today, I was just wanting to seek a pre-approval—just to find out how much we qualify for."

Trevor took some basic information from her and began entering it into the computer. As he typed, his mind wandered back to the day Brady was born. He remembered telling the officer his wife was in labor. He gave them an escort all the way to the hospital.

When they pulled up to the main entrance, a wheelchair was waiting on Roxanne. A nurse loaded her up and to the maternity ward she went.

Trevor remembered how excited he was when the doctor said, "Congratulations! It's a boy!"

He looked down and was amazed at how precious the little guy was. He had a head clear full of black hair and it was sticking up in every direction. His forehead looked slightly distorted, but other than that he was as cute as could be.

"Um, sir," the lady said, sounding a bit impatient. "Is

everything okay? You've just been staring at the screen for the last couple of minutes."

I cannot keep doing this, Trevor told himself. *I have to stay on task. I know better.*

After continuing the pre-approval process and sending his client on her way, Trevor walked to the restroom—not because he needed to go, but because he needed some alone time and if there was any place to get it, that was the place.

Locking himself in a stall, he put the toilet lid down, and sat on top of it. *I just need time to clear my head.*

He stared at the empty cardboard tube where the toilet paper was supposed to be hanging. *It's a good thing I didn't really need to relieve myself right now,* he thought. *Maybe I should call Roxi back. No, I can't do that. If somebody walks in and I'm in a stall talking and crying... no, no, I won't do that. I need to get this off of my chest. Something has to give.*

Suddenly, it felt as though a small voice spoke to him and reminded him of God's power. *Why haven't I thought about praying?*

In his heart, Trevor began speaking to his Creator. "Dear God, where do I start? Should I begin by telling you what a horrible husband and father I am? Well, I guess you already know about all of that, huh? I don't have a lot of time so I'm just going to cut right to the chase. My family's in trouble. The state thinks Roxi and I are abusive people. God, I know you've already shown us much more grace and mercy than we should ever even dream of receiving from you. But God, I can't even focus on my work. Those boys are a part of me."

Before his prayer could continue, the restroom door opened and footsteps could be heard coming across the floor. He had no idea if it was a co-worker or a customer in the restroom with him. He didn't care—as long as they didn't talk to him. As long as they left him alone.

Somehow, his prayer had come to an abrupt halt, but his thoughts continued. *So Brady knocked a kid out? And he's in the state's care. They won't even let me talk to him. I can't jump onto him for losing his temper. I can't even hear his side of the story.* Suddenly, from the next stall over, came an intense grunt followed immediately by the sound and foul odor of someone aggressively sharing their flatulence. The sound repeated over and over again for about thirty seconds. The smell was so bad Trevor thought about asking the guy if he was okay.

I guess my alone time is over, he told himself. He had to get out of there. No doubt about that!

14
SHELTER OF INSANITY

BEFORE A PSYCH EVAL could be scheduled and before they could be put in another placement, Ms. Simms took the boys to see a therapist.

"Hi Derrick. My name's Daphne and I'm here to be your friend," she said.

Derrick liked that idea. He didn't have any adult friends. It would be cool to have one her age. *Especially since she reminds me of Mom,* he thought. It was something about her smile. Or maybe it was the way she giggled.

Not knowing what else to say, Derrick simply replied, "Okay."

"Good. Now I'm going to ask you some questions so I can get to know you better. If you don't feel comfortable answering them, that's okay. Just tell me and we'll move on."

That sounded like a good idea. Derrick liked her. "Okay," he said once more.

"Let's start this way. Why don't you tell me how you ended up in foster care?"

What a horrible first question! *I can't tell my new friend that I lied about my parents to get into foster care. She'll change her mind about being my friend if she knows I'm not honest.* "I'm not comfortable with that question. Can we move on?"

Daphne looked disappointed. "Sure," she agreed. "How do you feel about being in the system?"

"I don't know. It's not too bad, I guess."

"Do you want to live with your mom and dad?"

"Yeah, but not yet. Dad was really mad when we left and he has a really bad temper. I don't wanna go home until I know he's calmed down."

Daphne took note of his answer. "I understand. How long does it normally take for your dad to calm down?"

"It just depends. Sometimes an hour. Sometimes two. Sometimes a whole day. I've even seen it take him a week."

"I see," Daphne continued. "We don't have a lot of time for our first meeting because I have other appointments coming in today. Do you have any questions or concerns you would like to discuss with me?"

"Yeah. Are Mom and Dad okay? When will we get to see 'em?"

"Your parents are fine. I'm not sure when you'll see them yet. We know it's too soon right now, but you will when the time is right," Daphne told him.

"You remind me a lot of Mom."

"Really? How so?"

"You have gentle eyes. Your perfume smells kind of like Mom's. You're almost as pretty as she is. I don't know. But somehow being here with you makes me realize how much I miss her."

"It's perfectly normal to miss your Mom. What do you miss the most about her?"

"Lots of things. The way she sings when she's washin' the dishes. The tickle fights. The pillow fights. The way she would always keep Brady from pickin' on me. The way she would make our breakfast. She always fixed way more food than we could eat and the frig was always jam packed with leftovers."

Derrick felt a tear beginning to trickle down his cheek. "I just miss her. And Dad too."

"It's okay, honey," Daphne told him. "Keep crying. Let it all out."

After a few more minutes of sharing fond memories of his

mom and dad, Daphne told him it was time to end their first session.

She explained that she had other appointments which had been previously scheduled, but she had agreed to work the Clark boys in between clients. Knowing Brady had just gotten out of a very bad fight, she had to talk to him before her next appointment arrived in ten minutes.

"Brady," she said as she and Derrick returned to the lobby. "I'm finished with your brother. Please follow me."

Derrick may have saw some resemblance to his momma when he looked at Daphne, but Brady saw her through an entirely different set of eyes. He found her quite attractive and had trouble keeping his eyes off of her chest. Her shirt was cut low and he could only imagine what she would look like if it was cut just a little lower. *I wonder if she finds me attractive as well?* he asked himself. Brady knew she was older than him, but he had heard that some women liked younger men. He couldn't wait to be alone with her in a room. *This might be the best experience I've had in foster care so far.*

"Brady, my name's Daphne and I'd like to be your friend," she began.

Really? That girl is hot. Maybe if we start out as friends, it'll lead to something more. "I'd love to be your friend," he said, unable to mask a huge cheesy grin that was building on his face.

"Good. I'm glad to hear that, Brady," Daphne replied. "I have some questions for you. If you don't feel comfortable answering me, just say so and we'll move on. Okay?"

"Sure."

"We don't have much time, so let's cut right to the chase. Tell me why things didn't work out at Samantha Hilton's place."

"I didn't like her. She was a boring old hag," Brady replied.

Daphne giggled.

That is the cutest laugh I've ever heard. She likes my sense of humor, Brady told himself.

"Well, what happened between you and Daniel? That is his name, right? The guy you got in a fight with?"

[114]

"Yeah, that's his name. I wouldn't really call it a fight though. Daniel wasn't much competition. I kicked his scrawny little butt," Brady bragged while flexing his biceps.

Again Daphne giggled. Brady loved it when she did that. He couldn't help but to smile even brighter.

She asked what the fight was about and Brady told her all about the alarm clocks.

"I understand," she said. "Do you think hitting him or 'kicking his scrawny little butt' as you put it was the best way you could have handled that situation?"

"Oh yeah," Brady said. "Daniel had it coming. He's a real jerk."

Daphne agreed that perhaps Daniel had provoked him, but she asked how he could have handled the situation in a better way. If he would have thought things through, he could have kept himself from getting punched on and getting his face bruised up.

Brady thought for a moment before joking with her about just tossing him through the window so he wouldn't have had a chance to fight back.

"That's not quite what I had in mind," Daphne giggled. "Do you think maybe you could have acted like you thought his prank was funny? You know, laughed along with him?"

"I guess I could have—if I was a sissy. But I'm not a sissy and I wasn't gonna pretend I thought it was funny," Brady said.

"Oh, I see. So tough guys like you have to fight? Is that it?"

Brady noticed what she said. *She called me a tough guy. She noticed my muscles and she liked what she saw.* "Exactly," he told her.

Brady didn't get to spend quite as much time with Daphne as Derrick had because her next appointment showed up right on time and was waiting in the lobby. She apologized for having to cut things so short, but promised to meet with him again the following week.

The session's over already? I just got started flirting. I haven't even had a chance to take my shirt off yet to impress her with my six pack. At least she said we can have another session next week. I'll make sure to do some serious working out before then. "Sure. I've really enjoyed talking to you," he said.

Daphne walked Brady back out to the lobby.

Ms. Simms was waiting on him with her keys rattling. "Good news guys. We found a shelter who said you can stay there for the night. They're full, but they have a couple of kids who went out for a family visit until tomorrow. You can take their beds until they return."

A shelter? What in the world is that? Derrick wondered. He had done what they called a "shelter-in-place" at school where he had to hide under his desk. Surely it wasn't a place they had to hide. Who would they hide from?

Brady knew exactly what a shelter was. He had heard of them before. It was kind of like an orphanage. Lots of kids and lots of rules. It was only for one night though; he could deal with it.

Ms. Simms loaded the boys into her vehicle again and drove about fifteen miles to the child shelter. It was huge. Both of the boys were amazed at how beautiful it was; it looked like a mansion. It was a white, three-story building, with a swimming pool out back and a huge yard out front that resembled a school playground.

Ms. Simms led the boys up the walkway to the enormous front door. It was locked, so she had to ring the doorbell. Brrriinnnggg... Brrriinnnggg.

In a matter of minutes, a nerdy looking man with a name tag that read "Alvin," answered the door. He looked like he was about thirty years old. His hair was as black as coal and it was greased down so much he looked like it was stuck to his head. His huge black-framed glasses didn't improve his appearance in the least. Alvin looked like a walking toothpick.

"Hello Ms. Simms," he said. "This must be the boys you were telling me about. Welcome aboard guys."

"I'm sorry I can't come in," Ms. Simms told him. "I've had a busy day and I have to get back to the office to get caught up on some paperwork."

[116]

The child shelter the boys were taken to could contain a maximum of twelve children. It was at full capacity. Unlike what they had imagined, each child did not have his own room. There were six beds in one room and six beds in another. The girls all slept in one and the boys slept in the other. Brady had thought it was bad before when he had to share a room with his brother. He couldn't imagine sleeping in a room with five others.

"Boys, my name is Alvin. I'm the director here. I understand you gentlemen were brought here after causing some problems in a foster care placement."

"We didn't start it," Brady told him.

"I've heard that before. Boys, you have a reputation now. I have to insist on your staying in the living room until bedtime. You will be under my constant supervision."

"Sounds like fun," Brady responded sarcastically.

Ignoring the wisecrack, Alvin continued, "Here are some basic rules while you're here. There will be no physical violence. We do not tolerate profanity. Whispering is not permitted. Your hands must stay completely visible at all times. While sitting on the sofa, you must keep one cushion between you and anyone else sitting on it. At no time should I see you having any form of physical contact with anyone else staying here. Is that understood?"

"Yes, Your Highness," Derrick said, remembering that's what his mom had said to his dad a few days before.

"You may watch television, play video games, or just sit there admiring one another if you wish. That's all you will be permitted to do today," Alvin continued.

Derrick wondered if Alvin was allowed to discipline him since now he wasn't technically in a foster home. He wondered if he could still get away with being disrespectful and doing anything he pleased. Could they do anything about it? Daniel had told him that as long as he was in foster care, no one could lay a hand on him.

"Don't you think he's a big geek? Derrick whispered.

"Excuse me," Alvin said. "Did I not say there is to be no

[117]

whispering?"

Brady started to take up for him, but decided against it. It wasn't his fault his brother had a big mouth.

"Yeah, so what?" Derrick asked.

"So what? Don't test me young man."

"Test you? What do you mean?"

"Fine. You want to play hard ball?" Alvin asked, before pushing a button behind the counter.

The next thing he knew, two huge men entered the room. Alvin pointed Derrick out and the men approached him.

"I'm sorry," Derrick said. "I won't backtalk anymore."

"Get up, boy," one of them said.

Derrick was afraid. What were they going to do to him? He just sat there for a moment, hoping everything would calm down. To his surprise, the second man grabbed a hold of his right arm and pulled him up to his feet. The first man grabbed his left arm to make sure he didn't run.

"You are going to learn real quick that we don't tolerate misbehavior. When you're told to do something, you do it," the man said.

Brady started to chuckle. Inside he was thinking, *Oh, I get it. So in foster homes nobody can touch us, but in facilities, they can. Derrick's about to get his butt beat. He's had this one coming to him for a while.*

Suddenly, Alvin came out from around the counter holding a needle.

Brady no longer found the situation funny. A spanking was one thing. A needle was an entirely different matter. "What are you doing to him?"

"You want a taste of it as well young man?" Alvin asked.

"No."

Alvin injected something into the lower part of Derrick's back, directly under the waistband of his blue jeans.

"Owww!" the boy cried.

Within seconds, he fell asleep. Brady didn't know what they had injected him with, but he didn't like it. *Are they allowed to do that? How is that not considered child abuse? Instead of discipline, they drug people to knock them out?* Brady had heard about child shelters, but this is something he had never heard of.

[118]

Once Derrick's body fell limp, one of the men picked him up and carried him out of the room.

"Where are you taking him?" Brady asked.

"To the same place we take all naughty children," Alvin replied.

"Bring him back. I mean it!"

"Who do you think you are, young man? You need to sit there and keep your mouth shut," Alvin snapped.

Getting angry, Brady felt his hands balling up into fists. His heart started pounding so hard he thought it was going to explode. Jumping up off the couch, he stomped over to Alvin. "You better bring him back!" he shouted.

Before Brady knew what happened, one of the men who had been holding onto his brother grabbed him from behind. He wrapped his big arms completely around the teen so that he couldn't move his upper body at all. Brady tried to kick, but the man wrapped one of his legs around Brady's. He was completely helpless.

While in that position, Alvin again pulled out a needle. "No, let go of me!" Brady screamed.

Looking up, he noticed some kids had just come in from the pool. They all gawked at him. They wondered who the new kid was and why he was being injected already. Brady was humiliated. He felt like a wimp being held down like that. Even worse, he hated needles. "Get that thing away from me!"

Alvin gently pulled back the waistband of Brady's jeans and the next thing he knew, he felt the sting of the needle. "What's in that thing?" he yelled.

Just like his brother had minutes before, Brady fell immediately to sleep. He had never expected that to happen. That was the first time in years someone had overpowered him.

Two hours passed before Derrick's eyes began to open. "Where am I?"

Unfortunately, no one was around to hear him. He raised

his head and looked to the side to see Brady sleeping like a baby. He started to get up, but he couldn't.

What's going on? Derrick looked down to find he had been strapped down like some kind of wild beast. What looked like giant rubber bands were tightly wrapped around his ankles, just above his knees, right below his belly button, and against his chest. He wasn't going anywhere.

Derrick was scared to death. What on earth had taken place? *Why am I in a room like this?* He began trying to wiggle his way loose, but quickly learned he couldn't move a muscle. Seconds later, Brady woke up. Before his eyes were even opened, he could hear his brother grunting and groaning.

"Derrick, are you okay?"

"I don't know," Derrick whimpered, starting to cry.

"What's the matter?" Brady asked, starting to get up. He couldn't move either. Just like Derrick, he had been strapped to the bed.

"Let us out of here!" Brady hollered.

"Help!" Derrick yelled.

Minutes later, Alvin entered the room. "Hello gentlemen," he said. "Looks like you're not quite so tough now, are you?"

Brady was furious. His hands balled into fists again.

Alvin noticed. "Look at those puny little hands," he teased.

"When can we get up?" Derrick asked.

"When you're told you can," Alvin laughed, before leaving the room.

Brady and Derrick just looked at each other. They couldn't believe Alvin had simply left the room. Who did he think he was? What gave him the right?

"Brady, what are you wearing?" Derrick asked.

Brady looked down to see that he was wearing what looked like an off-white colored hospital gown. Where had his clothes gone? Looking over at Derrick, he saw he was dressed in similar fashion.

These men were cruel. As soon as he got out of there, Brady was determined to report the child shelter for being so abusive.

Another hour passed before Alvin returned. "Have you

gentlemen calmed down yet?" he asked.

Derrick and Brady both looked at each other. If they smarted off, they would have to stay longer. They had not really calmed down. They were both still very angry, but they couldn't show it. At least not until they were out of that horrible place they called a shelter.

"Yes, sir," Brady replied.

"How about you, young man?" he asked Derrick.

"Yes, sir. We're sorry for bein' bad."

"Good, boys. It's time for dinner now. After I take the straps off, I expect you to wash your hands and come to the table with the rest of us. When we get there, you are to keep your hands on top of the table at all times. Don't forget the rules we went over earlier. Just like sitting on the sofa, you must keep one chair between you and the person on either side of you. No physical contact. No whispering," Alvin lectured.

"Yes, sir," both boys said.

Looking down, Brady asked if they could get their clothes back.

Unfortunately, Alvin told him that was out of the question. They would be required to remain in their hospital gowns until it was time to leave the next day.

Brady argued that it wasn't fair to expect them to go to dinner dressed like girls.

Alvin wasn't one to reason with. He said there were two options—go to dinner in their gowns or stay strapped to their beds.

"Fine. We'll come to the table," Brady agreed. He couldn't help but wonder how his clothes had gotten changed. Someone in that building had seen him without them on. He hoped whoever it was hadn't touched him inappropriately. He was sickened by even the thought of it.

Dinner smelled great. Its aroma made its way into their nostrils before they even entered the kitchen. It smelled like a

Thanksgiving dinner—but it couldn't be. After all, it was only September.

"Brady, you sit over there between Shawn and Melissa," Alvin said, pointing to an empty chair. "Derrick, you sit between Margaret and Allison."

The boys hadn't been seated long before Alvin jumped onto Brady. "Put your hands on top of the table."

Back at home, both Brady and Derrick had been taught that leaving their hands or elbows on the table was bad manners. Now Alvin told them they had to keep their hands on the table. It sounded absurd, but Brady did what he was told.

Seconds later, a woman showed up at the table and set down a huge golden looking ham. Next came a clear dish filled with macaroni and cheese. That was followed by a bowl of mashed potatoes. Everything looked and smelled wonderful.

"Time to dig in," Alvin said.

In no time, the table came alive. Kids all around the room started reaching across to get whatever they could get their chubby little fingers on. Everyone acted as if they were starved half to death, although it was obvious they had been well fed.

Right after dinner, Alvin told Brady and Derrick to get ready for bed. He took them to the boys' sleeping quarters and told them which beds they would be sleeping in. He assured them they would be leaving the shelter immediately after breakfast the following morning.

Brady couldn't wait. He didn't know where he was going when he left the shelter, but anywhere had to be better than this. Derrick agreed. He had never been treated this way before. He would rather live under a bridge somewhere than to have to put up with being treated like a dog by Alvin.

As the lights went out, Brady let out a sigh of relief. No one strapped him to the bed. No one stuck any more needles in him. The bed wasn't very comfortable, but at least he was free to move around as he needed to.

"Brady, I'm scared," Derrick told him.

"Scared of what?"

"I don't know. I'm just scared. I miss Mommy and Daddy."

"Me too. This'll all be over soon though. Just wait and see."

With that, the two stopped talking and managed to fall asleep.

15
A FRESH START

7:00 AM THE NEXT morning arrived sooner than either of the boys could have imagined. "Guys, what is taking so long? Everybody else is already sitting at the table waiting for you so they can eat their breakfast!" Alvin shouted from the hall.

"Already?" Brady mumbled.

"Hurry it up. The others are growing very impatient and I can't say I blame them."

Brady disliked that man the way he disliked going for a sports physical every year. *I can't wait to get out of this place. It's even worse than that horrible trailer Ms. Hilton kept us locked up in.*

Still, he decided he had better do what he was told. The last thing he wanted was to get another shot.

"You boys better be at that table in less than three minutes," Alvin commanded.

"Yes, sir," Derrick said.

Derrick was determined to stay out of trouble all day. It was a new day and a new beginning. He didn't care what it took. From the moment his eyes opened, he was going to be a good boy. No one could make him be anything less. At least, that was his plan.

In no time, the two brothers were joining the other children at the table. The food looked, and again smelled absolutely delicious. Sitting right in front of Derrick's plate was the biggest chocolate chip muffins he had ever feasted his eyes on. Brady's vision was drawn to the enormous pile of buttermilk pancakes directly in the center of the table. His nose, however, was telling him to pick up a handful of sausage links. Oh, what a meal it was going to be.

"Time to dig in," Alvin said.

Derrick couldn't wait. Just like the others, he scurried to get a little bit of everything on his plate. His stomach seemed to have grown by three inches in two days. He didn't mind though; he had decided he was going to start watching his weight—he just had to get fatter so he could see it better!

Brady wanted to dig in as well, but didn't want to enjoy himself in front of Alvin. He was still very angry about what had taken place the night before. If he could be alone with the man, he'd probably break his jaw. *The big wimp has his own set of bodyguards; if I beat him up, I'll end up with a needle stuck in me again.*

Slowly, Brady filled his plate while sporting a look of disgust on his face. On the inside, he couldn't wait to eat. On the outside, he was a zombie. *I'm gonna pretend this food means nothin' to me.*

"Brady, are you going to miss us?" Alvin asked.

"Yeah, sure. About as bad as I miss having the flu last winter."

"Still Mr. Funny Pants, I see. I guess I'll take that as a no."

Derrick smirked. He wished he had come up with something like that to say. He wasn't about to chime in though. What his brother said was funny, but he didn't want to chance ruining the day by getting himself punished.

As soon as the boys had finished their last bites, Alvin told them to get ready for Ms. Simms to pick them up. "You need to get your teeth brushed and hair combed, get your clothes back on, and be at the table in five minutes. Understood?"

Get our clothes back on? "Hallelujah," Brady mumbled. He was sick and tired of wearing a hospital gown. It made him feel slightly feminine—like he was wearing a nightgown like Samantha Hilton had on the night before.

"Your clothes have been folded neatly and laid on the beds you slept on last night," Alvin continued. "When you get your gowns off, you need to deposit them in the laundry basket next to the door in your room. Is everything clear?"

"As clear as a pile of fly-covered dog mess," Brady said.

"Excuse me? If you don't want to get yourself ready, I would be more than happy to call some friends of mine who will treat you like you're two. They will physically hold you down and brush your teeth. They'll comb your hair. They'll strip you all the way down to nothing and then put your regular clothes back on you. Is that what you want?"

I hate that man with everything in me, Brady thought. He felt his fists forming again. His heart started pounding almost uncontrollably. He wanted to knock every one of Alvin's teeth out one punch at a time. He wanted to make it next to impossible for him to keep barking orders at him. Then he remembered that needle and decided he had better behave himself.

"No, sir. I'm sorry," Brady lied.

"Very well then," Alvin told him. "Your five minutes begins right now!"

Brady took a run for it. *There's no way I'm gonna give Alvin any excuse to send his "friends" to humiliate me again. I'm gonna be ready in four minutes flat.* He knew it would be difficult, but he was an athlete. Athletes could do anything they set their minds to.

Derrick thought it was funny seeing his brother move about so quickly so he decided to join in. The two of them wouldn't have moved any faster if they were being chased by a stampede of flesh eating dinosaurs at dinner time. They quickly slipped out of their hospital gowns and into their own clothing, ran to the restroom and practically fought over the water faucet to get their teeth brushed and hair combed. Lastly, it was a mad dash back to the table.

"Very good, gentlemen," Alvin told them.

Brady was thrilled to see Ms. Simms being escorted into the building. "Good morning children," she said.

"Good morning," Derrick replied.

"I'm not a child," Brady told her. "But good morning nonetheless."

"As usual I'm on a tight schedule. I've got a million things to do today. Do you boys have all of your belongings?"

"We don't have any belongings, remember?" Brady said.

"Oh, silly me. Let's get going then. Shall we?"

With that, Ms. Simms and the boys got into the Mercedes. As soon as she turned on the key, an extremely loud burst of rap music, that is if a person could even call it music, attempted to destroy their ear drums.

"Where are we heading?" Derrick hollered over top of the radio.

"Anywhere but here would be fine with me," Brady shouted.

Ms. Simms could tell Brady had a chip on his shoulder. Turning her music down, she asked what was wrong.

Brady ignored her.

She looked at him with a questioning look in her eye. She didn't say a word though—just kept making eye contact, hoping for a response.

"You need to get that fixed," Brady told her.

"I need to get what fixed?"

"Your staring problem."

Ms. Simms didn't know what was going on, but she was not very happy about it. "Brady, if you don't tell me what's bothering you, I won't be able to help."

"You wouldn't help me even if I did tell you what was bothering me."

"Of course I will. Tell me all about it."

"Alvin and his goons ought to be arrested," Brady told her.

[127]

"Arrested? For what?"

"Assault. Drugging minors. Negligence. Humiliation."

"Brady, I've known Alvin for years. He's not abusive."

"Not abusive, huh? Jabbing needles into kids rumps and pumping them full of drugs is okay with you? Stripping boys naked while they're unconscious, then dressin' 'em up like little girls, and strapping them to beds... all of that is okay? None of that is abusive?"

"Brady, I believe you're exaggerating things just a tad. The shelter doesn't just inject people with drugs for no reason. When kids are out of control, they do sometimes help them by giving them some medications to help calm their nerves. It's not a punishment. It's something they do to keep that child from hurting himself or others. Sometimes they do have to use force. I know that's hard, but it's just the way it is. As far as the gowns, I know they're uncomfortable. It's no different than when a person has a surgery. It's just common procedure."

"So if I have kids some day and I decide to strap them to a bed when they misbehave, is that okay?"

"That's different. You know it is," Ms. Simms insisted.

"See. I knew you wouldn't help me. Let's just drop it. Can we?"

"Sure, why not," Ms. Simms replied. She told the boys they were being taken to a new foster home—together. She said they would be moving in with a family with the last name of Adams.

Brady couldn't help but to give her a hard time about that one. He asked her if she was referring to the same family of Adams's who were known as monsters.

Ms. Simms told them they had nothing to worry about. Mr. and Mrs. Adams were about the nicest foster parents they would ever meet. They were a lovely couple and all of the other children in the home were more than happy to be there.

The drive to their new foster home lasted forty-five minutes. The Adams's lived out in the sticks. As they pulled up the gravel driveway, Brady was quick to point out that there weren't any neighbors even in sight of the house.

The front door was propped wide open. Ms. Simms led the boys up to the door. "Hello?" she called.

"Howdy," Mr. Adams said. "Hold on a sec and I'll get the rest of the bunch."

"The rest of the bunch? How many people live in this dump?" Brady asked.

"Brady, behave yourself. Do not louse this up," Ms. Simms snapped.

The three of them stood on the front porch for what seemed like ten minutes before a line of children began marching down the stairs. Brady watched them all very closely.

The first one down the stairs was a girl of about thirteen years of age. She had red wavy hair and freckles across her nose and on both cheeks. Behind her was a boy of about nine years of age. He was practically bald, extremely thin, and was wearing a three-piece suit and tie. Behind him was an older teenage boy. Brady guessed he was close to the age of seventeen. He was wearing a pair of bifocals, had a pineapple haircut, and had socks that came up to just below his knees. He was a goofy looking character to say the least. Behind him was a girl of approximately five years of age, carrying a baby doll. The girl was wearing a blue dress that said "Daddy's Girl" on the front of it and her baby doll had a dress that matched hers.

Mr. Adams introduced himself as Tim and his wife as Alice. "Boys, I hope you'll like it here. All of the larger bedrooms have been taken, but we still have two small ones left—one for each of you."

Brady was loving it. Finally, his own room again. He didn't care how big or how small it was; he just wanted some privacy.

"Let me introduce our children," Alice said. "Starting with the red head—this beautiful young lady is Wendy. Next, we have Greg. Before you ask, I'll go ahead and answer your question—he has no hair because he has cancer and he's been going through some chemo treatments. It's not contagious."

Brady was in shock. He had known people to die of cancer. Never though had he seen such a young victim. If Greg could get cancer, that meant he could too. He had never even given that any thought before. What a scary world he was living in.

"Next we have Ralph. Ralph is the braniac of the family. And last, but certainly not least, we have Ginger," Alice said.

"Don't forget about Helen!" Ginger spoke up.

"That's right. We must not leave out Helen, Ginger's baby doll," Alice said.

Ginger grinned from ear to ear as she cradled the doll as if it was a true infant.

Derrick looked at her with a funny expression on his face. He hadn't been around many little girls in the past. Of course, he had been in class with them at school, but that was different. At home it was always just him and his brother. All of his friends were boys and most of his cousins were boys as well. He didn't understand why Ginger didn't seem to notice that the baby she was holding was nothing more than a ball of material someone had made to look like a baby. It wasn't real. He thought about telling her so, but he remembered the promise he had made to himself earlier. He was not going to say or do anything that could get him in trouble.

"Which one of you boys is Derrick?" Tim asked.

"I am!" Derrick said excitedly.

"Derrick, welcome to our home. How old are you, twelve?" Tim asked.

"No. I'm eleven," Derrick said, feeling good that someone thought he was older.

"What grade are you in?" Alice asked him.

"Sixth."

"How about you, Brady? How old are you?" Tim asked.

"Fourteen. My birthday's next week though."

"I should've known. Look at that peach fuzz under your nose. You're going to have a moustache before long," Tim told him.

Finally, someone noticed. Usually when Brady pointed that

[130]

out to people, they said, "Where?" He knew it was visible. None of the guys at school or in his neighborhood wanted to admit it because they were jealous.

"Would you young men like to see your bedrooms?" Alice asked.

"Yes, ma'am," Brady said.

"Follow me then."

As they reached the top of the stairs, Alice pointed to the right. "The room there at the end of the hall is where Tim and I sleep. If you ever need anything in the middle of the night, please don't hesitate to let us know. All we ask is that you knock before you come in."

"Yeah, I've already learned that lesson," Derrick chimed in.

Turning to her left, she began leading the boys toward their rooms. "Here's the restroom," she said, pointing to her right.

Derrick glanced inside. It was the biggest bathroom he had ever seen. It had a Jacuzzi tub and a separate room for the toilet and sink. A huge mirror stretched from the ceiling to the floor. The walls and the floors were made out of a deep blue ceramic tile. It was the most awesome restroom he had ever laid eyes on.

A few more feet and they arrived at Derrick's room. "Come in here and have a look," she said.

Not knowing what to expect, Derrick walked in first with Brady right behind him. "Have you ever slept on a waterbed?"

"No, ma'am," Derrick said.

"Well, I think you'll like it," Alice told him. "It's very comfortable."

"This room's kind of tiny."

"Yes, I know. You won't be spending much time up here anyway. It's just a place to lay your head down to get some shut eye every now and then."

Derrick wanted a bigger room, but still it was nice. He wasn't going to complain anymore. It could be a lot worse. It was much better than the shelter he just came out of and nicer

[131]

than the room he shared with Brady at Ms. Hilton's trailer.

"Can I see my room now?" Brady asked.

"You most certainly can. It's right this way," Alice said, heading down the hall. "Oh, I forgot to tell you. You will be sharing a room."

Brady got furious. *There is no way I'm gonna share a room. Especially not considering Derrick has one all to himself.* "That's not fair. You and your husband said we each get our own rooms."

"Come in and see for yourself," Alice said as they approached the next bedroom.

When Brady walked in, he saw something he had never expected. Half of one wall was nothing but a fish aquarium. The tank stretched from one end of the room all the way to the other and went from the floor to about half way up the wall. It was full of huge fish. He had never really been a big fan of marine life, but it was different. Maybe sharing a room wouldn't be so bad after all.

"Brady, since this is your room now, I will teach you how to take care of the fish and it will be your responsibility to care for them daily," Alice told him.

"Yes, ma'am," Brady agreed. For once, he wasn't angry. He kind of liked the idea.

Before Brady had a chance to explore his room any further, someone came in behind him. He turned around to see Greg standing there. The boy was no longer in his three-piece suit. Apparently he had only worn it to make a good first impression. Now he was wearing a pair of dark blue gym shorts and a black tank top. "Like your room?"

"Oh, it's all right," Brady replied.

"Wanna see out back?"

"Sure. Can my brother come along?"

"Yeah," Greg answered. "Let's go get him."

Brady and Greg stopped by Derrick's room together. There, they found him keeping himself busy tossing and turning on the waterbed, trying to make waves.

"I think I'm gonna get sea sick," Derrick laughed.

"Derrick, come on. Greg wants to show us out back," Brady said.

"Out back? Why should we go outside? I wanna keep playin' on the waterbed."

16
MUD DIVING

GREG TOLD him the waterbed was nothing.
The three boys galloped down the stairs and out the back
door. Brady nor Derrick had ever seen anything like what met
their eyes. The backyard seemed to stretch for miles. It had a
pond in the middle with two small rowboats floating in it. A tire
swing hung from the branch of a tall oak tree. There was a jungle
gym like one would expect to see on a playground. The most
interesting thing of all was a huge area that looked like a muddy
mess.

"What's that?" Derrick asked.

"Come here and I'll show you."

Together the three amigos walked to the edge of the mud.
"Bend down and look really close; you'll see some little critters
hiding in there," Greg told him.

Derrick and Brady both bent down trying to see. "Where?"
Derrick asked.

"I don't see anything but mud," Brady complained.

"Look closer. Here, let me help you," Greg said as he
walked around behind Derrick. Greg took a step back and then,
with all of his might, shoved Derrick face-first into the mud.

Derrick was stunned. *What on earth did he do that for?* "You're
gonna make me smash the critters!" he yelled.

"The only critter in there is you," Greg teased.

"Not for long," Brady chuckled.

Grabbing a hold of Greg's waist, Brady picked him up.
"Let's see how you like it!"

Before he could get loose, Brady threw Greg straight into

the slime pit. Greg had forgotten just how deep it was. Lying down, it nearly covered him up. It was kind of gooey, but fun!

"Let's get him!" Derrick hollered, while picking up handfuls of mud and bombing them toward his brother.

"We can do better than that!" Greg squealed.

The two younger boys went running toward Brady. Brady laughed louder than he had ever laughed in his life as he tried to get away.

"You can't out run me," Greg yelled.

In no time, Greg caught up to him. He grabbed his waist and Brady kept on running. Greg fell, but still didn't let go. His arms were now wrapped firmly around Brady's ankles which caused Brady to fall forward.

"Come on, let's drag him back to the mud!" Greg yelled.

"I have a better idea," Brady suggested. "What if we all run and dive into it? We'll see who can slide the furthest!"

Derrick was surprised. It was rare that he saw Brady have so much enthusiasm about doing something he would normally consider to be childish. He liked Greg. *Maybe he can help me and Brady get along better.*

Mud diving sounded like a great deal of fun so Derrick was all for it. "Last one in's a rotten egg!" he yelled.

"On the count of three," Greg called. "One... two... two and a half... two and three quarters... THREE!"

On three, all of the boys ran as fast as they could. As they reached the edge of the mud, they jumped into the air with their arms stretched out in front of them. After their bellies hit, they slid toward the center.

Mud went everywhere! It was in their hair, all over their faces, all over their clothes. It was what being a boy was all about.

"I won!" Brady proudly announced.

"Time to tackle the winner!" Greg yelled.

"Yeah, let's get him!" Derrick agreed.

They quickly grabbed a hold of Brady and knocked him into the mud. Actually all three of them fell back down into it. They

[135]

were laughing hysterically. While Brady was lying face first in the mud, Derrick and Greg climbed on his back and started burying him in it. Brady squirmed around trying to get loose, but with all of that mud he couldn't get much leverage. The boys were having the time of their lives.

All at once though, their fun came to an end. "Dinner time!" Alice yelled.

Dinner time? Already? The boys all looked at each other. Mr. and Mrs. Adams probably wouldn't appreciate them being so dirty when it was time to go in and eat.

"What are we gonna do?" Derrick asked.

"I don't know, but we have to think fast!" Brady said.

"Come on," Greg told them. "There's a water hose hooked up over on the other side of the field."

The boys slipped around all over the mud as they made their way out, each of them falling at least one or twice before getting back onto dry ground. They then raced off toward the hose. "First one there gets to hose off the other two," Greg announced.

Being the oldest and most athletic, Brady won the race by a long shot. He quickly turned on the hose and said, "Who wants to get it first?"

Neither boy volunteered. Even though he hadn't felt it before, somehow Derrick knew that water was going to be ice cold. Greg knew it too, but he knew from experience.

"Okay, no volunteers? Then I'll choose. Get up here, Derrick!" Brady said.

"No! Let Greg go first, please!"

"Nope. I won the race so it's my choice," Brady said. "Get up here."

Brady couldn't wait to get a little taste of sweet revenge. Derrick slowly walked in front of him. "Start with my back," he said, turning his back toward his older brother.

"Sure, no problem!"

Brady aimed the hose high in the air above Derrick and squeezed the trigger as hard as it could squeeze.

"Eww... That's cold!" Derrick whined, dancing from foot to foot.

Loving every second of it, Brady lowered the hose so it was

[136]

spraying full force on Derrick's neck. His whole body seemed to cringe. He almost looked like a turtle, the way his head tried to sink down into his body as if it was a shell. His feet were still dancing ninety miles per hour. "Ewww... Cold, cold, cold," he whined.

Greg couldn't decide if he should laugh or not. After all, he was going to be next. It was hilarious watching Derrick squirm around like that and listening to his fussing. He knew though, that before long it was going to be him hopping up and down and freezing half to death.

"Here guys, let me help you with that," a voice called from behind them. The voice belonged to Tim.

"We're sorry, sir," Brady said. "We didn't mean to get this dirty."

Brady was scared plum to death.

Derrick remembered the promise he had made to himself earlier about staying out of trouble. *What have I done? It's too late now. Tim's going to punish all three of us.* "We were just having fun," he whined.

"I know you were, guys. Boys will be boys. We've got to hurry up and get you three cleaned up though so you can have some dinner. Alice cooked some lasagna and believe me, you don't want to miss it!"

Brady nor Derrick could believe it. Tim didn't seem to care at all that the boys were covered from head to toe in mud. It was almost as if he had expected as much.

"Brady, give me the hose please," Tim said as he took it out of his hand. "Now, I need all three of you to line up and face me."

Tim had completely ruined the fun for Brady. He had planned on taking a good twenty minutes to spray off each of them. The longer they squirmed, the more he would have enjoyed himself. Now though, the tables had been turned. He much preferred to be on the giving end than being in the line-up himself.

"Everybody ready?" Tim asked with a smile on his face.

[137]

They all nodded without saying a word. Mr. Adams began by spraying the hose at their feet to get their bodies used to it before he went any further. He went back and forth, spraying all three of them. Then he brought the hose up and soaked their legs, their stomachs, their chests, their faces, and eventually their hair. Next, he repeated the process, but started at their faces and worked his way back down to their toes. Afterwards, he made them turn around and began spraying off their backs.

The boys could not believe how cold they were. Their bodies were trembling from the wetness. In a way though, it felt good. After all, it was summer time.

"Let's go get some food," Tim said, turning the hose off.

"I'm starving," Greg agreed.

Then Derrick remembered. "Sir, my brother and I don't have any dry clothes. All we have is what we're wearing now."

Tim gave them a look that let the boys know he understood and that it was going to be okay.

Greg spoke up. "Derrick can probably wear the same size as me. Brady might be able to fit into something of Ralph's."

Tim thought for a moment. "Boys, I have a better idea. What do you say we all eat outside in the sun today? Kind of like a picnic?"

"Awesome!" Greg said.

"You boys go sit down at the picnic table and the rest of us will bring the food out," Mr. Adams said.

As he left, Brady asked Greg if Mr. Adams was always so kind.

He was glad to hear that most of the time he was. Even if Greg did add that one little detail about Tim knowing how to yell when he got angry enough.

In a matter of minutes, the rest of the Adams family began bringing out the food, plates, cups, and silverware. It was the first picnic Brady or Derrick had been on for two years. They couldn't help but notice that everyone was happy. They all came out of the house with smiling faces. They talked and laughed with each other. It was like a dream world they were living in.

As soon as she finished eating, Ginger asked, "Can we give 'em their presents now, Daddy?"

"Whose birthday is it?" Derrick asked.

Tim and Alice both gave Ginger a dirty look. "Ginger, you weren't supposed to say anything yet," Alice scolded.

"It's not anyone's birthday," Tim replied. "When we heard about you boys coming and that you didn't have anything, we bought you a few items. It's nothing much; just little welcoming gifts."

Derrick's face lit up with excitement. He loved presents. He didn't care what he got; anything was better than nothing. He didn't understand why complete strangers bought him things, but that didn't matter. He was glad they did.

Brady was excited, yet confused at the same time. This foster family wasn't treating him like the others had. He wondered why. Perhaps they were up to something.

While the boys were busy thinking about that announcement, Tim and Ralph went inside to get their gifts. It seemed like twenty minutes passed before they returned to the table. By the time they got there, Derrick's pulse was racing. He loved receiving presents as much as goats loved stealing chicken feed.

"Brady, this first gift is for you," Ralph said with a dorky looking smile on his face.

Nervously, Brady took the package from him—it was wrapped in Christmas paper. Apparently they didn't have any other packaging lying around, so they just used what they had. That didn't matter to Brady though. It was still nice of the Adams family to buy him and his brother things.

As Brady picked up the package, he was shocked with how heavy it was. He wondered what it could be. At first when they had said gifts, he had imagined it would all be clothing. Slowly and carefully he unwrapped the present. To his amazement, it was a punching bag. Not a child's punching bag that he would fill up with air and sit on the floor. It was the real deal—the kind that hung from the ceiling. And there was a set of boxing gloves included in the package as well.

Brady's eyes were filled with surprise as he thanked them for their generosity.

"We heard you like to work out," Alice replied, "so we thought you might enjoy that."

"This next one's for you Derrick," Ralph said.

"I know what that one is! Can I tell him, Mommy?" Ginger asked.

"No, shhh!" Alice told her.

Unlike his brother, Derrick tore his wrapping paper to shreds. He couldn't wait to see what he got.

"Yes! Yes! Yes!" he screamed, looking inside of the wrapper.

"What is it?" Brady asked.

"A chemistry set!" Remember, I wanted one for Christmas last year and nobody bought me one?"

Everyone at the table was excited for both of the boys. They seemed like they really appreciated what they had gotten.

"Derrick, here's another one with your name on it," Ralph said.

"What is it?"

"Open it and see," Wendy told him.

Derrick felt the package and could tell it was clothing. He quickly ripped the paper as quickly as he could. It wasn't just a shirt. It was a whole outfit! There was a pair of brand new shoes, a package of socks, a package of underwear, a pair of cargo pants, and a nice looking shirt with three buttons at the top. "Can I go try it all on?"

"Not yet, wait until you and your brother get the rest of your gifts," Tim said.

"Can I pass out the next one?" Greg asked.

"Sure buddy," Ralph told him. "Which one do you want to give them?"

Greg looked at the remaining packages and chose one for Brady. "Here you go," he said with an expression of pride on his face.

Brady felt the package. It didn't feel like clothing. It didn't feel like athletic equipment. He shook it. Nothing rattled. Nothing jingled. He didn't have a clue. Taking his time again, Brady slowly unwrapped the package. Inside, he found a leather wallet.

"I've never had one of these before," he said excitedly.

"You guys are alright."

"We figured you are getting to the age where you might want a billfold," Tim told him. "Did you look inside?"

Inside? Why should he look inside? Brady opened it to find a ten dollar bill.

"Whoa! Thank you!!!!" Brady was beginning to sound as excited as Derrick.

"Brady, you get one more," Ralph said.

From the way the package was wrapped, Brady knew it was something similar to what Derrick had gotten moments before. Usually he didn't care much for new clothes, but in light of the circumstances, he appreciated them now. He didn't take his time with this one—he turned that wrapping paper into ancient history.

Inside, he found a black leather jacket, a white muscle shirt, a regular t-shirt, a pair of blue jeans, a belt, a package of socks, and a package of underwear.

"I'm with Derrick. Can we go try on our new clothes?" Brady asked.

"In just a minute," Tim said. "There is one present remaining. This one is for both of you to open together."

Now both Brady's and Derrick's curiosity was overwhelming. What kind of gift could they share? They had two separate bedrooms. They wore different sizes of clothing. They were total opposites. There was only one way to find out.

"Ready? Get set! Go!" Brady said.

The two boys quickly unwrapped the last present. They looked at the gift, then at each other with puzzled looks on their faces.

"What is this for?" Derrick asked.

"It was my idea," Wendy said. "Before Tim and Alice adopted me, I was moved around from foster home to foster home. One of my moms gave me a scrapbook. She helped me put it together. We took pictures of all of the things I was doing while in her home and put some papers I did in school in there. I took that book with me to my next foster home and kept updating it with new pictures. I moved again and took it with me and still kept filling it up. Now I like to look back and it helps me remember the different families I stayed with and what I did while I was waiting to be adopted. I thought you might like to do that too," she said.

"Adopted? We're not being adopted," Brady said.

"That's not what I meant," Wendy replied. "I just gave it to you so you can keep a scrapbook of the time you spend in foster care. If you end up getting adopted, you can take it with you, but if you get to go back with your parents, you can share it with them. I'm sure they'd like to see what you've been doing while you've been away from home."

"I like that idea," Derrick said. "When can we take some pictures?"

"Maybe tomorrow," Alice told him. "For now, why don't you boys run upstairs and try on those new clothes?"

"Yes ma'am!" Brady said. He didn't give it a second thought. He couldn't wait to get out of his wet clothes and put on something brand new.

Derrick was excited too. If he had to be in foster care, this was the family he definitely wanted to stay with!

17
HONEYMOON PERIOD

ARLY THE NEXT morning, Alice tapped on Brady's
door. "Time to get up."

"Why?"

"We have to get you enrolled in school this morning."

"I'm already enrolled in school—where I was living before."

"You don't live there now. We have to get you signed up at a new school," Alice told him as she opened his door.

"We're not gonna be here very long. We'll probably be movin' back home with our parents in a few days."

"I don't know, Brady. Usually things don't go quite that quickly with foster care. Go ahead and get dressed and come downstairs for breakfast."

Brady was upset. He liked Mr. and Mrs. Adams and their family. He liked staying there, but only on a temporary basis. He did not like the idea of staying there long term. *I don't want to change schools. I've never had to be the "new kid" before and I don't want to start now.*

After giving it more thought, Brady knew he had no choice. He got out of bed and got his clothes down from their hangers. As he was starting to get dressed, he heard Alice knock on Derrick's door.

"Good morning," she called.

Derrick was dead to the world. "Derrick, it's time to get up."

[143]

After the second call, Brady was afraid something was wrong. Under normal circumstances Derrick was a light sleeper. Brady finished getting his pants on before heading into the hall. "Do you want me to get him up?"

"I would appreciate that, Brady," Alice replied.

Brady tapped on the door. "Derrick, it's me. Is everything okay?"

Derrick still didn't answer.

Brady opened the door and went in to find Derrick out like a light. His mouth was wide open, his blankets were thrown in the floor, and one leg was dangling over the side of the bed. Brady walked over and started to shake him.

"Derrick, come on, you have to get up," he said, placing his hand on Derrick's shoulder.

His shoulder seemed rather warm. Derrick still didn't move. Brady felt his forehead and sure enough, it was hot. Derrick had a fever. Brady shook him a little bit harder. "Derrick, time to get up."

Slowly, Derrick lifted his heavy eyelids. "What's goin' on?"

"We have to go get signed up for school."

"I don't feel so good," Derrick whined.

"Do you want me to get Alice?"

"Yeah."

Brady ran downstairs as fast as he could.

"Did you get that sleepy head up yet?" Alice asked.

"I think he's sick," Brady told her. "He feels really warm and said he doesn't feel well."

"You go check on him," Tim said. "Brady, you go ahead and sit down and have your breakfast with the rest of us. After we eat, I'll take you to get registered for school and if your brother's sick Alice will stay here to care for him."

"I don't want to leave my brother here alone," Brady said.

"He'll be fine. I'll take good care of him," Alice said as she started back up the stairs.

Brady was not very happy about the whole idea of starting a new school. Especially now that Derrick was sick and got to stay home. He wished he was sick too. *Now there's an idea.*

"You know what, Mr. Adams? I'm not feeling very well either," Brady lied.

[144]

Tim stood from the table and walked over to Brady. He put the palm of his hand against Brady's forehead. "You feel okay to me. What's wrong?"

"I don't know. I just don't feel good," Brady lied again.

"It's probably just butterflies since you're starting a new school," Tim told him. "It'll be all right. Just wait and see."

He's not buying it, Brady thought. *I'm going to have to do a lot better than this.* "Sir, I think I might throw up."

Mr. Adams had taken in a lot of foster children in the past. He could usually tell when one of them was lying to him. "Come on then, I'll walk you to the restroom," he said.

"No, you don't need to do that. I can go by myself."

Mr. Adams told him he would have to go to school unless he actually vomited. He said it was his understanding that Brady had not been in school since entering "the system" and he was going to have no part of his truancy on his record.

Brady didn't know what to do. He certainly did not want to go to school. Then another light bulb went off. *Mr. Adams said I can miss school if I throw up. Fine. I can do that.*

The fourteen year old slowly walked to the restroom, making sure to hold his stomach the entire way just in case anyone was watching him. He went in and closed the door. He opened the lid to the toilet and knelt down in front of it. Opening his mouth, he leaned forward, shoved his forefinger way back in his throat, and wa la!

Standing up, he moseyed back to the kitchen, still purposely holding his stomach. Using the whiniest voice he knew how to muster, he told Tim he was right—he had thrown up indeed.

Tim looked him over closely. Brady didn't look pale. There weren't any tears in his eyes. He didn't feel too warm or too cool—he was faking.

"Good. That should make you feel better. Sometimes all we need to do is get that stuff out of our systems once and then the rest of the day we're good. Come on, let's get you to school."

As Tim stood from the table, Alice came back down the stairs. "Derrick is sick all right. I'm going to have to keep him

[145]

home from school today."

Brady was furious. *How did Derrick manage to get sick already?* Especially right when it was time to start his first day of school? He wished he knew his secret. Maybe later, if no one was looking, Brady could go in and spend a lot of time by Derrick's bedside and he would catch whatever was ailing him.

From the look on Tim's face, Brady knew he did not have a chance of cutting class. He too stood from the table and walked toward the front door.

"I'll see you later, dear," Tim said as he headed out. "You kids be sure to get out to the bus before it runs."

Brady did not utter a word all the way to school. Even though Mr. Adams was seated right beside of him in the car, he felt all alone. His stomach was really starting to hurt. He felt like he might really have to hurl. Then again, he figured it was just nerves. He had been going through a lot of changes lately and starting a new school scared him more than the rest of it. He wasn't sure why it scared him more than changing homes did, but supposed it had something to do with being separated from Derrick. At least when Derrick was with him, he wasn't completely alone.

When they pulled up to the middle school, Brady's heart sank deep into his chest. As slow as he could possibly move, Brady unbuckled his seatbelt and got out of the car. He followed Mr. Adams inside to the office.

"Hi, I need to enroll a new student," Mr. Adams told the secretary.

"Sure. Let me call Mr. Hendricks, our new school counselor, so he can help you get started on the paperwork."

Brady felt like he could pass out at any time. *I'd much rather be sick in bed than being here any day.*

"Hello men," Mr. Hendricks said as he entered the room. "Son, why don't you and your dad follow me back here to my office?"

"He's not my dad. He's my foster parent," Brady grumbled.

Mr. Hendricks knew he had just torn open an anthill. "I'm sorry about that. Would you mind bringing your foster parent

[146]

inside and sat down. Mr. Hendricks closed the door and asked
Mr. Adams to walk to the other side of the hallway.

Mr. Hendricks attempted to whisper, but Brady could hear
every word. "How long has this child been living with you in
foster care?"

"A couple of days."

"What kind of issues are we going to have with him?"

"Brady seems like a good boy. Like I said, he's only been
with us for a couple of days though, so I really don't know.
We're still in the honeymoon period right now," he heard Tim
say.

"Honeymoon period?"

"In foster care, that's what we call it when a new kid moves
in. Generally speaking, the kids are always on their best behavior
for the first couple of weeks. After that, that's when we get to
meet the real demons inside of them."

Brady couldn't believe what he was hearing. Mr. Adams had
been so nice to him. Now he was talking about him like he was
just another foster kid; not a human being. He spoke as if he
expected him to become a hoodlum in a couple of weeks. Brady
was furious.

That was okay though. He didn't plan on being there but
for a few days anyway. He would not forget what he just heard.
If that's how Mr. Adams felt about him, that's how he would act.
*But why should I wait a few weeks? Maybe I'll let him meet the 'demons' he
spoke of today!*

Moments later, the door to the office whipped open. "All
right, are we ready to get things moving?" Mr. Hendricks asked.

"Yeah, I'd like to get things moving. I'd like to get back in

[147]

the car and get moving back home," Brady replied.

Mr. Adams told Brady he knew he was nervous, but he was certain he was going to like his new school. He just needed to give it some time.

"You don't know anything about me. Like you said out in the hallway, we're still in our honeymoon period. Remember?"

Mr. Adams didn't say another word. He didn't mean for Brady to hear him. He didn't really mean it the way it sounded either. Guilt started settling in. He knew the Clark boys had gone through a lot. They didn't trust adults. They had been taken from their parents, thrown into a foster home, thrown into a shelter, and now had moved in with him and on top of everything else, now they were changing schools. He couldn't believe he had said something so calloused that could be so easily overheard.

"Brady, I have met a lot of foster children in the past," Mr. Hendricks said. "I'm very familiar with the types of problems you may be facing. I want you to be honest with me. What can I do to make things easier for you? I don't want you getting in trouble here. Can you behave well in a regular classroom setting?"

"Only one way to find out."

Mr. Hendricks could tell he was going to have his hands full. "I'll tell you what. Let me just call your old school and get your records and then I can get your schedule made up. Mr. Adams, would it be okay with you if we don't have him start classes until tomorrow?"

"That's fine," Mr. Adams said. "I just want to get him enrolled as soon as possible so he doesn't miss any more school."

"I'll only be here a few more days anyway."

"We'll see."

"I'm going back with my parents," Brady mumbled hatefully.

"Maybe you will. Maybe you won't," Mr. Adams replied.

Brady's blood was boiling again. He wanted to regain control of the situation, but he didn't know how. It seemed that no matter how hard he tried, things never went his way anymore. If he could have only one wish, it would be to take back the lies

[148]

he had told about his parents. It was too late for that now; even if he wanted to tell the truth, he couldn't. There was no way he could admit to telling such vicious lies.

"Before you go, I almost forgot to ask," Mr. Hendricks said. "Is Brady taking any kind of medication that we need to be aware of?"

"Not currently. However, his case manager has scheduled him for a psych eval and I'm taking him there later this afternoon," Mr. Adams told him.

Brady was shocked. He knew Ms. Simms wanted him on medicine, but he didn't know he had an appointment already. *So, what?* he wondered. *The deal was for me to start school today and then be pulled out later this afternoon for a doctor's appointment? How stupid is that!*

"So more than likely he will be medicated when he comes to school tomorrow?" Mr. Hendricks asked.

"I'll call you and let you know," Tim replied.

When the meeting ended, Brady stomped his way to the car. He got in the front seat and slammed the door with all of his might, then glared at Mr. Adams.

"What's wrong, Brady?"

"What's wrong? What do you think is wrong?" Brady yelled.

"I don't know. You tell me."

"I'm not telling you anything."

"Okay, fine. I can't make you talk to me. When we get home, you are going to be disciplined for the attitude you're showing me," Tim said.

"You can't discipline me. You're not my father!"

Tim didn't say another word all the way home. He let Brady sit there and stew. He had been parenting long enough to know there was no point in trying to reason with a teenager who was that upset. He wasn't yet sure how he was going to discipline Brady, but he knew he had to get him under control immediately to prevent problems in the future.

As they pulled back into the driveway, Brady began unbuckling his seatbelt. Tim told him he was expected to go

[149]

straight to his bedroom and to wait for him there.

"Whatever," Brady replied, rolling his eyes.

Before the car was completely stopped, Brady opened his door and jumped out. He stomped into the house, slammed the door shut behind him, and stomped up the stairs to his room. He slammed the door as hard as he could.

"What happened?" Alice asked as Tim entered the house.

"The boy has a bit of a temper," Tim replied. "Let me deal with him."

Alice had no problem with that whatsoever. Most of the time when it came to older foster children, she dealt with the girls and Tim dealt with the boys. They both felt that was the safest way to handle things.

Tim took a few deep breaths and then walked up the stairs. When he got to Brady's room, he started to turn the doorknob; it was locked. "Open this door," Tim ordered.

"No, I won't!"

"Brady, listen to me. I'm sorry if I said anything that offended you. I just want to talk."

"Talk?" I thought you said you're gonna punish me?"

"I am going to punish you, but not yet. First I just want to have a man to man chat."

"I don't feel like talkin'," Brady said.

This might just turn into a long evening, Tim thought. *It looks like the honeymoon period ended sooner than I thought it would. I hope things don't get ugly.*

"Brady, I am not going to keep standing here talking to this door. Open it now, please," Tim repeated.

Still angry, Brady walked to the door and swung it open. He didn't even look at Tim. He just walked back to his bed and sat down. Tim walked in, leaving the door open behind him. He didn't want to do anything to make Brady uncomfortable.

"Is it okay if I sit here?" Mr. Adams asked, pointing toward the opposite end of the bed.

"I guess so. It's your bed."

Tim told Brady there were rules in the Adams's household and those rules were expected to be followed. Children would

[150]

show respect to the authority in the house.

It wasn't hard to figure out that Brady was not ready to take any rules to heart, so Tim moved on to the discipline part. He said Brady had lost all privileges. He would eat at meal time only. If the rest of the family got ice cream or a special snack, Brady would not be permitted to join them. Anytime the others were outside playing, he would be sitting on his bed doing nothing. Brady would not leave that room for any reason without permission.

The grounding would remain in effect until Tim felt the boy was being more respectful. He further explained that Brady would be required to eat his meals in his room. He said the rest of the family would eat at the table and when they were finished, he would bring Brady's meals up to him. If the food got cold while the rest of the household was eating, that was just going to be Brady's problem.

"Whatever!" Brady mumbled.

"One more thing. Your bedroom door is to stay open the entire time you're grounded. If I walk by even once and find it closed, I will take it off its hinges and you'll no longer have one," Mr. Adams said sternly.

18
TOUGH LOVE

APPARENTLY DANIEL had been mistaken. Foster parents may not have had the authority to physically discipline them, but Tim was not afraid to provide consequences. Brady didn't care. He wanted to stay as far away from that family as possible. The only family he had was his mom and dad and his bratty little brother. The rest of them could all just wander off and die for all he cared.

As Brady sat on his bed, he heard Mr. Adams enter Derrick's room. "Feelin' any better, bud?"

"A little," Derrick whined.

"Would you like me to read you a story?"

"A story? Would you really?" Derrick loved books almost as much as he loved one-on-one attention.

"Okay, let me see what I can find downstairs and I'll be right back," Mr. Adams said.

I don't believe what I'm hearing, Brady thought. *Tim's in there acting all nice to Derrick, but then when he thinks we can't hear him, he'll probably talk about him like trash.*

Before Mr. Adams had a chance to return, Derrick had to use the restroom. When he started walking down the hall, Brady whispered, "Come here a second."

"Why?"

"Keep your voice down. Just come here."

"What do you want?"

"Did you hear our conversation? I'm grounded. Tim won't let me come out of my room for any reason until he thinks I've learned my lesson," Brady whispered.

"So?"

"What should I do? I don't wanna be cooped up in this tiny

room forever."

"Don't do it then."

"What do you mean?"

"Remember what Daniel said? No matter what a foster parent tells you to do, you don't have to listen. They can't make you."

"You know what? You're absolutely right. I'm going outside and he can't stop me!"

What the boys didn't know was that Mr. Adams was already reaching the top of the stairs. Just as those last words dripped from Brady's tongue, Mr. Adams said, "Oh you are, are you?"

Derrick turned around and headed back toward the restroom.

"Derrick, you have just lost your privilege of having me read to you," Tim told him.

"What did I do?"

"You told your brother to not mind me. I won't put up with that. When you get out of the restroom, go back to your room."

"You can't lie to him like that," Brady said. "You told him you were gonna read him a story."

"I can do whatever I feel is necessary," Mr. Adams replied.

"Oh really? What are you gonna do if I go outside?"

"How do you think you're gonna get there? I'm between you and the steps young man. What are you gonna do? Jump out of a window?"

"I'll knock you out of my way and I'll run out that door."

"If you think you're man enough, try it! I dare you!" Mr. Adams said hatefully, spreading his feet apart to get himself ready just in case Brady lunged at him.

Brady stared him right in the eye. His hands curled into fists and his blood started boiling as his body began rocking back and forth. "I'm serious. You better get outta my way."

"I'm serious too. You better go back to your room."

"What if I don't? You gonna kick me out?" Brady asked.

"It doesn't matter what will happen if you don't. I told you to go to your room and I want you to do it now," Tim demanded.

"Forget it!" Brady said, running toward him.

Brady attempted to shove his way past Mr. Adams. He had no idea just how stout Tim was. Tim didn't move a muscle; he blocked the hallway so there was no way Brady was going around him.

"Get outta my way, old man!"

"Go back to your room, little boy!"

"Oh, that does it!" Brady hollered.

He made a fist and swung at Mr. Adams.

Mr. Adams caught his hand and spun him around backward. Grabbing both of Brady's arms, he crossed them firmly across his chest and placed him in what was known as the basket hold restraint.

"Let me go!" Brady screamed. "You let me go now!"

Tim didn't let go; he held on tight. Brady tried to kick him with his right leg. He kicked backward as hard as he could. With that, Mr. Adams used his own right leg and swept Brady's feet out from under him, knocking the boy into a seated position.

"Come on, you're hurtin' me," Brady grumbled.

"Are you going to go to your room?"

"No, I'm not!" Brady yelled, bringing his head backward and busting Tim's lip.

Even with a busted lip, Tim refused to let go.

From her post at the bottom of the stairwell, Alice hollered to see if Tim wanted her to phone the police.

Brady fully expected to hear him say yes, but he didn't. Tim said he had everything perfectly under control.

"Call them! Tell her to call the police. Have them take me outta here. You don't want us here anyway!"

Tim didn't say a word. He just held Brady longer as the boy begged to be let loose, claiming Tim was hurting his arms. The longer he was restrained, the angrier he was becoming.

Brady spit on Tim's arm—over and over again.

"Stop that right now!"

"And what are you gonna do about it if I don't?"

With Tim again ignoring him, Brady tried to wrestle around to free himself, but he couldn't do it. "Fine. You win! Let go of me and I'll go to my room."

[154]

Mr. Adams said, "Okay, but you better not be lying to me."

Slowly, he let go of the boy's arms. Before Tim had a chance to get on his feet, Brady spun around and punched him in the mouth. "I told you to let me go, old man!"

Mr. Adams grabbed Brady's ankles as the boy attempted to make a run for the stairs. Brady toppled to the ground and Mr. Adams again had to restrain him.

"Is everything okay up there, Tim?" Alice called.

"Go ahead and call the police, honey. If this boy wants to go to jail that bad, maybe it'll teach him a lesson."

"Jail?" Brady hollered. "I don't wanna go to jail! Please don't call them. I'll be good! I'm sorry!"

"Do you mean it this time?"

"Yes, sir. I do. I am really, really, really sorry. It'll never happen again. Please don't send me to prison."

"Honey, I'm giving him one more chance. If you hear any more struggling, you call them," Mr. Adams said while releasing Brady for a second time.

This time, Brady stood up and gave him dirty looks. His hands were still curled into fists. Mr. Adams stood up and told Brady to get to his room.

Brady went alright—and slammed the door behind him.

That was a mistake! Tim was quick to remind him what he said about taking the door off the hinges if he slammed it again.

Brady swung the door open as far as it would go. He held onto the top of it with both hands and lifted his feet off the ground so that all of his weight was pulling on one corner of the door.

Mr. Adams demanded he let go, but Brady refused, sarcastically claiming he had only been trying to help Tim get it off its hinges faster.

Tim ordered him to sit on his bed until he was told otherwise. About that time, he glanced down at his watch. He couldn't believe it. It was already time to leave for Brady's psychological evaluation.

"Never mind. Come on. I have to take you to your

appointment."

Brady started to insist on not going, but he was too tired to fight anymore. He stood up and walked to the car, getting into the front seat again.

"Get in the back" Mr. Adams said.

"The back? Why?"

"You've lost all of your privileges and sitting up front is one of them.

Fine. Whatever, Brady thought, unbuckling his seatbelt and opening the door.

As he got in the back, Mr. Adams walked around the car and turned on the child safety locks just in case he got any ideas.

Driving toward the doctor's office, Tim gave Brady a good talking to. The boy had it made. He and his brother were living together in a home where there was enough love to go around for everyone. Tim said he liked Brady and his brother, but violence could never be tolerated. If he wanted to stay in their household, his rebellion needed to stop immediately.

Brady was in no mood to reason. With a chip on his shoulder, he accused Tim of looking for an excuse to kick them out.

Tim assured him nothing could be further from the truth. As long as Brady accepted consequences when he misbehaved, they could work through things. If he kept misbehaving and refusing consequences, he would have to leave. Because it was Brady causing the problems, it wouldn't necessarily be both of the boys who would move on—it would be Brady hitting the road by himself.

"You mean you will let him stay and make me leave? You would separate us?" Brady asked.

"It would not be my choice to separate you. That would be a choice that's made by your behavior."

Tim did not want to ask Brady to leave; he liked the young man. Even through everything that had taken place just moments before, Tim saw potential in him. He didn't always see that in kids. Sometimes he could look into their eyes and see nothing but hatred or evil—Brady was different. There was something about him. Tim truly believed he could turn around and be a pretty decent kid.

[156]

"Do you hate me?" Brady asked.

"Hate you? For what?"

"I don't know. You just don't like me. Do you?"

"I do like you. I like you and your brother. What I don't like is the way you've been treating me today."

"You don't know what it's like."

"What do you mean?"

"Never mind," Brady replied.

"Come on. Out with it. What do I not understand?"

Brady accused him of having no clue how it felt to be tossed around like a sack of rotten potatoes. He didn't know what it felt like to be taken away from his parents. To have one hundred different sets of rules to follow. To change homes two or three times in the same week.

Tim helped Brady realize he had just crammed his big fat foot right in that mouth of his. Tim had been a foster child himself.

At first, Brady thought he was making it up. That is, until Tim told his story. He had been six years old when he entered foster care. Never had anyone decided to take him into their home and keep him. He had watched as several children he met in different homes either returned to their biological parents or were given forever families. Over and over again, his heart was broken. That's why he had become a foster parent—to make a difference.

Brady didn't know what to say. He never would have expected that. It did make sense though. It would explain why the Adams's were so much friendlier than the other foster homes. Tim really did know how it felt; he had been there himself.

"Why did you get put in foster care?" Brady asked.

"My mom abandoned me."

"What about your dad?"

"Mom killed him—right before she ran out the door. Stabbed him right in the chest in the middle of the night while he was sleeping."

[157]

"Why?"

"I don't know. Mom did a lot of crazy things. I was just a little boy back then, but looking back I would suspect she was taking some kind of drugs. She probably doesn't even remember doing it."

Tim said his mom had never sent him a birthday card. Never called him. Never mailed him a letter. She had left as if he didn't even exist.

Brady was stunned. He could not even begin to imagine how that felt. He had been put in foster care by his own doings. He had lied because he had been mad at his parents for disciplining him. He figured Tim would have been thankful if his mom had stayed around—even if she punished him five or six times per day. Tim probably would have gladly traded places with him. It actually made Brady sick inside to imagine that something so horrible actually happened in real life.

"Now I've told you my story. Wanna tell me yours?" Mr. Adams asked.

"Do I have to?"

"No, you don't have to. I just thought you might want to talk about it."

"Not right now. Maybe another time."

Brady didn't know what story to tell. If he admitted the truth, what would happen to him? It may have even been illegal to tell such a horrible lie. He had already been threatened with going to jail once and it terrified him. He definitely did not want to go there.

"That's okay, Brady. We're pulling into the doctor's office now anyway," Mr. Adams said.

19

THE DRUG TEST

PEOPLE SAY THINGS get easier with time. For Roxanne and Trevor, however, every hour that passed seemed to be more difficult than the previous one. Not being able to see their boys every day was hard. Not being able to talk to them on the phone was even harder.

The couple, determined to regain custody of the children God had given them, began making phone calls and doing research on fighting Child Protective Services and the foster care system. Roxanne worked from home while Trevor did his research during his down time at the bank.

Unfortunately, their digging only made the case seem impossible to win. They found dozens upon dozens of websites and social media groups filled with members who were just like them—desperately seeking reunification with their children.

The people were angry. They vented their frustrations. They had turned into hatemongers—despising anyone affiliated with such agencies. Anyone who called themselves a social worker or a foster parent was clearly an enemy.

It was easy for the Clarks to understand why the other parents felt the way they did, but their case was different. They knew they had appeared guilty. They had indeed made some poor choices. The boys had, at least supposedly, made false allegations against them.

The chances of regaining custody anytime soon? Slim to none. That's what various attorneys they contacted had to say.

Roxanne, becoming discouraged once more, found herself slipping off to sleep on the couch again—for the third time that day. And for a third time, her sleep was haunted by memories.

She had flashbacks. She could see Brady and Derrick as happy little boys. Derrick, sitting on her lap being read to as a toddler, and Brady snuggling up on the couch next to them. She read them book after book and the boys loved every second of it. Then there were the birthday parties. Trevor had always made sure the boys' birthdays were something special. All of their classmates from school were invited, their friends from church, kids in the neighborhood. They had a blast! Then, as always, came the nightmare.

They were in the woods. The thunder was hollering. The lightning was flashing. Roxanne was angrier than ever—making a mountain out of a mole hill. The household beat up the van. Then, there came the police officer. Roxanne had tears rolling down her face as she continued dreaming.

A sudden knock on the door suddenly woke her. *Who could that be?*

Wiping the tears from her face, she walked to the front door to see a younger woman, who appeared to be fresh out of college, standing on the porch. "Hi, I'm Ashley, with the Department of Social Services. I'm here to do a drug screening."

"A drug screening? On who?"

"It's standard procedure, ma'am. The ultimate goal of foster care placements is reunification. It takes time and there's a lot of red tape, but this is something we have to do—that is, if you're willing to cooperate."

"And if I refuse?"

"That's your choice. We'll just note that in our files. It won't look very good on you in court though. I can tell you that much."

In court? What is that supposed to mean? Roxanne thought. *Oh, I get it. They're going to make it look like I'm a drug addict and refuse to allow my kids to come home.*

"Sure, come on in," she said.

When Trevor came in from work that evening, he had a similar story to tell.

Apparently, Ashley had paid him a visit at the bank. He said it was absolutely humiliating and he hoped it wouldn't cause him to lose his job. Ashley told him she would be coming by on a weekly basis to make sure he was working and to make sure he was drug free.

"Do you have any idea how that makes me look?"

"This just isn't right," Roxanne replied. "There has to be a better way."

"It doesn't make sense. They didn't find any drugs in our vehicle or on our person. There were no allegations of drug involvement. Why are they even testing us?"

Roxanne turned to look out the window. "It's just standard procedure. I guess there's nothing we can do about it."

20
FIRST DAY OF SCHOOL

BRADY DID NOT like the idea of taking medication. After his psychological evaluation, it was determined that he had what was known as Attention Deficit/Hyperactivity Disorder, better known as ADHD. The doctor explained to Brady that it was a treatable disorder and it simply meant that he was having some issues with being too hyper and impulsive and not being able to stay focused on any one thing for a very lengthy period of time.

For fourteen years Brady had been at home with his biological parents and had done well in school without ever being on any kind of medication. His grades were normally average or above average and he rarely got in trouble. He didn't understand why everything was changing. His whole world seemed to be spinning out of control.

"I don't like this," he said. "I don't need medicine."

"I'm sorry you feel that way bud, but the doctor says you do," Tim replied.

"Can't you talk to him? Can't you tell him that I don't need it? Of course I can't focus on anything right now. I miss my parents. Anybody taken away from his family would have trouble focusing. That's not something pills are gonna fix."

"I can talk to him, yes. Can I tell him you don't need your medicine? Unfortunately, no. Brady, you have some problems with your temper. I'm sure you're aware of that."

"Didn't you have a problem with your temper when you were put in foster care against your will?"

[162]

"Yes, I did. I too was put on medication to help me deal with it."

Brady decided there was no reason to argue. If he had to take the medicine, he would take it. *I won't be very happy about it, but it's only until I'm back with Mom and Dad. I can handle it for a little while.*

That night, Brady fell right to sleep. Once again, he had been completely exhausted from the activities of the day. He knew he would have to go to school the next day and he definitely needed his rest before then.

Soon after drifting off, he had a dream. In it, he was back at home. He and his family were sitting around the table playing a game of Scrabble, one of his favorite board games. It wasn't so much his favorite because he enjoyed playing the game as it was because of the way it made his parents laugh. His dad would almost always spell out some incredibly odd word that his mom would insist he was making up. They would open up the dictionary and about half of the time, his mom would be right. She would say, "Busted!"

In his dream, his mom was laughing hysterically, as she often did. His dad was grinning from ear to ear. Derrick, on the other hand, appeared to be in deep thought as he studied the letters before him.

The dream was short-lived. Brady woke up and immediately realized it wasn't real. A lone tear trickled down his cheek. *Man, I'm such a moron. I have really loused things up. I would give just about anything to be sitting around that table again right now.*

Homesickness was hitting and hitting hard.

In the morning, Brady woke up before Alice even knocked on the door. He wasn't sure why, but for some reason he was excited about going to school. Without being told, he got out of bed, got dressed, brushed his teeth, combed his hair, and then went and woke Derrick up.

Derrick's temperature had disappeared over night.

"What's going on?" He asked when Brady started shaking him.

"It's time to get ready for school."

"School? Are you sure?"

"I'm positive. I got enrolled yesterday and you're going to get enrolled today now that you're feeling better," Brady told him.

Without an argument, Derrick got up and got himself dressed as well.

"Derrick, time to get up!" Alice called as she walked by his room.

"We're both already up, ma'am," Brady replied.

"You sound awfully chipper this morning."

"I know. Sorry about yesterday."

"What's different? You haven't even taken the new medicine yet."

Brady came out of Derrick's room so his little brother could finish getting ready for school. "I don't know. I guess it just hit me that you and Tim are being so kind to us. You guys are giving us a place to stay and you bought us gifts. I was wrong to act like that," Brady told her.

Alice was surprised to say the least. *It's like Brady switched from dark to light and there's no reasonable explanation for the change.*

"Do you think maybe I shouldn't take the medicine then?" he asked her.

That's it. Now Alice understood. *Brady's being good and pretending to be on his best behavior to get out of taking his pills.* "I'm sorry, Brady. We have to follow the doctor's orders."

"I know. Couldn't you please talk to the doctor though and explain how well I'm behaving without it?"

Alice reminded him about the violent outburst he had the night before. Even though he seemed to be in pleasant spirits at the moment, she had no way of knowing how long that was going to last. If she called the doctor claiming he didn't need medicine and then he flipped out again, she would look foolish to call him back to say she had made a mistake. They could not continuously call the doctor, toggling their opinions back and forth.

Brady was disappointed. He was not really being good just

[164]

to get out of medicine. He had realized that he was acting foolish the day before. He knew the Adams's had every right in the world to boot him out of their home for the way he had acted, yet they decided to give him another chance. Overall, they had been nothing but kind to him and Derrick.

Alice told him to go downstairs and have Tim get him his meds. Once he took them, he could eat breakfast.

Reluctantly, Brady followed her instructions.

As soon as he reached the bottom step, Tim asked if everything was okay.

"Everything's great. I was just talking to your wife about how much better I feel this morning. I'm really sorry for the way I acted yesterday."

"I'm glad to hear that. Today is a new day and you have a fresh start. The day will be whatever you make of it," Tim said.

"I'll be good today, sir. I promise I'm going to stay outta trouble."

"Me too!" Derrick announced, jogging down the stairs. "I'm trying to do better too."

"Good boy."

Before long the whole house was buzzing with excitement. All six of the children were up and about, trying to get ready for school.

Brady told Tim he was ready for his meds.

Tim, being the next-to-perfect foster parent he was, walked toward the living room. He had the medications locked up, per agency directives, to make sure no one ever got into them when they weren't supposed to.

Looking at his prescription, Brady cringed. "Sir, I'm not very good at swallowing pills."

"At the age of fourteen?"

"My parents don't believe in taking medicine for anything unless we are really sick," Brady said. "Usually I don't take anything except for vomiting or diarrhea."

"Really?" Tim asked, sounding surprised. "How unusual in this day and age."

[165]

Tim told him he would catch on in no time. All he had to do was take a glass of water, tilt his head back, place the pill on the back of his tongue, and it would slide right down.

Brady didn't like the idea. He knew his parents would not approve. At the same time, if he refused he knew it would only start another war in the household and he definitely did not want that to happen. He followed Tim's instructions to a T, but the pill refused to make its way into his throat.

Tim told him that was okay. He would just have to try again.

Brady tried again, and again, and again. Finally, after the fifth try the pill went down. It hurt going down his throat and his stomach was already beginning to ache. "I don't think this was such a good idea. I don't feel so well now," Brady whined.

"Let's not start this again, young man."

"I'm not lying this time. I really think I'm gonna be sick."

"Brady, you have to go to school today and that's final," Tim said.

Just as he said the word "final," Brady hurled. It went all over the living room floor.

"I am so sorry," he apologized. "I didn't think that was gonna happen."

"It's okay. I'll clean it up. Feel any better?" Tim asked.

"Nah. I don't think so."

"Then go to the restroom and I'll be in to check on you in a second."

Brady did as he was told. Once he knelt down in the restroom floor, his stomach seemed to feel better. He wasn't nauseous anymore.

In no time, Tim knocked on the door. "Do you need to stay home today?"

"No, sir. I'm okay. I wanna go."

Tim was shocked beyond imagination. He just knew Brady was going to use this for a reason to skip another day of school. He was prepared to let him too because he felt bad for not believing him about not feeling so well.

Tim told him he still had time to catch the bus with the others. He would have to get his backpack on and head out to the road immediately so as to not miss it.

[166]

Brady went outside and just as he opened the door, the rolling banana stopped out front. Scared of missing it on his first day, he ran full speed ahead. Out of breath, he climbed on board and looked around for an empty seat—there weren't any.

"You can sit with me," a heavyset girl with the worst case of acne he had ever seen said when she saw him walking up the aisle. She winked as she spoke to him and Brady thought he was going to hurl again. Her face looked like a toad and her body was shaped like an enormous potato.

There's no way I'm going to sit with her, he thought. "Thanks, but I'd rather sit toward the back."

As he continued walking, a guy close to his age scooted over by the window. He didn't say anything, but Brady knew that in his own way, he was telling him it was okay to sit there.

Brady plopped himself down and uttered a quick word of gratitude.

"You're new here, aren't ya?" the boy asked.

"Yeah, today's my first day."

"How long you gonna be stayin' with the Adams family?"

"I'm not sure yet. Probably just a couple of days."

"A couple of days? Man, you've gotta be kidding. The Adams's have been doing foster care for years. I've never seen a kid stay there less than a couple of months."

"Well, now you have. We're not staying that long," Brady insisted. "What's your name anyway?"

"Mike."

Brady introduced himself and the two seemed to become friends right away. They had a lot in common—working out, being outdoors, and picking on their little brothers.

"Maybe you can come over to our house and hang out tonight?" Brady asked.

"Sounds like a plan."

When the bus pulled up to the school, the nervous feeling crept all down Brady's spine again. This was the real thing. No more just getting enrolled and starting tomorrow. *Today, I have to*

[167]

go to class. Today, I have to make new friends. Today, I have to establish a name for myself. Today, I will get my homework assignments at my new school. Today, if I'm lucky, I will find a new girlfriend.

As he stepped off the bus, he found Ms. Simms waiting for him. "Hi Brady," she said. "How are things going?"

"Fine, but why are you here? Are we moving again?"

"No. I'm just here to make sure you get started in school today without any more delays. Let's go in and see Mr. Hendricks."

"Sure."

"By the way, I talked to your foster parents and I heard you had a pretty rough day yesterday."

"Yes, ma'am, but I'm feeling better now."

"So that medicine has kicked in already, huh?"

"No it hasn't. Actually I was feeling better before I even took the meds. The pill made me barf."

"Sorry to hear that, Brady. You'll get used to it though. It'll help you. I just know it," she said.

Before long, Brady found himself sitting in Mr. Hendricks's office. "Good morning," he said.

"So, are you ready to start school?"

"I suppose," Brady told him.

"I have your schedule all made up and printed out for you. I've been reviewing your records from your previous school and everything looks great. I know you've been an excellent student in the past and we expect that to continue with us as well."

"It will, sir."

Brady stayed in the counselor's office until the first bell rang. "That bell means it's time for you to report to homeroom," Mr. Hendricks told him. "Do you think you can find it or do you need me to have a student give you a tour?"

"I can find it," Brady said, looking down at his schedule.

It didn't take him much effort at all to locate his homeroom. It was only five classrooms down the hall from the office.

His teacher was the kind he was hoping not to have. The kind who expected new students to introduce themselves to the class.

I knew there was a reason I didn't want to be a new student. I hate talking in front of people.

Turning to face the class, he said, "The name's Brady Clark. I just moved to this area a couple of days ago. I'm in foster care and I'm stayin' with the Adams's."

"Very good," his teacher said. "Does anyone have any questions they'd like to ask the new student?"

"I have one," a girl said from the back of the class. "Do you have a girlfriend?"

Brady's face turned as red as a beet. *She's drop-dead gorgeous,* he told himself. She had long, straight blonde hair, a full figure, and a very cute accent.

"Not yet," Brady said.

"I have a question," a boy said. "Why are you in foster care? Your parents abuse you or something?"

"Not hardly," Brady replied. There was a lot more he wanted to say to that student, but he knew it was his first day and he needed to bite his tongue. "I'm not going to be in foster care very long. It's a short-term placement."

21
FAMILY VISIT

The teacher said, "Well, I guess we should get started with our work now. Brady, please take your seat."

Brady looked around the room to find only one vacant desk—the closest one to his teacher. He walked over to sit down and as soon as his behind was about to connect with the chair, the girl sitting behind him kicked it sideways with her feet. Brady fell flat on the floor.

Everyone in the classroom started laughing—everyone except for Brady that is. He was humiliated. *How could someone do that to me on my first day? Especially in a class where a beauty queen was just checking me out?*

"Sorry about that," the girl said. "It was an accident."

Again, the class erupted in laughter. *If she was a guy, I would have socked her right in the throat.* But she wasn't a guy. She was a very attractive member of the opposite sex and Brady knew better than to hit a lady.

"Are you okay?" the teacher asked.

"Yes, ma'am," Brady told her.

Slowly and carefully, Brady managed to sit down. This was not the way he had wanted the day to start. He knew it would not be an easy day, but he had hoped there wouldn't be any embarrassing moments or bad situations.

As soon as class was over, Brady stepped into the hall to begin searching for the next room.

"Hey, you never did answer my question," someone said from behind him.

"What was that?" Brady asked, turning to face him.

"I asked why you're in foster care."

"I really don't wanna talk about it."

"You do realize that only losers get stuck in foster care, right?"

"You better shut your mouth before I shut it for you!"

"I see you're good at flapping your gums. You able to back it up?" The boy said, shoving Brady up against some lockers.

"Look, punk," Brady said, returning the shove, "I don't want any trouble. Just get outta my way if you know what's good for you."

"Now I'm insulted," the boy said. He shoved Brady into the lockers again before punching him in the gut so hard that it took Brady's breath away and he fell onto the floor. A crowd had begun to gather and everyone seemed to be pointing and laughing at him.

Brady managed to get back to his feet where he put the boy in a choke hold.

Mr. Hendricks rounded the corner just as he did and asked what was going on.

One of the bystanders lied and claimed "the new kid" had started a fight with Joey.

The crowd dispersed instantly as it was school policy that anyone standing around watching a fight could be suspended for three days.

"You two come with me," Mr. Hendricks said.

As they walked down the hall, everyone seemed to know what had happened. They all laughed and some even cheered as the boys entered the office.

"You fellas have a seat while I have a talk with Mr. Jenkins," the counselor told them.

A few moments later, Mr. Jenkins called both boys into his office, where he shut the door behind them. "Gentlemen, I am very disappointed in you. I don't know what happened between the two of you and quite frankly I don't care. I do not believe in violence and it will not be tolerated at this school. Joey, you have never gotten into any trouble here that I'm aware of. Brady, from what Mr. Hendricks tells me, you have a very clean record from your last school as well. I don't want there to be any more issues like this in the future. Understood?"

"Yes, sir," both of the boys said.

"This is a very nice school that you are attending. You should find it a privilege to be enrolled here. That goes for both of you. Most schools in this area are at least one hundred years old. You are in a fairly new building that is well maintained and you should be treating it with respect. This is one of the nicest schools—" Mr. Jenkins was saying before he saw a roach crawl across the floor.

As if it was an everyday occurrence, Mr. Jenkins pulled out a bottle of roach spray and drenched him within seconds. The roach turned over on its back and Brady watched his legs scurrying as if he was running for his life. Mr. Jenkins stood up and stomped him with his shoe.

Brady tried not to laugh. *A nice school, huh? A nice school with a roach infestation.*

"Now boys, what was I saying?" Mr. Hendricks asked.

"You were just telling us what a nice school this is, sir," Brady told him.

"So I was. Boys, I'm going to have each of you call your parents and tell them what happened. I do not plan on suspending either one of you at this time. Instead, I'll be assigning each of you to lunch clean-up duty for the next two weeks. That means after everyone is finished eating, you will be scrubbing down the tables and throwing away any trash that is left behind. Is that clear?"

"Yes, sir," Brady agreed.

"How about you, Joey? Did you understand what I said?"

"Yes, sir," Joey mumbled.

"Good, gentlemen. Brady, you go first. What's your phone number and I'll dial it for you?"

"I don't know it. I just moved in with the Adams family."

"The Adams family, huh? They have had children in this school for the last ten years. I have their number programmed into my speed dial," Mr. Jenkins chuckled. "Here, you take the receiver while I dial the number."

Brady was a nervous wreck. *I sure hope nobody picks up.* The phone rang once. No answer. It rang a second time and still there was no answer. On the third ring, however, Alice's voice came on the line. "Hello?"

"Alice, it's me, Brady."

"Brady? Did you vomit again? I can come get you if you're sick."

"I got in a fight."

"In that case, hold on a minute. Tim's home right now and this kind of call is something I think I'd rather have him handle."

Brady had to hold the receiver and wait for at least three minutes before Mr. Adams answered the phone.

"Brady?"

"Yes, sir."

"What's going on?"

"I got in a fight and I'm in the principal's office," Brady said.

"Who started it?"

"Not me. Honest."

"Brady, don't lie to me. I know what kind of a temper you have. If you started that fight, I want to know right now."

"I didn't start it. I promise. Please believe me," Brady pleaded.

"Is there a way you could have gotten away from the situation without fighting?"

"I don't know. Probably."

"Then why didn't you look for a way out?" Tim asked angrily.

"I'm sorry, sir. I don't know."

"I'll deal with you when you get home son," Tim said sternly.

Brady didn't know what Tim meant by dealing with him when he got home, but it didn't sound good. He was nervous. He didn't like Tim referring to him as a "son" either, but he didn't feel it would help his cause any to bring that up while Tim was already yelling at him. *I'll save that for a safer time,* he thought.

Brady stayed in the room while Joey called his parents. Of

course, they weren't home so Joey just had to leave a message. Things always worked that way. *Why don't I ever get off that easy?*

After school that day, Ms. Simms met Brady out by the bus and told him she heard he had ran into some more trouble. She begged Brady not to jeopardize his placement. After a short lecture, she told him she hadn't come by because of the fight. She was there to take him and his brother to a visit with their parents.

At first, Brady was excited. It had been a week since he had seen, or even talked to his mom or dad. He wondered how they had been doing. If they missed him as much as he missed them. He couldn't wait to hug his mother's neck and to hear his dad say, "I love you, son." Then reality set in.

Dad and Mom are probably not very happy with me. By now, they've most certainly heard about the lies Derrick and I told. They're probably downright angry. Dad might give me that whipping he started to give me in the woods. Knowing him, he probably won't even care if that social worker is in the room.

Brady felt like he was riding an emotional roller coaster. He was happy, sad, excited, and scared all at the same time. He wondered how Derrick would take the news. It didn't take long to find out since their schools were only located two miles from one another.

"There he is," Brady said as they pulled into the lot in front of the school.

Derrick was still busy playing on the playground. It looked like he had already made some new friends.

"Hey, what are you doing here?" he asked.

"Come with me and I'll explain in the car," Ms. Simms said.

Brady, not thinking it was fair to make his brother wait to find out, said, "We're going to see Mom and Dad."

"Oh no," Derrick replied.

"Oh no?" Ms. Simms asked. "You don't want to see your parents?"

"I want to see them, but—" Derrick paused.

"But what, dear?"

Derrick didn't know what to say. He was even more

[174]

terrified than Brady. He wasn't necessarily scared of his folks, but he didn't want to face them. He knew he had done some things that were horribly wrong, but he didn't want to admit them. He had never felt more ashamed of himself until that very moment.

"I don't know," Derrick said. "I forgot what I was gonna say."

As the car continued down the street, the boys were silent. Both of them knew how evil they had been—how they had caused their parents a lot of problems. They deserved to be punished severely. Their parents had done nothing but treat them right and they had let them down. They could only wonder what their parents thought of them.

Minutes later, they arrived at Charlie's Coffee House. Trevor and Roxanne were standing on the sidewalk watching for them. Roxanne had tears running down her cheeks as she saw her boys getting out of the car. Trevor showed no sign of emotion. He did not look angry, but he did not look thrilled to see his sons either.

"Mom!" Derrick hollered as soon as he opened the door. He took off running toward her.

She met her little boy with open arms, picked him up, and held him as tight as she could. "I have missed you so much," she whispered.

"Me too, Mom," Derrick said. "I love you."

"I love you too," his mom said, kissing him on the cheek.

Brady took his time walking toward his parents. He wanted to feel as free as Derrick did to run and jump into their arms and say, "I love you." He couldn't do it though. He had a guilty conscience. He and his parents knew what he had done wrong. Ms. Simms was standing right there too though and none of them could discuss it with her around.

"I missed you too, Brady," Roxanne said, setting Derrick down and opening her arms for a hug from her older son.

[175]

"I missed you," Brady said, giving her a very quick hug before backing up and looking at Trevor.

"It's nice to see you again, son," Trevor said.

Ms. Simms interrupted their mushy talk by telling them it was time to accompany her inside. She said Charlie was a good friend of hers and he had a room where they could be alone.

"You're coming in to?" Trevor asked, sounding somewhat disappointed.

"Yes, sir. I thought that had been explained to you already. I have to supervise any family visits that take place in the beginning of this attempt to reunify your family," Ms. Simms said.

Trevor did not look happy. Nor did Roxanne or the boys. They all wanted some time to talk openly about what had been going on, but now their conversation had to be very limited.

Ms. Simms led the four of them to the private room she had talked about. They sat down at a round table where they could see one another's faces. "I want you all to pretend I am not here. Talk to each other and not to me. I don't plan on saying a word until this visit is over in an hour."

At first, the room was silent. That is, until Derrick told his parents Brady had been put on medicine.

Confused, Roxanne asked him if he had been sick.

Brady explained to her about his diagnosis of ADHD.

Looking furious, Trevor said, "Who says you have ADHD?"

Ms. Simms shifted in her chair. It had been her idea to have the psychological testing done. She had spoken to the doctors about why she felt it was so imperative that Brady be placed on medication. She didn't say a word.

"The doctor," Brady told him.

"Who gave anyone permission for you to go to the doctor and be put on pills?" Trevor asked.

Trevor glared at Ms. Simms. He could tell from the look on her face that she had something to do with it. "I know you said to pretend you're not here," Trevor said, "but I know you're behind this. You have no right to put my child on medicine without my approval."

"I have every right, Mr. Clark," Ms. Simms told him. "As

[176]

hard as this may be for you to grasp, at the present time I am Brady and Derrick's legal guardian. I make all legal decisions regarding what's best for them."

"And you have known these boys for how long? A week? A week and a half at the most? And you already think you know Brady well enough to make decisions like this without even consulting the people who have been raising him for the last fourteen years?"

Trevor was angrier than he had ever been before. *First these people take my children. They don't let us talk to them, even after a fight breaks out. They put them in three different living environments in just a few short days. They interfere with my job. They harass us at home. They tarnish our reputation in the community. Now, they're drugging our son?*

"Sir, with all due respect, I am not going to sit here and argue with you during your family visit. You have not seen your children for a while. You need to be focusing your attention on your boys instead of wasting your family visit trying to argue about something as minor as medication," Ms. Simms said.

"Something as minor as medication?" Trevor repeated. "This is not a minor issue. I have taught my boys that they can be anything they want to be. That they can do well at anything they put their mind to. Yes, my boys have a lot of energy. They are boys for crying out loud. God made them that way. Look at Brady's face. Do you see much energy there? Whatever pill you've put him on is taking away his personality. It's turning him into a zombie. Can't you see that? You're not helping him, you're drugging him," Trevor said.

"This visit is now over. Come on boys, get in the car," Ms. Simms said.

"Wait, please," Roxanne pleaded. "I really want to visit with my boys."

"I'm sorry, Mrs. Clark. I cannot continue this visit with the level of hostility that's in this room. We can reschedule for a week from today at this same time if that would work with your schedule," Ms. Simms said.

Trevor felt horrible. *My wife is going to kill me. This is the first opportunity we've had to visit with our boys and I blew it.* It was hard not to. He loved his boys more than he loved himself. He knew, from many years of observation, what happened to kids who were put on medications for hyperactivity. Brady would calm down for a little while and then when his body adjusted to the medications, they would up the dosage or prescribe something new. He was a man who loved to research. There were a lot of unknowns when it came to mind-altering drugs. There was even some controversy as to whether or not ADHD was even a true diagnosis. *None of that matters right now though. It is important, but more important is getting our boys back.*

"Look, I'm sorry Ms. Simms. Please let the visit continue," he said.

Ms. Simms was determined to show she was in charge. "I can't do that. However, I will ask the foster parents your children are staying with to allow you to talk to the boys on the telephone for no more than twenty minutes each day between now and the next visit."

Trevor was angry. Roxanne was hurt. Derrick's secret hope of going back home with his parents after the visit had been shattered. Brady felt relief that he no longer had to be in the presence of the parents whom he had treated so poorly.

Both of the boys hugged their mom and dad and followed Ms. Simms back to the car. Roxanne and Derrick both had tears staining their faces. Trevor and Brady each had a solemn look—coldness in their eyes and on their faces.

Still crying, once they were in the car Derrick asked when he and his brother would be able to return home.

Ms. Simms said she doubted it would be anytime in the near future. She explained that what his parents had done to him was wrong. They neglected and physically assaulted him. Not only that, but his father had just demonstrated to her that he had a very serious issue with his temper. Ms. Simms said there were too many issues going on for reunification to occur in the near future.

Listening to her angered Brady. He demanded she stop speaking negatively of his parents. "My folks are the best parents in the world," he said. "I wouldn't trade them for anyone."

"That's nice to hear, but unfortunately all children like their parents. We have seen it time and time again. Children who have been physically and even sexually abused still want to be close to their moms and dads. That doesn't always get to happen though. Now that you are in the state's custody, we have to make sure you are protected and taken care of. What happens now is we have to work with you and your brother and also work with your parents—we need to retrain everyone so if and when you return home, you will be able to get along with each other better and be in a much safer environment than the one you left."

The ride back to the Adams's place was not a very pleasant one for Brady or Derrick. The whole way home Brady just kept thinking about those tears he saw running down Roxanne's cheeks. He remembered all the times he had seen her cry because of him letting her down. The times when he had been downright mean to her. She would always say, "I'll love you no matter what you ever do wrong."

Then he would picture the coldness in Trevor's face. He wanted to feel some affection from his father. To have the close relationship back with him that he once had. To tell him he was sorry for what he had done.

Derrick kept his mind on the visit as well. Why did Ms. Simms end the visit? They had the right to see their family. How come Tim and Alice could take care of him and his brother, but his parents couldn't? Why did they have to change schools? Why did they not get to go back home where they belonged? How much longer would this go on?

When they arrived back at the Adams's household, they found everyone outside playing. They had water guns and water balloons and were running around all over the place yelling, screaming, and laughing. Brady nor Derrick wanted to join the fun. They had too much on their minds.

Tim and Alice walked toward the car. "How'd things go?" Tim asked.

"Not very well," Ms. Simms replied. "We had to cut the

[179]

visit short because of some anger issues on the part of one of their parents."

"I told you not to talk about my family," Brady said, glaring at her.

"Brady, that is no way to speak to an adult," Tim scolded. "You go ahead in the house and go up to your room. Don't forget you're grounded until further notice."

"You're not my father. I don't have to listen to you," Brady said. "I'll go to my room though. Not because you told me to, but because I need to be by myself for a while."

"Can I go to my room too?" Derrick asked.

"Sure. Just stay away from Brady. Understand?"

"Yes, sir."

"Tim, you know you're not supposed to provide any consequences which are going to last for more than the one day the offense occurred, correct?" Ms. Simms asked.

"I know, but we're running out of options with this boy."

"I understand, but rules are rules."

"So you're telling me I have to unground him?"

"I'm telling you that there are policies in place that all of our foster parents are required to adhere to."

He didn't say so just then, but Tim had no intention of honoring that request, or order, or whatever Ms. Simms wanted to call it.

22
BEAR HUGS

NEARLY AN HOUR before bedtime Alice hollered, "Derrick, your dad's on the phone!"

"Really?" Derrick yelled excitedly. He never dreamed he would get to talk to his parents again so soon.

Derrick galloped down the stairs as fast as he could. He quickly took the receiver from Alice.

"Hi buddy, how are you?" his dad asked.

"I'm good. Where's Mom?"

"I'm right here, sweetie. I'm on the other phone so we can all talk. We miss you."

"I miss you too," Derrick replied.

"Your dad has trouble expressing himself in words sometimes, but I don't think he would mind if I told you he has been absolutely heartbroken not being able to see you guys every day."

Sniffling, Trevor interjected, "Mom's right. I find myself going into your bedrooms on a regular basis to check on you in the middle of the night and then I have to ask myself why I forgot yet again. This house sure is quiet without you fellas."

Derrick grew quiet for a moment.

"Where's your brother?" his mom asked.

"Hold on and I'll get him," Derrick said, before screaming, "BRADY, MOM WANTS TO TALK TO YOU!"

Brady bounded down the steps even faster than his brother had.

"Hold on right there, mister," Tim said, stepping between Brady and the telephone.

"Get outta my way, I wanna talk to Mom."

"Brady, I'm sorry but you are grounded. Remember?"

"You can't stop me from talking to my parents."

"I'll do whatever is necessary to teach you to behave like a civilized human being," Tim scolded.

Brady balled his fists up again.

"Undo those fists right now and get back upstairs," Tim demanded.

"He doesn't have to," Derrick yelled. "Here's the phone, Brady." Derrick tossed it into the air.

Tim intercepted the pass and put the phone up to his ear. "Mr. Clark, I'm sorry, but Brady is not available to talk to you at the moment. He's grounded."

"Let me speak to my son," Trevor ordered.

"I can't do that. If your son wants to speak with you, he is going to have to start showing me some respect," Tim replied before hanging up the phone.

Seconds later, the phone rang again and Alice answered. "Put my son on the phone right now!" Trevor screamed in her ear.

Tim grabbed the phone and shouted back, "Don't you ever talk to my wife in that tone of voice!"

"What are you going to do about it?" Trevor asked hatefully.

"Sir, you need to calm down. I'm going to notify Ms. Simms of your behavior and tell her I don't think these phone calls are a very good idea. If you can't control yourself any better than this, you have no business being a parent at all!" Tim shouted. With that, Tim unplugged the phone to ensure there would be no more interruptions.

Derrick started crying because once again the conversation he was supposed to have with his parents had been ended.

"I hate you!" he yelled at Tim before kicking him in the shin and running upstairs.

"You're the meanest person I've ever met in my life!" Brady told him. "Someday I hope they take your kids from you and see how you like it."

[182]

Brady marched upstairs to his room and slammed the door. He couldn't believe the nerve the Adams's had. Who were they to tell him he couldn't talk to his parents? What gave them the right?

He had no time to think before Tim whipped the door open, with a screwdriver in hand. "This door is coming off now," Tim said.

"You can't do that! I'm entitled to my privacy!" Brady replied.

"You're entitled to a roof over your head and food in your stomach—that's it! I warned you about this door. I have told you more than once it has to stay open while you're grounded and you have deliberately disobeyed me."

In less than one minute, Tim had the door completely off its hinges and carried it back downstairs with him. Brady was furious. Now anyone who walked down the hall could see him at any given time and there was no place for him to hide.

A few minutes after Tim went back downstairs, Wendy entered his room. "Sorry about your door," she said.

"Leave me alone. You're not supposed to be in here," Brady snapped.

"I know, but I wanted to tell you that I understand how you feel. It hurts to be away from your family, doesn't it?"

"Yeah."

"I still hurt inside sometimes too. You remind me a lot of how I felt when I first went into foster care. I don't know anything to say that will make you feel better, but you can talk to me any time you want to."

The room was dead silent for about a minute before Brady spoke up. "Can you keep a secret?"

"You can trust me."

"I haven't told anybody this, so if word gets out, I'll know you're the one who told and I'll kill you if you tell. Got it?"

"I won't tell. I promise!"

"We have to whisper," Brady told her, lowering his voice. "We're in foster care because we lied about our parents."

[183]

"Brady, what are you talking about?"

Brady began to cry. "It's a long story, but our family went camping and Derrick and I had both gotten in some trouble and—" Brady's tears began flowing faster and he began sniffling, having trouble getting the words out. "I punched Derrick and then Dad tried to talk to me about it. I smarted him off and he was gonna whip me."

"Then what happened?" Wendy asked.

"I shoved him, knocked him down, and took off running. My brother ran away too. We ran as hard as we could. We ended up lying down in the woods and a game warden found us. He called the police and as soon as they saw us, they automatically assumed we had been mistreated."

"What'd you tell 'em?"

Still sniffling and with his voice cracking with every word, Brady finished his story. He explained about everything he had said and about how Derrick had gone along with his story. He told her how sorry he was and that he knew what he did was wrong.

"Why don't you tell the truth? Why don't you tell an adult and maybe they can fix everything?"

"I can't. I'm scared," Brady cried.

"Scared of what?"

"I don't know. Just scared. I shouldn't have even told you. Promise me you won't tell anybody."

"I promise. But Brady, I think you'd feel a lot better if you told the truth," Wendy said.

"Maybe, but I'm not ready yet. I'll think about it though."

"Shhh… I hear someone coming," Wendy said.

Brady started trembling. He was sobbing hard and if Tim or Alice saw him, they would be suspicious. Wendy turned to run out the door so no one would know she was in there, but then she recognized the sound of the footsteps. "It's okay, it's only Greg," she said.

"Are you okay?" Greg asked, seeing Brady's bloodshot eyes. "Have you been crying?"

"Yeah, but I'm okay."

Greg gave Brady the biggest hug he had had in a long time. "It'll be okay. I cry sometimes too."

Brady started crying all over again. He couldn't believe a kid that was quite possibly dying of cancer was able to provide him with so much warmth and comfort.

"It's okay. Please don't cry," Greg told him.

"Lights out everybody!" Tim hollered from downstairs.

Wendy said good night and left the room.

"Are you going to be okay in here by yourself?" Greg asked.

"Yeah man, I'll be fine. Thanks."

Greg left the room, but only for a moment. He returned in a matter of seconds with a fluffy brown teddy bear. "Here, he always makes me feel better when I'm sad or scared," Greg said.

"I'm too old to sleep with stuffed animals."

"Please do it. I want you to."

"Fine," Brady grumbled. "Give him to me."

Greg gave Brady another hug and told him good night.

When Greg left the room, Brady pulled the teddy bear up to his chest and hugged it as tight as he could. The tears flowed down his cheeks like a waterfall after a rainstorm. He didn't know what he could do to fix the situation he had caused, but somehow he had to.

Back at the Clark residence, Trevor was fuming. Ms. Simms had promised him and his wife that they would be able to talk to the boys on the phone since their visit had been cut short.

He tried to call her at the office, but she had already went home for the night.

"Roxi, we're going to get through this," he told his obviously upset wife.

"I know. I know. I just wish we could hurry up and see the light at the end of the tunnel."

Roxanne didn't feel like her husband had blown this phone call. It was one hundred and ten percent Tim Adams's fault. *He had no business depriving our son from speaking to us on the phone. He crossed some serious lines here,* she told herself.

Roxanne decided not to voice her inner frustration. Trevor

was already upset enough. Telling him what she thought was only going to add more fuel to the fire and would inevitably make it even more difficult for them to be able to see the boys.

All night Brady sat on his bed thinking. He was determined to get everything straightened out. The problem was, he didn't know where to begin. He thought and thought and thought. *The first step needs to be to talk to my parents. Somehow, I have to get myself ungrounded so I can talk to them.*

He watched the clock and when it got to being thirty minutes before everyone else would be up, he trotted downstairs to the kitchen. Getting a wet wash cloth, he scrubbed down the kitchen table and countertops. He got enough bowls out of the cabinet for everyone in the family. He got out spoons for everyone and wrapped them neatly in paper towels just like he had saw them do at restaurants. Taking the milk out of the refrigerator, he placed it along with three different brands of cereal in the center of the table before sitting down to wait.

Ten minutes later, he heard Tim and Alice's alarm clock go off. He felt a grin spread across his face as he listened to them getting up and moving. He couldn't wait to see the look on their faces.

A few more minutes passed and Alice entered the room. "Brady? What's going on? Why are you up so early?"

"I couldn't sleep."

Alice then looked at the table and said, "You are so sweet. You got breakfast ready for everybody, didn't you?"

"Yes ma'am."

"Tim, come here! Hurry up! I want you to see what Brady did."

"What has that boy done now?" Tim hollered, stomping down the hall.

He looked at Brady and the boy's smile caught him off guard. Then he looked at the table. Then at the pleasant expression on his wife's face.

"Brady, you did all of this?"

"Yes, sir. I want to start over. I was mad yesterday about the visit. I've been upset about being away from my parents and

[186]

that's why I've been acting the way I have. I'd like to have another chance."

"I'll tell you what, Brady," Tim replied. "If you stay out of trouble today at school and come home with that smile on your face, I'll let you be ungrounded."

"Thank you, sir." Brady turned to Alice, "Would you like me to go upstairs and wake up the others?"

"Yes, please," Alice replied.

As Brady walked toward the stairs, he heard Tim asking what that was all about.

Brady felt like a huge burden had been lifted off of his chest. Even though he had been up the entire night, he wasn't sleepy at all. He was thankful Wendy had listened to him, thankful Greg hugged him, and thankful for the teddy bear that kept him company all night.

Before waking anyone up, Brady went back to his room and picked up Greg's teddy. Then he walked down the hall to the boy's room. Opening the door, he went in quietly and sat next to him on the bed. Looking down, he wondered how Greg must have felt about having no hair, about having a disease, about not living with his biological parents, about his whole life. *How can he be so happy with everything going wrong for him?*

Brady took the teddy bear in his hands and made it give Greg a kiss on the cheek. "Good morning."

Greg opened his eyes and looked at the bear. Brady made the bear kiss him all over his face.

Greg started giggling. "Stop it!"

"What's going on in here?" Tim said suddenly, sporting a look of astonishment.

"I was just waking Greg up," Brady told him.

"I see that," Tim replied. "You know what, boy? As of this minute, you are ungrounded. Thank you for getting yourself turned around."

Brady's smile had never felt so good. He stood, walked over to Tim, and gave him a hug. "Thanks for taking me in."

Tim was not an emotional kind of guy, but with a tear in his

[187]

eye he said, "Our pleasure."

Tim left the room and hollered, "Time to get up. Everybody needs to rise and shine!"

The house instantly filled with the sounds of everyone getting up and ready for school again. What a circus the place was with six kids and two adults running around like a bunch of monkeys who had eaten nothing but plain sugar for breakfast. That is, if monkeys like sugar.

When Derrick got up, he was surprised to find Brady in such a good mood. He, himself, was not in such good spirits. He had not slept much during the night at all. He kept thinking about everything that had happened and he was beginning to feel homesick. More than anything in the world, he wanted to be back at home like nothing had ever happened.

"Why are you so happy?" Derrick asked.

"I don't know. I just am," Brady replied.

"What were you and Wendy whispering about last night?"

"Don't mention that. It was nothing."

"Do you have a new girlfriend?"

"No, I don't have a new girlfriend. Wendy's a girl and she is a friend, but that's as far as it goes. Now you need to get moving so you can eat breakfast and catch the bus on time," Brady said in a fatherly sounding tone.

23

THE CONFESSION

THE WHOLE DAY went by smoothly. Brady and Derrick both seemed to calm down and relax. They both had a great day at school and made some new friends. Both boys brought their homework home. Neither one had a hateful word to exchange with anyone all day for the first time the whole week.

"Brady, since you and your brother have been behaving so well," Tim said late that evening, "I'm going to let you call your parents."

"Thank you, sir," Brady told him.

For once, Brady couldn't wait. He took the phone out onto the front porch and called his folks. His mom answered.

Brady was nearly speechless. Simply hearing her voice made him feel much more emotional than he had ever expected. Within a few seconds, he managed to find his words. "Hi Mom. It's me, Brady. I love you."

Roxanne could hear the calmness in his voice. "It sounds like you feel better today. I love you too," she replied.

"Can you put Dad on the phone, please?"

"Sure," his mother agreed before handing the phone to his dad.

"Are you allowed on the phone or did you sneak to call me?"

"I'm allowed, Dad," Brady said.

"That man you're staying with is an idiot!"

"Dad, let's not talk about that, okay?"

"What do you want to talk about then?"

"About what happened," Brady said. "I'm sorry, Dad. For everything I did. For everything I said. Can you ever forgive me?"

"Son, you know I will always forgive you. I love you with all of my heart and nothing will ever change that."

"What can I do so we can come back home?"

"I don't know any more Brady," his dad said. "The state thinks your mother and I are horrible parents. Unless we can somehow prove to them that we're not, it looks like you're stuck where you are."

"I'll figure something out, Dad. I promise."

"I hope you do, son. By the way, happy birthday!"

Brady had completely forgotten. He wished he could be there with his parents for such a special occasion. But he couldn't and he knew it was his own fault. "I don't deserve any presents, Dad."

"No, you don't," Trevor told him, "but we bought you a few anyway."

"Why'd you do that?"

"The same reason God gave us His son as a present even when we didn't deserve it," Tim replied.

"You didn't have to get me anything, Dad."

"Yes I did, son. Yes I did."

"How are you and Mom doing?"

"We're doing okay. We both miss you guys an awful lot, but other than that we're fine," Trevor told him. "How about you? How are those jerks treating you?"

"They're not jerks, Dad. They're really good people once you get to know them. They have a really nice house and a lot of land. There's a pond out back and they even let us play in the mud!"

"It sounds like you're really happy there," Trevor said. "Do you like them better than you like me and your mom?"

"No Dad, of course not. I just mean they're treating us good. That's all."

"Where's your brother?"

"Let me get him," Brady said. "DERRICK! DAD'S ON

[190]

THE PHONE!"

"Next time, please cover up the mouthpiece when you're going to do that," his father said. "You almost busted my eardrum."

"Sorry, Dad."

Derrick took his time coming down the steps and walking to the porch. "I don't want to talk to him," he complained.

"What did he just say?" Trevor asked.

"He said he doesn't want to talk to you, Dad."

"Tell him to pick up the phone."

"Derrick, Dad said you need to pick up the phone. He wants to talk to you."

"I don't want to and I don't have to!" Derrick said loudly before bolting back upstairs.

"What's all that shouting about?" Tim hollered, walking in the front door.

"Sorry, sir, my brother refused to talk to Dad on the phone."

Tim had no idea what that was all about. It seemed a bit unusual and he hoped nothing was wrong. Still though, he could not let Derrick start screaming every time he didn't want to do something. He was going to have to deal with the situation as soon as possible.

"Brady, let me talk to your foster parent," Trevor said.

"Dad, do you promise not to yell?"

"Do it Brady, now!"

"Yes, sir," Brady said. "Mr. Adams, my dad wants to speak with you."

Tim gave Brady a dirty look as he picked up the phone. "Hi Mr. Clark."

"Hey, I need you do to me a favor."

"What's that?"

"I need you to go get that boy of mine and put him on the phone. I need to talk to him."

"I can't make him get on the phone if he doesn't want to."

"You can't? Now wait a minute. This boy is only eleven

years old. You're a grown man. You can make him. That's a parent's job. I thought you were a foster parent?" Trevor snapped.

"He is his own person. If he wants to talk, he can. I can't jump inside of him and make him do anything."

Trevor did not like this situation at all. At home, he would have never tolerated such disrespect from a little boy. He found it absurd that any adult would not make a child do something. He had been raised that adults were supposed to tell kids what to do, not just allow children to do as they pleased.

"Fine. Put Brady back on the phone," Trevor said.

"I'm sorry, but the boys are only allowed to talk to you for twenty minutes a day and the twenty minutes is up for this evening."

"I have not talked to him for twenty minutes. So not only do you not know how to raise children, you don't know how to tell time either. I'll tell you what I think. I think you deliberately turned my son against me. You need to—"

His sentence was interrupted by the sound of the phone being slammed down in his ear.

"Did you just hang up on my dad?" Brady asked.

"Yes I did," Tim replied. "He deserved it. I am not going to let someone sit there and scream at me like that."

"You had no right," Brady snapped. "You're just jealous because he's my real dad and you wish you were!"

Brady ran back upstairs to his room. On the way there, he heard Derrick mumbling, "I hate my life. Nobody loves me. Nobody cares about me. Nobody even knows I'm alive anymore. I wish I was dead."

Brady paused at his doorway and said, "Awww... poor little baby."

Derrick picked up one of his shoes and bombed it at Brady's face. "Shut up!"

"Hey, don't you throw things at me!"

In no time flat, Tim was standing right behind them. "How did this shoe get in the hallway?"

"Derrick threw it at me!" Brady said.

"Derrick, I don't know what's going on with you all of the sudden, but it has to stop immediately," Tim said. "Brady, go to

[192]

your room."

As Brady stepped aside, Derrick picked up his other shoe and threw it right at Tim. "I hate you! I hate your wife. I hate your kids. I hate your stupid house. I hate your stupid yard. I hate you, I hate you, I hate you!"

"That will be enough of that," Tim scolded.

Derrick did not agree. He grabbed a hold of the chemistry set the Adams's had bought him. He threw the box as hard as he could right at his bedroom window. It cracked!

The sound of breaking glass quickly brought Derrick back to reality. It was too late though. Tim was already in the process of wrapping his strong arms around the boy's waist and pulling him to the ground. He held him tight and said, "Don't even think about fighting me!"

Brady ran back to the room. "What are you doing to my brother?"

"Brady's nothing but a big pile of white trash!" Derrick shouted. "He has skid marks on his underwear. He dates the ugliest girls in school. He's a dork! I hate him!"

His brother didn't know what was going on, but he hollered, "Shut your trap you little geek before I come over there and shut it for you!"

"That'll be enough of that," Tim said.

"Brady, get back to your room. I'll take care of this."

Before Brady had a chance to even start toward his room Wendy, Greg, and Ginger all appeared at the door. "What happened? What's all the noise about?"

"I hate all of you!" Derrick screamed. "I hate Greg's bald head! I hate the freckles plastered all over Wendy's face. I hate Ginger's stupid baby doll! I hate all of you!"

"Hey, what's going on up there?" Alice called, coming up the stairs from the living room.

"Derrick said he hates my baby!" Ginger said with tears running down her face.

"And he made fun of me for not having any hair," Greg added.

[193]

"He said he doesn't like my freckles," Wendy cried.

"You children go back downstairs," Alice said. "Tim, is there anything I can do?"

"I don't know. Why don't you go fill the bathtub with some nice warm water and some bubble bath? Maybe after he calms down a bit we can get him in the tub and he'll be able to relax."

Relax? Why would he want to relax when everyone in the world hated him? No one even cared that he didn't get to see or talk to his family. No one seemed to notice how hurt he was inside. No one took the time to hug him or talk to him. No one took the time to say they were sorry his life was such a mess. How did they think a warm bubble bath would fix any of that?

"I'm not taking a bath and you can't make me!" Derrick screamed.

"Just calm down," Tim told him in a quiet voice.

"I will not calm down! I hate you! I hate your wife! I hate your family! I hate everyone!"

"Derrick, you need to stop this."

"I can't stand it anymore. Somebody just kill me!" Derrick yelled.

Tim held him tighter without uttering a word. He decided there was no use in trying to talk him out of this one. He could tell Derrick was close to having a mental breakdown and he had to just let all of his thoughts out. He let him yell and scream as long as he needed to.

"My life sucks!" Derrick continued. "This whole world sucks! I don't know why I even had to be born!"

Derrick screamed for two hours straight before finally quieting down. Tim was able to relax his grip after about thirty minutes, but he still held onto him because he wasn't sure what Derrick might do to himself or others. Not to mention what additional damage could be done to the house.

When he finally quieted down, Tim said, "Derrick, I need you to go take a bath now. I know the water has probably cooled down, but it will help you relax."

"No! I'm not taking a bath! You can't make me!" Derrick screamed.

"You are going to take a bath young man," Tim said. "Whether you like it or not."

[194]

"No I'm not!"

About that time, Brady appeared at the door again.

"I thought I told you to go to your room?" Tim snapped.

"I have a question, sir," Brady replied.

"What is it? It had better be important!"

"It is important. Didn't you tell my dad you couldn't make Derrick talk to him on the phone? That you couldn't get inside of him and make him do anything? Didn't you say he is his own person and he has to make his own decisions or something like that? Why is this any different? How come you'll make him take a bath, but not talk to our father?"

"Yeah!" Derrick screamed. "Leave me alone! Let me go! I'm not takin' a bath!"

"Brady, see what you've done. You've just made the whole situation worse! Go to your room and stay there!"

"No!" Brady argued. "No, I won't!"

"Brady, do you want to have to move again? I cannot have you and your brother staying here and disrupting the rest of our household like this. I can't take it."

"I knew you were just like the others. I thought maybe you actually cared about us. You don't though, do you? You're just looking for a reason to get rid of us, just like everybody else! No wonder Derrick hates you. I do too!"

"Alice, call the social worker!" Tim yelled. "Tell her what's going on and see if she can get these boys admitted into a psychiatric hospital. They need some serious help and we can't help them here any longer."

"We're not goin' to no hospital. We'll run away first," Brady yelled.

In no time Wendy appeared back at the door. "Daddy, there's something you should know."

Brady glared at her. "Don't say it."

"I'm not going to say anything. Brady, you need to. Now is the time. Please, Brady. Tell him for yourself and for your brother. He needs to know.

"Tell me what?" Tim asked.

[195]

Brady glared at Wendy. She promised she wouldn't say a word about what he told her. Now she just blabbed and Tim knew something was up. He didn't want to tell, but he felt he had to do something. If he and Derrick had to be put in a hospital, they might not ever get to see their parents again.

"I'll tell you, but only if you let my brother go," Brady said. "Derrick, will you promise to be good if Tim lets go of you?"

"I promise."

"If you don't, I'm going to give you a whipping like Dad used to."

Ordinarily Tim would have told him he couldn't do something like that, but this time he didn't say a word.

"I'll be good. Really, I will," Derrick said.

Slowly, Tim turned him loose.

"Can we talk in my room, Mr. Adams? I really need to talk to you alone," Brady said.

"Sure son," Tim said, walking toward the hall.

"Please don't call me 'son.' I'm not your son and to be honest, once you find out what I've done, you wouldn't want me to be."

Before he even made it to his bedroom, Brady's face filled with tears again. He told Tim everything that had happened. He told him how guilty he had been feeling and how he saw how his lies were ruining his and his brother's lives and probably his parents' lives as well. His lies not only affected his own biological family, but they had affected the other foster family he lived with and the shelter he stayed at. It had caused Ms. Simms a great deal of headaches trying to locate places for them to stay. It had caused the school system to transfer all of their school records to a different school. His lies had caused a lot of people a lot of grief and a lot of work and he was truly sorry and ashamed of what he did.

"Brady, you know I have to report this information to Ms. Simms?" Tim asked.

"I know, sir. I want you to. I want to go back home."

"I understand. I'll call her first thing in the morning."

24
UNCOMFORTABLE CONVERSATION

T HE NEXT MORNING, Tim and Alice kept the Clark children home from school per Ms. Simms's directives.

After all of the other children had gone off to school, Ms. Simms came over for a visit. She said she needed to talk to each of the boys individually, beginning with Brady.

She decided to take him for a walk outside to have their discussion. "Brady, when you first entered foster care I sat down and questioned you and your brother for hours. You told me some pretty horrible things about your parents. Why did you tell me all of that if it wasn't true?"

"I don't know. I guess I was mad at my parents and wanted to pay them back."

"Pay them back for what?"

"I don't know. For bossing us around all of the time."

"Brady, I'll tell you what I'm afraid of. I'm afraid you were telling me the truth the first time around and that you're lying to me now because you want to be back with your parents so badly."

"I'm not a liar," Brady said.

"Did you lie to me when I questioned you the first time?"

"Yeah."

"And what are people called who tell lies, Brady?"

"That's not fair. I'm telling the truth now."

"How would I know that? How can I know you're telling

me the truth now?"

"Please believe me. Do you not see the tears in my eyes? Do you know how hard it is for me to admit what I've done?"

"I don't know, Brady. I'll talk to your brother and I'll talk to your parents and we'll go from there."

Ms. Simms was more confused than ever. Brady looked as if he could really be telling the truth. But she had been a social worker for years and in that time she had seen many kids come up with lies in efforts to get placed back with their parents. Sometimes she could tell when they were lying and sometimes she couldn't.

After taking Brady back to the house, she asked Derrick to accompany her outside.

"Derrick, do you know why I'm here?"

"Because of the window I broke last night?"

"I heard about that, but no," Ms. Simms said. "Derrick, why are you in foster care?"

"You already know. Remember, we told you all about that when we came to your office the first time?"

"Yes, I remember. But Derrick, Brady is saying that some of those things you fellas told me weren't true. I want you to be honest with me. What happened?"

"Did Brady tell you EVERYTHING?"

"Everything! I just need to talk to you too to make sure I get all of the details straight."

Derrick was scared. He felt like this was some kind of trap. What if Brady hadn't already told the truth? What if he squealed and then Brady beat him up when he found out about it? Then again, if Brady didn't tell, how would Ms. Simms know anything? If he told her, maybe he could see his parents again.

"It all started when we went camping," he began. He told her detail by detail exactly what had taken place.

Ms. Simms was impressed that the boys' stories seemed to agree, however she was still worried. After all, when the boys were answering her questions the first time around, their stories matched as well. Maybe they had come up with this tale together and it was just a plot. If so, they were very good liars!

After questioning and re-questioning the boys for the majority of the day, Ms. Simms called Mr. and Mrs. Clark and told them what was being said.

"So we get to have our boys back?" Roxanne asked.

"I'm not so sure," Ms. Simms replied. "I have talked to the head of our department here at Social Services and he said we will have to let a judge make a ruling on this case.

"This is nonsense," Trevor said. "The boys told you they lied. They told you what really happened. You now know they weren't abused or neglected. Why can't you give us our children back?"

"Mr. Clark, it's not that simple. We don't know for sure that the children are telling the truth now. Maybe they were telling the truth before and they're lying now," Ms. Simms said.

"The state will appoint you a lawyer and they will have an attorney as well. We are going to request an emergency hearing take place as soon as possible so we can get to the bottom of all of this."

The whole situation was ugly, but Mr. and Mrs. Clark felt very confident that the horrible ordeal they had been going through would soon be over. Both of them had been missing out on a lot of sleep since everything took place. They spent many dark nights crying on each other's shoulders and reminiscing about when the boys were born and about everything they had gone through together as a family. Other nights had been spent arguing about whose fault it was that the boys had been taken away from them. Finally, they felt the chaos may soon come to an end.

25
IT WAS BOUND TO HAPPEN

THE NEXT MORNING, Brady was called to the office during homeroom.

When he got there, Ms. Simms was waiting for him. "Good morning, bud. I'm here to take you to a new foster home."

A new foster home? Why are we moving this time? Brady thought.

He stood speechless for a few seconds before asking, "What? Do the Adams's not want us anymore?"

"No, Brady. It was my decision. There are going to be some legal battles going for a few weeks. Your parents and the Adams's don't get along very well and I don't want matters to get any more complicated than they already are."

"Where are we going? Please tell me we're not going back to Ms. Hilton's."

"No, you're not going back to Ms. Hilton's. But, Brady, there's something else you need to know. You and your brother are going to be separated for a little while."

"Oh, no! Absolutely not. I won't let that happen," Brady insisted.

"It already has. Derrick has already been taken to his new foster home."

"Where? Where is he?"

"I can't disclose that information. Until the court makes a decision, you and your brother aren't going to have any contact with each other or with your parents. That's just the way it's going to have to be."

"That's just the way it's going to have to be," my behind, Brady thought. *She can't do this. I hope Mom and Dad sue her and her entire*

department for all they're worth. Scumbags!

Hesitantly, he followed her out to the car to find his things had already been packed in garbage bags and were sitting in the backseat. *I didn't even get a chance to say goodbye to the Adams's, to the kids, or even to my classmates or teachers.*

An hour later, they pulled into a grocery store parking lot where a wealthier looking black lady was leaning against the hood of a newer BMW.

As they pulled in, the lady strolled over to the vehicle, looking as though she owned the world. "Hi kiddo. I'm Miss Shantel. Looks like we're gonna be roomies for a while."

"Guess so," Brady said. "How many other foster kids do you have?"

"None. It'll just be the two of us. Well, the three of us if you count Droopy, my beagle."

Brady got his belongings from the back and started to climb into the passenger seat of the BMW.

"I don't think so, honey," Miss Shantel barked. "That's Droopy's seat. You'll have to sit in the back."

Ms. Simms smiled and told Brady everything was going to be fine. She said she hated to rush off, but she had a lot to do, as usual.

Their fifteen minute drive to Miss Shantel's house was spent in silence—well, not really. She conversed with Droopy the entire way there. She told him he was a good puppy and asked him if he was excited to have a big brother for a little while. She told him it was going to be okay. She promised to not like Brady better than him just because Brady walked on two legs.

What kind of nut is this? he asked himself. *Her dog rides up front, while I have to ride in the back? I'm not good enough to talk to, but her furry little friend is?*

Eventually, they pulled up to her gorgeous two-story log home. "I'll tell you what, bud," she said. "I'll take your things in the house. I need you to get the mower out from under the deck.

The grass is getting pretty high and if you're gonna stay here, you're gonna have to pitch in and help out a little bit."

"I can take my own stuff inside," Brady told her.

"I didn't ask you what you could or could not do. I'm telling you—get your rear over there and get that mower and I mean NOW."

Brady gave her an evil stare. *Who does she think she is?*

"Fine. Whatever. I'll mow the grass, Shantel."

"That is MISS Shantel to you."

Oh, this is going to be a fun placement! Brady thought.

Tired of fighting and having no one to show off for, he hustled to the mower and got it fired up. About ten minutes into mowing the lawn, he caught sight of Miss Shantel watching him from the window. It looked like she was stuffing a slice of pizza in her mouth while gabbing on the phone.

Being hungry himself, the sight of food made his mouth water. *That looks so good,* he thought, even though he could barely even see it from where he was standing. *Maybe if I hurry up, I can get some while it's still warm.*

Fifteen minutes later, he was finished. He walked inside and allowed his nose to lead him to the kitchen.

"I'm finished, Shantel. What's for dinner?"

Covering the mouthpiece on the phone, she yelled, "How many times do I have to tell you, boy? You call me MISS Shantel!"

"Sorry."

"And can't you see I'm on the phone? Don't interrupt people. That's rude!"

Brady sat down on a barstool to wait for her to finish her conversation. She talked for at least an hour, sharing every detail of her life with whoever was on the other end of the line. Her aunt was in the hospital with pneumonia, the ladies at her church were planning a cook-off, one of her coworkers had just gotten fired. Wow, did she ever have an interesting life.

Then, it happened. Staring out the window and forgetting he was in the room, Miss Shantel said, "Oh, I forgot to tell you. The agency finally listened to me. You know how I've been asking them to get me a teenage boy? They finally did! Finally, I have somebody who can cut the grass and do some of the maintenance around this place. I thought they were never going to listen... Yes, he's already mowed the lawn. Doesn't look like he did a very good job. Just lookin' out the window I can see some spots he missed. Looks like he left the mower sitting right in the middle of the yard... I know, I know... He'll learn... Yes, he's a doll baby. Cute as a button."

Finally turning around, she nearly dropped the phone. "How long have you been sitting here, baby?"

Brady didn't speak. He was too busy giving her the stare of death.

Miss Shantel told whoever she was talking to that she had to go.

"Sorry, sweetie. I know I said some things that probably didn't sound very nice. I didn't mean them that way. You'll just have to get to know me to understand."

"Sure. No problem," Brady said. *I can do this. I can do this. Bite your tongue, Brady.* "What's for dinner?"

"Oh," Miss Shantel said. "I completely forgot about dinner. It's been a crazy day. Look, there's a loaf of bread up there in the cupboard. Just get that and help yourself to some peanut butter and jelly. I don't have any potato chips or anything like that, but you can have some saltine crackers on the side if you'd like."

She gets pizza and I get stuck with peanut butter and jelly? Brady was one very unhappy camper. *Why me? Why does this always happen to me? Why would I be the one to get sent off to some rich, stuck-up snob?*

Derrick found himself in an awkward position as well. He was also staying with a single foster parent—a man by the name of Dexter.

Dexter was twenty-three years old and had only recently been approved to foster. When Derrick first met him, he was scared to death. He could tell Dexter wasn't very confident. And he was a little too excited about being a foster parent.

As the day had went on though, Derrick had begun to appreciate him. It seemed like Dexter was going to be a kind man who would cater to his every whim. Derrick could wrap him around his little fingers in no time.

"Thanks for letting me help you make dinner," Derrick told him. "I love to cook."

"No problem, little man. I know you've been through a lot and I'll do whatever I can to make you feel more comfortable."

"Anything?"

"Well, almost anything. Watcha got in mind?"

"Can I stay up late tonight?"

"How late?"

"All night?"

"Well, not all night, but how about 'til midnight?"

"1 am?"

"I suppose," Dexter told him.

26
THE FUN BEGINS

WHILE THE CLARK family sat on pins and needles waiting on the court date to arrive, the state was busy preparing their case. They had a lot of hard questions. They wanted to know how the van had been destroyed out in the middle of the woods. The reason Brady had been running around practically naked. How often Trevor and Roxanne had violent temper outbursts.

Since they had received a tip from Katherine Ryan, Dalton's mother, they decided to call her as a witness. They would also call Tim and Alice Adams to the stand to testify about the temperament of Trevor and the boys.

Mr. and Mrs. Clark's state appointed attorney was busy gathering evidence himself. He was going to call Dalton Ryan to the stand to tell his side of the story. Because Dalton was a minor though, they could not force him to testify. He had to agree to it voluntarily and have parental consent. The attorney planned to call each member of the Clark's household to the stand to tell what had happened and how they felt they had been affected by the tragic separation.

It was obviously going to be a very difficult hearing. One filled with emotions of bitterness and tears. It was going to be a life-changing experience whichever way the verdict would fall. Everyone concerned could only hope and pray the right decision would be made.

The night prior to the hearing, none of the Clark family was able to get even a wink of sleep. They all wondered what the next day would hold. Their entire future rested upon the decision of one man.

The boys had never stepped foot inside of a courtroom. Walking in, they were filled with anxiety and fear. The judge's platform looked intimidating. The attorneys appeared ready for a battle. Ms. Simms seemed angry with them. Mrs. Ryan was there, looking as though she thought she was a queen. She looked very angry—like she wanted to see their parents fry like bacon.

Trevor and Roxanne came into the courtroom dressed nicer than the boys had ever seen them. Trevor had his hair cut and was wearing a suit and tie. Roxanne was wearing a fancy dress that came all the way down to her ankles. Neither of them appeared very happy. They looked as though they had been arguing all the way to the courthouse.

Trevor and Roxanne were told to take a seat next to George Dorcas, their attorney. The boys were instructed to sit next to their parents.

"Whatever happens today, boys, your father and I both love you very much," Roxanne whispered.

"Will all rise as the honorable Judge Theodore Raines takes the bench," the bailiff announced.

Everyone stood to their feet at once and the room was filled with silence.

As soon as he was seated, everyone else was permitted to sit as well. "We are here today to decide the case on the State of North Carolina vs. the Clark family. The State of North Carolina is being represented by Attorney Jordan L. Hively and the Clark family is being represented by Public Defender George R. Dorcas. Mr. Hively, would you like to make your opening statement?" Judge Raines asked.

"I would, Your Honor," Mr. Hively said, rising to his feet and walking to the front of the room. "On September the 3rd, Brady and Derrick Clark were found wandering in the woods. Brady, who was fourteen years old at the time, was found with no shirt or pants on and was missing his shoes and socks as well. His feet were covered with cuts and blisters. His whole body was filthy. Derrick, at the age of eleven, had no shirt on. His toes were hanging out the front of his shoes. He looked as though he had not slept in days. Both boys looked and smelled as if they had not had a bath for a very long time. When questioned, the children reported being abused both physically and verbally. Both boys admitted to having their needs neglected by their parents. It is our belief that the juveniles should remain in foster care until Mr. and Mrs. Clark are able to improve their living situation so that the boys could have a safe and happy home," Mr. Hively said.

Brady felt the weight of the world on his shoulders. *What have I done? Why did Derrick go along with my story?* He really wished he could take back everything they had said, but it was too late for that. It was time to move forward.

"Mr. Dorcas, would you like to make an opening statement?" Judge Raines asked.

"Yes, Your Honor," Mr. Dorcas said, standing and making his way to the front of the courtroom. "On the weekend in question, Trevor and Roxanne Clark took their children on a camping expedition to spend some quality family time together. The weather grew fierce, knocking a tree down on top of the family's vehicle and causing their tent to leak. The family was unable to get much rest that night. The campground did not have bathing facilities so it was impossible for anyone at the site to bathe.

"Brady and Derrick Clark, normally well behaved children, were exhausted by the following morning. As most boys their ages do, they got into a lot of mischief and yes, in that time frame they did get dirty and covered with sweat, which may have caused them to appear as if they had not bathed in quite some time. In our defense, we plan to prove that these children were not neglected or abused. The children were upset because when they had gotten out of line, their father and mother corrected them. They attempted to escape correction by making false allegations against their parents, which they now admit, and those allegations landed them in the custody of the state of

[207]

North Carolina. These children should never have been placed in foster care and should be returned to their biological parents at the conclusion of this hearing."

Trevor and Roxanne gave each other a look of approval. They had heard that Public Defenders were useless, but Mr. Dorcas seemed like he knew what he was doing. With his help, surely they could regain custody of both Brady and Derrick.

27

COURT BATTLE RAGES

JUDGE RAINES asked Mr. Hively if he was ready to call his first witness.

"Yes, Your Honor. I would like to call Ms. Katherine Ryan to the stand please."

Trevor and Roxanne cringed. They knew Ms. Ryan hated them. She had warned them that she would get Child Protective Services involved. She had even threatened to hire an attorney. Seeing her take the stand infuriated both of them.

After being sworn in, Ms. Ryan was asked to take a seat at the witness stand.

"Ms. Ryan," Mr. Hively said, "Tell us what you remember about the events that took place on September 3rd."

Ms. Ryan looked nervous. She was shaking, but just a little. "Mr. and Mrs. Clark had invited my son to go along on a camping trip with them. At first I said no, but Dalton begged to go with them. Dalton does not have a father in his life to do things like that with, so I decided to let him go along.

"I received a phone call early that morning telling me that Mr. and Mrs. Clark had been fighting and that Mrs. Clark left the rest of her family as well as my son and disappeared into the woods where she was later found by a search party. Not long after that, I was driving by the local middle school and I saw a group of students gathered around a flagpole. I saw a friend of mine so I stopped and asked what was going on. She pointed to

[209]

the top of the flagpole and there was a pair of pajama pants hanging from it," she said.

"And who did the pants belong to?"

"The pants belonged to the Clark's older son, Brady," Ms. Ryan said.

"Okay, so after you received the phone call about Mrs. Clark and then saw their son's pants flying on a flagpole, what did you do?"

"At that time, I was worried. I decided to go find my son. It took a while to find them, but when I did I was shocked. As I pulled up to the campsite, I saw the Clark's van. Not only did it have a huge tree lying on it, but all of the windows were knocked out. The headlights and taillights were busted out. There were scratches all up and down the sides of the van."

"Hold on just a moment," Mr. Hively said. "Your Honor, we have pictures of the van that we would like to enter as evidence." Mr. Hively walked back to his table and returned with an envelope full of photographs.

The judge admitted the photographs as evidence.

"What did you see next?" Mr. Hively asked.

"I saw Mr. and Mrs. Clark. Trevor looked filthy, but he didn't look anywhere near as bad as Roxanne. Roxanne's hair was a mess. She looked like a sick woman. Appeared like she had been beaten. I really don't know how else to describe her."

"What next?"

"Then I saw the boys. My son, Dalton, was the best looking of the three. He was pretty dirty but he didn't look nearly as bad as the other two. I was the most concerned about Brady. He was walking with a limp, wearing nothing but boxer shorts. I cannot imagine anyone allowing their child to walk around in the woods dressed that way. The boy had cuts and scrapes and bruises on him. His hair was covered with sweat and his whole body looked filthy dirty. Derrick didn't have a shirt on. He was holding a rag in his hand that was covered with blood. Like his brother, his hair was filthy and so were his clothes. He looked like a homeless child who no one had been taking care of," Ms. Ryan said.

"What did you do when you saw all of this?" Mr. Hively asked.

[210]

"What any mother would have done. I told Dalton he was coming home with me. I didn't want him to be put in danger by those people any longer. I told them I was going to call Child Protective Services and maybe even a lawyer."

"And how did they react to that statement?"

"They applauded me like a bunch of wild school children!" Ms. Ryan snapped.

"No more questions, Your Honor," Mr. Hively said.

Again, Roxanne and Trevor glanced at each other, this time though they were not so confident. They realized Ms. Ryan's testimony was a strong one and made them look like very unfit parents. They had no idea if or how Mr. Dorcas might be able to turn things around.

"Mr. Dorcas, would you like to cross examine the witness?" Judge Raines asked.

"Yes, Your Honor," Mr. Dorcas replied, approaching the witness stand. "Ms. Ryan, how long have you known the Clark family?"

"Three and a half years," Ms. Ryan said coldly.

"Have you been to their home in the past?"

"I have."

"Did you ever see any signs of neglect or abuse when you visited their home?"

"No. If I would have, I would not have allowed Dalton to go camping with them," Ms. Ryan snapped.

"So prior to September 3rd, you had no reason to doubt the parenting skills of Trevor or Roxanne Clark. Is that correct?" Mr. Dorcas asked.

"Yes, that is correct, sir."

"Ms. Ryan, you earlier stated that after you saw the Clark's van, the next thing you saw was Trevor and Roxanne Clark. Is that correct?"

"Yes, sir."

"What were Trevor and Roxanne doing when you saw them?"

"They were helping Brady walk back to the campsite. Brady

was limping and he was standing in the middle of his parents. He had one arm around each one of them and was holding onto them for support."

"So you didn't see Mr. or Mrs. Clark abusing the boys? Instead, you saw them helping their injured child make his way back to the campsite. Is that correct?"

"Yes," Ms. Ryan said, although she really wished there was some other way she could have thought to answer that question.

"What was Dalton's reaction when you told him he had to go back home with you?"

"He asked if he could continue to stay with them."

"Didn't you find it odd that if those children were in danger of being abused or neglected, that your son would want to stay there, Ms. Ryan?"

"Kids don't think that way."

"I have no further questions for this witness, Your Honor," Mr. Dorcas said, returning to his seat.

Brady and Derrick were shocked. Never in their life had they seen anything like this. They had seen court shows on television, but they had always seemed boring. This was so intense they just wanted it to be over and done with.

"I would like to call my next witness, Your Honor," Mr. Hively said. "Will Alice Adams please take the stand?"

Alice looked a lot more nervous than Ms. Ryan had. Her face was almost as white as a ghost. She stepped forward, was sworn in, and took her seat on the witness stand

"Mrs. Adams," Mr. Hively began. "You and your husband cared for the Clark children for several weeks. What can you tell me about their behavior in your home?"

Alice trembled. She had trouble finding the words to say. "They are good boys, sir. They make some bad choices sometimes, but they have worked out well in our home."

"What kind of bad choices would you say they have made?"

Alice looked like she could cry. More than anything she wanted to sit back down with everyone else. She hated everyone looking at her and she didn't like testifying. "Back talking, temper tantrums, breaking things, that type of thing," she said.

"Can you tell me what kind of temper tantrums you're referring to?"

[212]

Again, Alice was quiet for a moment. "I'll give you an example of one. A couple of weeks ago, Derrick came home from school without his homework. Tim told him to write, "I will do my homework every day" one hundred times. Derrick refused to do it. He screamed that my husband couldn't make him do anything. He took the ink pen Tim had handed him and broke it in two. He wadded the paper into a ball and threw it in my husband's face. That's the type of thing I'm referring to. They're not horrible behaviors. They just have some anger they need to let go of."

"I see," Mr. Hively replied. "So the children have learned some very aggressive behaviors and have not been taught how to deal with their emotions. What about their parents? Have you had much contact with them?"

"Very little. In fact, I don't believe I have ever had a conversation with Roxanne. Trevor has called our house a couple of times and he always ends up yelling at me or my husband or at the boys. We've even had to turn the ringer off on the phone and have had to hang up because he would not calm down on several occasions," Alice said.

"Would you say Trevor has some anger management issues?"

"Objection, Your Honor," Mr. Dorcas interrupted. "This is clearly speculation. Mrs. Adams is not a psychologist and is not qualified to pass this type of judgment."

"Objection sustained," Judge Raines said. "This question shall be removed from court documentation."

"I have no further questions, Your Honor," Mr. Hively said.

"Mr. Dorcas, would you like to cross examine?" Judge Raines asked.

"Yes, Your Honor," Mr. Dorcas said, quickly rising to his feet. The tension in the room was mounting. Everyone was so quiet a person could have heard a pin drop.

"Mrs. Adams, you said when Trevor calls he usually ends up being very upset before the phone calls have ended. Can you tell me what has set him off? What has been said during the

[213]

conversations that has made him so angry?"

"Usually, it's because one of the boys can't talk to him. If one of them is grounded for misbehavior or is busy, he will not accept that. He insists on speaking to both of them every time he calls and will not simply take 'no' for an answer," Mrs. Adams said.

"So Mr. Clark loves his boys so much that he needs to hear from them on a daily basis? It sounds like he is determined to make sure his children are okay and wants to talk to them as often as possible. Would you say that statement is correct?"

"Yes, sir."

"Mrs. Adams, on occasions when these children have thrown temper tantrums, what is done about them? Like in the example you gave us, when Derrick refused to write the sentences your husband told him to write. Was any disciplinary action taken against Derrick for that?"

"Sir, we do the best we can. There are so many regulations we foster parents have to abide by that it is sometimes very difficult to enforce consequences."

"What do you mean by that? Can you give us a few examples?" Mr. Dorcas asked.

"Yes, sir. We're not allowed to ever provide corporal punishment. If a foster child refuses to do what we tell them to do, we're not allowed to lay a hand on them. The only exception is if the child is acting out violently. If they are hitting us or attempting to hurt us or another member of the household, we are allowed to restrain them. Even then, we have to be careful that the child is not hurt in the process. We are not allowed to make the child go to bed without dinner. We are not allowed to make them sit in a room by themselves with the door closed. We are not allowed to make them do manual labor as a punishment. Our hands are really tied," she said.

"I see. So that is why they are grounded. You don't have any other punishment you can give them? Does grounding seem to work?"

"To be honest, sir, we're not even supposed to ground them. According to the rule book, whatever punishment we give them must be carried out in its entirety on the same day of the offense. We do not deny that we have broken that rule, but we didn't see any choice in the matter.

"But to answer your question, sometimes the groundings have been effective and at other times they have not. We can tell the guys they cannot use the phone, watch TV, use the computer, etc. If they do those things anyway, there's not a whole lot we can do about it. We can unplug the item they're using, but that hurts the rest of the family—not just the one who is being disobedient. The kids in foster care learn very early on that while they're in care, the foster parents have very little rule over them."

"I understand completely. Back to the question though, what consequences did Derrick face for not doing the writing assignment?" Mr. Dorcas asked.

"He was told to go to bed early."

"Did he accept that consequence?"

"No, sir, he did not."

"Your Honor, I have no further questions for this witness," Mr. Dorcas said.

"I have one more witness I would like to call to the stand," Mr. Hively said. "Mr. Timothy Adams, will you please approach the witness stand?"

Mr. Adams did not appear as nervous as the prior witnesses had. With confident strides he made his way to the front of the courtroom where he was sworn in just as the others had been.

"Mr. Adams, I understand you have had a few physical altercations with each of the Clark boys. Would you mind telling me what has been taking place?"

"Yes, sir. The first physical altercation that comes to mind is a couple of days after the boys moved in. Brady was back talking me and I told him to go to his room. He told me I couldn't make him go there and that he was going to go outside one way or another. I stood between him and the path to the door and he tried to bowl me over. He tried to use force to get around me—even went so far as to try to punch me. I had to physically restrain him and during that time he head-butted and spit on me. More recently, I had to physically restrain Derrick after he broke

[215]

out the window to his bedroom with the chemistry set we had purchased for him as a gift. He was screaming that he hated me and all of my family. He screamed that he wanted to die and wished he had never been born."

"It sounds like you have had your hands full," Mr. Hively responded. "Do you think the boys have improved any since they have been staying with you?"

"No, sir. As a matter of fact, I feel they have gotten worse. They have both had their good days and their bad days, but I do not feel that their behaviors are improving."

"I have no further questions, Your Honor," Mr. Hively said.

"In that case, I would like to cross examine the witness," Mr. Dorcas said, approaching the witness stand. "You stated that these boys are not improving in your household. From your experience as a foster parent, do you feel these children would improve in any other setting the state could place them in?"

"That's a tough question, sir," Tim replied. "These boys have a lot of hostility. They are very angry and bitter about being in foster care. They miss their parents and feel the world is against them."

"That is understandable. I'm sure we could all imagine what it would be like to be torn away from our families because of a false allegation we had made against them."

"Objection, Your Honor," Mr. Hively shouted. "The defense has not proven that any false allegations have been made."

"Objection sustained. Please strike Mr. Dorcas' last comment from the record," Judge Raines said.

"Mr. Adams," Mr. Dorcas continued, "when Brady told you he had originally lied and that's how he ended up in foster care, did he seem sincere?"

"Yes, sir," Tim said. "There is no doubt in my mind that Brady was telling me the truth. He cried his eyes out as he told me what he had done and I could tell his own guilt had been eating at him for a long time."

"I have no further questions, Your Honor."

"Ladies and gentlemen," Judge Raines announced, "the court will take a recess and we will resume these proceedings at 8:00 am tomorrow morning."

[216]

With that, everyone stood to their feet as Judge Raines left the courtroom.

When he was out of the room, everyone began to murmur. No one knew what to think about the many testimonies they had just heard. They were all very interested in seeing this case resolved.

Roxanne cried as she told her boys goodbye. "I love you. I'll see you both first thing in the morning and hopefully take you back home with me when it's over," she said.

"Boys, I love you too," Trevor added. "Let's keep our fingers crossed."

"Wouldn't praying work better than crossing our fingers Dad?" Derrick asked.

"You're right. That would help a lot more," Trevor said. "As a matter of fact, why don't we pause to do that right now. Is that okay, Mr. Dorcas?"

"Quickly," he said.

"Let's all join hands and bow our heads. I'll pray," Trevor said. "Dear God Almighty, you saw what took place here today. You know what's been going on for the past few months. We have admitted our faults and failures to you. We have confessed our sins and we've sought you with all of our hearts. God, my wife and I are crazy about these guys. We love them and want to have the opportunity to nurture them. To raise them according to your will. We won't be able to do that unless you help. Father, I know all of us probably have a little bit of doubt. But overall, we believe. We know you are able to do something mighty. Please show us your power! Please remove our unbelief."

Before he could continue, Mr. Dorcas tapped him on the shoulder. "Sorry, Mr. Clark, but our time is up. The next case is ready to be tried."

28
THE VERDICT

Bright and early the following morning, the judge announced court was back in session.

Trevor and Roxanne were more tense than they had been the previous day. They were one day closer to finding out whether or not the state of North Carolina would find them suitable as parents. They hated being treated like common criminals, but at the same time they could understand why everything was taking place.

"Yesterday," Judge Raines said, "we heard several testimonies from witnesses called by prosecuting attorney Jordan L. Hively. This morning we expect to hear more testimonies— this time from witnesses called by defense attorney George R. Dorcas. Mr. Dorcas, would you like to call your first witness?"

"Yes, Your Honor," Mr. Dorcas said. "For my first witness I would like to call on a minor, Mr. Dalton Ryan."

Dalton had not only agreed to be a witness, but had managed to talk his mother into consenting to it. Dalton nervously approached the witness stand and was sworn in as he had seen so many others do the day before.

"Mr. Ryan, how old are you?"

"Fifteen."

"At the age of fifteen, how many camping trips have you been on?"

"Only one," Dalton said sheepishly.

"And that one camping trip is the one you went on with the Clark family? Is that correct?"

"Yes. That's correct," Dalton replied.

"Did you enjoy that camping trip?"

"Yeah."

"How did you feel when your mother came to pick you up early?"

"I was upset. I wasn't ready to leave yet."

"So you were enjoying the trip. You weren't ready to leave. Can you tell me what you enjoyed the most about camping?" Mr. Dorcas asked.

Dalton didn't say anything for a moment. It was clear that he was trying to think of the perfect answer. "I liked everything about it. I enjoyed sleeping in the tent. Spending time with Brady and Derrick. Throwing Derrick in the river—"

"You threw Derrick in the river?"

"Yeah," Dalton chuckled. "Brady and I threw him in the river—you know, just playing around."

"Is there anything you did not like about the camping trip?"

"I didn't like leaving early. Does that count?" Dalton asked.

"Anything else? Like, for example, did you have any fights or arguments? Did anything scare you? Did you ever feel threatened?"

"I was kind of frightened when I thought Brady peed on me when I woke up in the morning and found my sleeping bag wet."

"Did anything else scare you?"

"Yeah. It was pretty creepy when Roxanne disappeared. I didn't know what had happened to her and I felt like it was partially my fault because I had been making fun of her for drooling in her sleep."

Roxanne's face turned as red as a beet. Why did that have to be brought up again?

"Did you ever feel like you were in any danger?"

"No, never."

"Did you ever see Brady or Derrick be abused in any way or did they ever tell you they had been abused?"

"Nah. Mr. and Mrs. Clark are always good to their kids."

"I have no further questions for this witness, Your Honor."

"Would you care to cross examine, Mr. Hively?" Judge

Raines asked.

"I would, Your Honor," Mr. Hively said, approaching the front of the courtroom. "Dalton, would you mind telling me how the Clark's van got so tore up? Obviously the tree damaged the top of the van. What happened to the rest of it? You know, the headlights, the taillights, the windshield, the back glass. What did all of that damage?"

"We all did it, sir," Dalton told him.

"You all did it? How?"

"Mr. Clark started it. He took a rock and threw it through a window. Then Mrs. Clark kicked out the headlights. Then we all took turns kicking it and throwing things at it. It got a little bit out of control."

"So you all basically disabled the only mode of transportation you had to get out of the woods?"

"Yes, sir. I guess we didn't think about it like that."

"I can understand you not thinking about it. After all, you're still a boy. However, do you feel Mr. and Mrs. Clark should have allowed this to take place?" Mr Hively asked.

"No, sir. They shouldn't have."

"Tell me what you had to eat on the day your mom picked you up."

"Cookies and brownies, sir," Dalton said. "My mom made them."

"Was that a snack?"

"Well, Mom sent them as a snack, yes. But we ate 'em for breakfast."

"Is that all you had for breakfast? No eggs, no bacon, no sausage, no toast, no cereal, nothing like that?"

"Nah. None of that. All we ate was cookies and brownies."

"Can you tell me how Brady's pants ended up getting on top of a flagpole?"

"Sure. Brady's ex-girlfriend Cindy and her new boyfriend showed up at the campground. They knocked Brady down and took his breeches."

"Where was Mr. and Mrs. Clark at this time? Were they not supervising him?"

"Mr. Clark was gathering firewood. Mrs. Clark was sitting

on a log near the tent. She was out of it and didn't even realize what was taking place," Dalton said.

"Mrs. Clark didn't hear anything?"

"Not a thing. She almost looked like a ghost. She just sat there motionless, staring off into space."

"I have no further questions, Your Honor," Mr. Hively said.

Roxanne gave Trevor a fearful look. She did not like the way Mr. Hively got Dalton to make things appear. She knew Dalton had to answer the questions, but his answers made them look like really bad parents.

"Call your next witness," Judge Raines said.

"Your Honor, I would like to call Trevor Clark to the stand," Mr. Dorcas said.

Trevor was surprised, but not shaken. He quickly made his way to the bailiff to be sworn in.

"Mr. Clark, I'm going to cut right to the chase here. Have you ever done anything to intentionally place your children in danger?" Mr. Dorcas asked.

"No, sir."

"Have you ever allowed your children to go hungry or naked?"

"No, sir."

"Have you ever beaten your children?"

"I haven't beaten them. I have spanked them, but that's perfectly within my legal rights," Trevor said.

"Have those spankings ever left any lasting marks? Have they ever cut the skin or caused any bruises that you are aware of?"

"Not that I know of."

"Do you know of any occasions of which your wife abused or neglected your children?"

"No, sir."

"I have no further questions, Your Honor," Mr. Dorcas said.

"You may cross examine the witness, Mr. Hively," Judge

Raines said.

Mr. Hively wasted no time at all. "Mr. Clark, you stated you have spanked your children, but not beaten them. Is that correct?"

"Yes, sir."

"Now when you say that you have spanked your children, did you spank them with your open palm?" Mr. Hively asked.

"Sometimes," Trevor said, "but I used whatever was necessary to teach my boys to be in subjection to me and their mother."

"Whatever was necessary? Please elaborate on that."

"When the boys were younger, I would spank them with my bare hand. Now that they have gotten older, I feel that more force is needed in order to get their attention," Trevor said.

"What kind of force do you use?"

"Usually my belt."

"Usually? That's kind of vague. So what else do you use?"

"I've used a shoe, a ruler, and on a few occasions I've taken a switch to them."

"I see… Do you think the boys are afraid of you?"

"I believe they have respect for me. I believe they know that if they get out of line, they are going to get a whipping. You can call that fear if you want to, but I want my children to know how to behave."

"Dalton previously testified that you busted out a window of the van with a rock. Is that true?"

"Yes, sir," Trevor said.

"How did that come about?"

"I needed to vent. We had been having a rough weekend and I needed to do something to break the tension."

"Oh, I see," Mr. Hively replied. "When you get angry or feel tense, you break things. Do you think maybe that's where Derrick got the idea to bust out the window in his bedroom at the Adams's residence?"

"Could be. I really don't know."

"I have no further questions for this witness," Mr. Hively said.

Trevor and Roxanne looked at the boys and in their minds

they could already hear the verdict and it wasn't in their favor. Things were not going well. The previous day everything seemed to be going their way, but all of that had changed.

"For my next witness," Mr. Dorcas said, "I would like to call Mrs. Roxanne Clark to the stand."

Roxanne started crying before she even left her seat. Had she been such a horrible mother that it had come to this? She only hoped she wouldn't be made to look like a total failure in front of an entire courtroom full of people.

"Mrs. Clark, how would you describe your relationship with your children?" Mr. Dorcas asked.

"We are very close."

"Do you ever argue with them?"

"Sometimes. Not very often though. They know better."

"Have you ever beaten them?"

"No, sir. Never."

"Have you ever allowed your children to go hungry or naked or to be placed in harm's way?"

"No, sir, I have not," Roxanne said.

"Do your boys know you love them?"

"Yes, sir. I'm sure of it. I tell them all of the time."

"Have you ever known of your husband to abuse the boys in any way?" Mr. Dorcas asked.

"No, sir. Trevor is a loving husband and a wonderful father. He would never do anything like that."

"No further questions, Your Honor," Mr. Dorcas concluded.

"I'd like to cross examine," Mr. Hively spoke up. "Mrs. Clark, are you afraid of your husband?"

"No, sir," Roxanne said. "I love my husband."

"Where do you work, Mrs. Clark?"

"I am a stay at home mother."

"Have you ever considered working outside of the home?"

"I have thought about it, but Trevor would not permit that."

"So Trevor makes your decisions for you?"

"Trevor is the man of the house. I am the woman of the house. I am supposed to be in subjection to him and that's the way I like it to be. I'm not afraid of him. It's just the way people were created. That's what the Bible teaches," Roxanne preached.

"And I suppose next you're going to tell me the Bible says it's okay for your husband to beat your children with a belt. Is that correct?"

"There is an enormous difference between beating children and disciplining them," Roxanne lectured. "The Bible does say that we are to correct our children and it does provide specific instructions as to how that discipline is to be carried out."

Roxanne's tears had dried up. She suddenly had the courage of a lion.

"Would you do anything in your power for your husband?" Mr. Hively asked.

"Yes, sir, I would."

"Does that include lying to protect him?"

"Normally, I do not tell lies. However, it would depend on the situation. I love my husband very much. If you're asking me if I'm lying for him now, I will tell you I most certainly am not. I would be willing to take a lie detector test if you need me to."

"There will be no need for that, Mrs. Clark. Is it true that you had a part in destroying your vehicle?" Mr. Hively asked.

"That is true. I did. It's something you would have had to have been there to understand. We have been married sixteen years and in that time, nothing like that had ever happened before. We were all very frustrated. Our tent had leaked, a tree fell down on top of the van, and everybody was grumpy. Our food was locked up inside of the vehicle and Brady's clothes and shoes were in there.

"We tried everything we could think of to get our things out of the van and then Trevor busted out the window. When I asked him why he did that, he said he needed to vent. I realized I needed to vent too so I followed his lead and then the boys joined in. It was harmless. That old van needed to be replaced anyway," Roxanne said, beginning to laugh.

"Have you ever been to counseling?" Mr. Hively asked.

"I have never been to any type of counseling and never will be. I am as sane as anyone in this courtroom."

"I have no further questions for this witness," Mr. Hively said.

Roxanne was proud of herself. She had stood up to him. She didn't cry. She didn't let him make her look like a bad mother.

"Your Honor, I have no more witnesses at this time," Mr. Dorcas said.

"Let's commence with closing arguments," Judge Raines said. "Mr. Hively, please step forward."

Mr. Hively walked to the front of the room again. "From what we have heard here today, Mr. and Mrs. Clark both admitted to destroying their means of transportation because they were having a bad day. They both admitted that Trevor has control issues. We have learned that Roxanne is willing to lie for her husband if the need arises. We have heard witnesses talk about the violent behaviors the children have learned from their parents. It has been a long two days, but I believe it has been proven that these children would be better off not returning to their biological family at this time," Mr. Hively remarked.

"And now Mr. Dorcas," Judge Raines said. "Please step forward."

Mr. Dorcas came to the front of the room as if he was a superhero. He stood with his back straight and his shoulders drawn back. "Over these past two days we have heard from witness after witness. Nowhere during this hearing has anyone proven that these boys have been physically abused or neglected. Brady was not wearing clothes when he was found because his clothing had been left in the van and a tree had fallen on it. He had pajama pants on, but some teenage pranksters took them from him. Derrick had on a pair of worn out tennis shoes because the family was on a camping trip where they were going to be roughing it.

"The family did destroy the van, which we might all agree

was out of the ordinary, but it did not harm anyone and no one was put in any danger by it. These parents love their children and the children love their parents. I have not seen any evidence that would even begin to suggest that Mr. and Mrs. Clark are incapable of providing for the needs of both Brady and Derrick."

It had been a grueling couple of days. The hearing was practically over. Now it was time for the verdict. Everyone was nervous. What would happen? Both sides had presented a solid case. There didn't seem to be any room for criticism. Both attorneys had done an excellent job of presenting the facts.

"I find in favor of the defense," Judge Raines said after a brief period of silence. "Effective immediately, Brady and Derrick Clark are to be released to the custody of Trevor and Roxanne Clark."

"YES!!!!" Roxanne screamed and burst into applause. "I knew it! I just knew it!"

"Thank you," Trevor said to Mr. Dorcas. "You did a great job."

Brady burst into tears. He couldn't say a word.

Derrick looked at Ms. Simms and smiled as if to say, "In your face you, old battle axe!"

"Furthermore," Judge Raines added, "the Department of Social Services will oversee this placement. They will ensure the children are being well taken care of. We will have another court date in sixty days to reevaluate this situation."

Trevor and Roxanne were outraged. They had never done anything wrong to begin with. How did the court system have the right to insist they be supervised in how they were raising their children? Still, it was either that, or continue to allow their family to be separated. Neither said a word.

"Dad," Brady spoke up suddenly. "Am I going to get a whippin' when I get home?"

"What do you think?"

"I don't know."

"I think you do know. Do you think you deserve a whippin'?"

Brady hated that question. Why did parents always ask questions they knew their kids would not be honest about?

For once though, Brady did tell the truth. "Yes, sir. I know I deserve a whipping—a good one."

"You're right, son, you do deserve one. But I'm not going to give it to you," Trevor replied.

"You're not? Why?" Brady asked, sounding a bit confused.

"For starters, I think you've already suffered enough for what you did wrong. More importantly though, I want to teach you a lesson about grace. Remember how we've talked about how all of us have sinned? About how all of us deserved to die and go to Hell? Jesus came in our place and took all of the punishment for us so we wouldn't have to go to Hell, didn't He?"

"Yes, sir, but what does that have to do with me getting a whipping?"

"I'm going to show you what grace is all about. It was God's grace that allowed Him to send Jesus here to take away our sins. It is that same word grace that is going to allow you to escape this punishment. You deserve a very hard butt busting just like we all deserve to go to Hell. You're not going to be punished though because I am giving you a gift of grace and am not going to make you pay any further for your sin. Understand?"

"Yes, sir," Brady said. "Thanks Dad!"

"There's a little more to grace than that though, buddy. Grace means not only did God forgive us of our sins without us having to pay for them ourselves, but Jesus paid for them for us. We're not going to take it that far. But sovereign grace would mean I would take the whipping for you and you would be free of that punishment."

Derrick chimed in, "Are you kidding? Come on, Dad, whip him. Please! He deserves it!"

"Derrick, shut up!" Brady said.

Some things never change.

[227]

CHECK THIS OUT!

Author JR Thompson has a new Christian mystery,
Hidden in Harmony, scheduled to be released on October 14,
2017. He's ecstatic about sharing it with you,
so he decided to share a preview.

CHAPTER 1 – UNFORESEEN COMPANY

"What is piled up on our porch?" Alayna squawked as the Russell family bumped along their rocky driveway.

Visible only in the dim headlights of their old, beat-up Jeep Wagoneer, was what appeared to be a heap of filthy blankets. Collin turned to their thirteen year old, "Remington, what kind of fort were you building this time?"

Remington answered with a powerful snore. He had fallen asleep just minutes before reaching their turn-off.

The dilapidated rags suddenly sprung to life, unveiling a helpless looking man who appeared to have been there for hours. *Oh, my,* Alayna thought. *What is going on here?*

Collin asked her to stay in the Jeep and not to wake Remington, while he stepped out and cautiously approached the stranger.

"Can I help you with something, buddy?" he called out.

A weak, exhausted voice barely managed to rasp, "Your assistance would be most beneficial. I'm drenched, cold, and ravenous."

Attempting to rise, the man tumbled back to his space atop the wooden stairs.

Grasping the door handle, Alayna started to get out. Then, she came to her senses. Apprehensively, she watched as her husband sprinted to the shivering, obviously homeless, middle-aged fellow. Collin knelt down next to the man, spoke a few words, and then motioned for his wife to join him.

Wasting no time, Alayna rushed to the porch. The stranger's gentle, needy eyes demanded her attention. *Looks can be deceiving,* she cautioned herself. *Stay strong.*

"Hon, this harmless guy is worn clean out. He's going to have to stay here tonight. Why don't you go inside and I'll get Remington?"

Alayna wasn't keen on the idea of a drifter dozing on her porch, not even for one minute. *We don't know this man from Adolph Hitler or Jeffrey Dahmer. This is definitely not the way I planned on spending my Friday night.*

Without a telephone, the internet, or even a close neighbor for that matter, if the transient wound up being a sociopath, the Russells were on their own. Alayna took comfort in knowing Collin was strong and courageous, but he didn't even own a gun. Right or wrong, she feared for her family's safety.

She had married an enormous hearted, yet incredibly obstinate salesman. Collin had already made a decision and it was set in concrete. It would be a waste of her sweet-smelling breath to try to dissuade him. Without uttering a word, she ascended the stairs — being sure to step as far away from the beggar as possible.

Opening his eyes, Remington knew he wasn't in his bedroom. *Where am I?* he wondered.

It only took a matter of seconds for his eyes to adjust. *Why did they leave me in the car?*

Putting his glasses on, Remington sat up. He looked through the windshield just in time to see Mom going inside. Then he caught sight of Dad and the unexpected visitor.

"Who's that, Dad?" the boy called as he opened his door.

"Don't worry about it right now, Remmy," Collin said, turning to face his son. "Just go inside and get into your pajamas. We'll do our devotion here in a few minutes."

"But Dad —," the inquisitive teen began.

Collin shut him down firmly, "Get inside, now!"

Dad had given him the look. Remmy knew what that meant. His toothpick frame bolted across the lawn, up the steps, and into the old farmhouse, where he was certain he would get the full scoop from Mom.

"Listen, buddy, I don't know what to do," Collin said. "I have a wife and a son that I'm responsible for — I can't bring you in the house. Surely you know that."

With disappointment forming in his eyes, the beggar slowly nodded. It certainly wasn't the first time he had been turned away. He had visited the only homeless shelter he knew of within a twenty-five mile radius; they were full. The Clayville Motor Lodge kicked him off of their parking lot. He had attempted to hide in a dumpster, but an angry store owner caught him and literally ran him out of town.

He fully expected Collin to turn him away — but he didn't. "For tonight, you can sleep out here on the porch," Collin told him. "In the morning, after you've regained your strength, you will need to be on your way."

Again, the transient nodded, this time with quivering lips. *At least I can get some sleep before I have to move on,* he thought, as he pulled the blankets tight around him, laid on his side, and curled himself into a tight ball.

He listened as Collin moseyed inside and locked the deadbolt behind him.

Collin didn't have time to inhale a single breath of air before Remington started in on him, "Mom wouldn't tell me what's going on. Who is that guy, Dad?" he asked.

To say Collin was annoyed would be like saying a woman

giving birth was slightly discomforted. *Does that boy's mouth ever close?*

Even though Remmy had already changed into his blue and white striped jammies, he was nowhere near ready for bed. Collin had no doubt his son had become obsessed with their mysterious guest. *Perhaps I should have had him take a bubble bath.*

Trying to refrain from hurting Remmy's feelings, Dad attempted to provide a simple answer to his question, "We don't know anything about the man, buddy. He's just a guy who is down on his luck. He'll be leaving in the morning."

Oh no, Collin thought, as he saw the expression that manifested itself on his son's face. *It's going to be a long night.*

"He's down on his luck? Do you mean he's homeless?" Remington asked.

Dad hesitated for a moment. "Yes, Remmy. He's homeless."

"How did he get that way?" Remington asked.

Collin explained the situation the best way he knew how, "Some people can buy a pair of shoes and have them last forever," he began. He went on to explain how caring properly for shoes was similar to a person maintaining their finances. Taking care of things made them last while acts of carelessness caused deterioration. He said people lost their homes for a variety of reasons. Sometimes, it was because of addictions to drugs, alcohol, or gambling. Other times it was just due to poor budgeting. Every person's situation was different.

Collin knew it annoyed Remington when he used shoes for an analogies. As a matter of fact, he annoyed himself by always talking about footwear. But what could he do? Shoes were his life.

Remington was anything but out of questions. He asked Dad why the man's family hadn't taken him in, how he had found their house when they lived three miles outside of Clayville, and how long he had been homeless.

Over and over again, Dad responded with as short of answers as he could muster. He knew Remington had a soft heart. With a lot on his plate already, the last thing he wanted to do was console a broken teen.

###

More than anything, Remington wanted to go outside to interview the stranger; Dad would never allow that. That is — unless he could come up with a clever way to do it. "Daddy, isn't it my turn to lead the devotion tonight?" he asked.

"It sure is. Do you have a message prepared?"

"Yeah, let me get my Bible," Remington replied, before running to his bedroom.

He grabbed his Bible off of his dresser and flipped to the concordance. *Where is it?* he asked himself. *What should I look under?*

It didn't take him long to find the passage he was hunting for. With a persnickety expression on his face, he scampered back to the living room and began his message, "Tonight, I'm going to read from Matthew 25. Verses 42 and 43 say, 'For I was an hungred, and ye gave me no meat: I was thirsty, and ye gave me no drink: I was a stranger, and ye took me not in: naked, and ye clothed me not, sick, and —'"

Alayna placed her pointer finger tight against her lips before softly saying, "We understand how you feel, Remmy, but we aren't living in Bible times anymore. We can't just bring a homeless man into our house; he could rob us blind. He could murder us. We don't know anything about him."

Her reasoning made no sense to Remington. *We don't live in Bible times anymore? Then why do we have to obey other parts of the Bible?*

This was one time when he couldn't keep his thoughts to himself, "So, you tell me I have to go to church because the Bible says I should. You want me to pay tithes, even on my birthday money, because that's what the scriptures say to do. You tell me it's not right to talk bad about people behind their backs, that I'm supposed to be careful what kind of friends I hang out with, that I should go soul-winning with the youth group — and you tell me the reason for all of this is because I should always do what the Bible says.

"Why is this different? The Bible says we're not supposed to send people away on empty stomachs; we're supposed to take people in who don't have places to stay; we're supposed to give people clothes when they don't have any. So what are you saying, Mom? We can just pick and choose which parts of the Bible to obey now that we're not living in Bible times?"

Standing to her feet and crossing her arms across her chest, Alayna bellowed, "That's enough, Remmy! Go to bed!"

The tension in the room could have been cut with a plastic butter knife. Not being a whiner or complainer, Remington stomped to his bedroom, nearly tripping over his drooping bottom lip.

He didn't understand — his parents had dragged him to Sunday School since he was in diapers; they had taught him to never fear man more than he feared God. *What ever happened to practicing what you preach?*

Remington slammed his rugged door shut and threw himself face down on his bed to sulk. Unlike a lot of kids his age, he thought highly of his parents. Generally speaking, they were fun-loving, sweet, and kind-hearted. They didn't have a lot of money, but that didn't matter to them. Through the years, they had learned that having faith in God was more important than anything money could buy.

Their way of handling this situation, however, was disheartening. A human being was stuck outside with no place to call home. He could catch a cold or even wind up with pneumonia. *Oh, but they're being charitable. They're letting him sleep on their porch.*

HIDDEN IN HARMONY is scheduled to be released on October 14, 2017.

Thank you for reading REVENGE FIRES BACK.

If you enjoyed the book and are interested in learning about more of Thompson's writings, please visit www.jrthompsonbooks.com

If you would like to contact the author, please search for his official Facebook page where you are free to comment on any of his posts. He loves to hear from his readers so don't hesitate to get in touch.

66120571R00145

Made in the USA
Lexington, KY
04 August 2017